# JERRY F. WESTINGER

# A Bad Price to Pay for Love

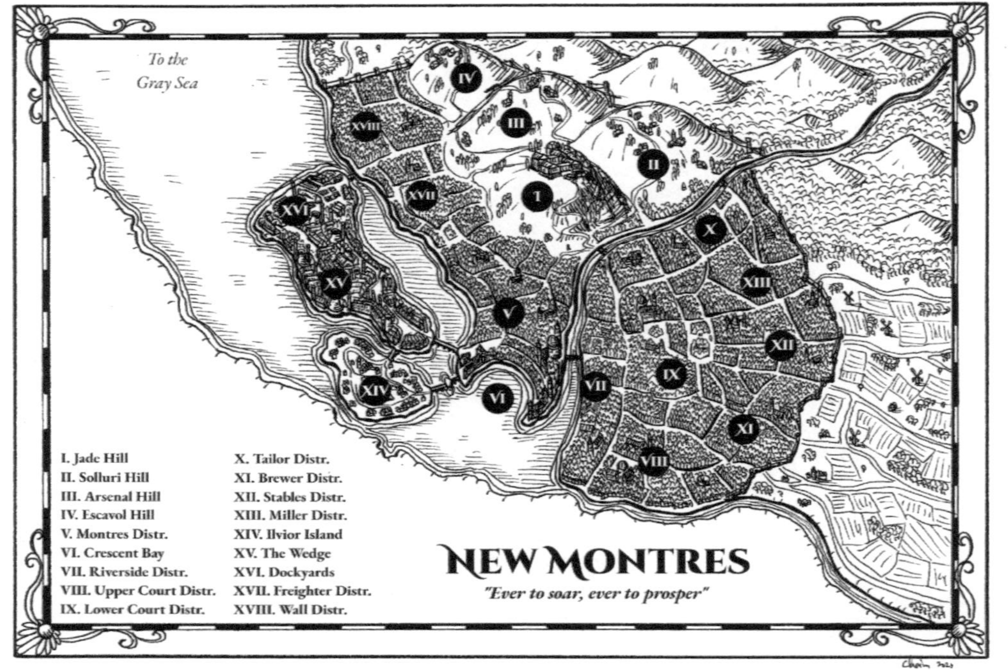

To the
Gray Sea
NEW MONTRES
"Ever to soar, ever to prosper"
I. Jade Hill
II. Solluri Hill
III. Arsenal Hill
IV. Escavol Hill
V. Montres Distr.
VI. Crescent Bay
VII. Riverside Distr.
VIII. Upper Court Distr.
IX. Lower Court Distr.
X. Tailor Distr.
XI. Brewer Distr.
XII. Stables Distr.
XIII. Miller Distr.
XIV. Ilvior Island
XV. The Wedge
XVI. Dockyards
XVII. Freighter Distr.
XVIII. Wall Distr.

# I

# Part One

# Chapter 1

If anybody asked, Argiey would have insisted that on some days it should be unlawful to get out of bed. Those cold autumn days, with rain that was thick enough to make him open an umbrella, but thin enough to make him feel a coward for doing so. Days when all he wanted was to stretch his feet by the fire, lazily sip a tumbler of caraway brandy, and leaf through a two-bit rag filled with dreadful stories.

But nobody asked Argiey. In fact, as luck would have it, a customer rolled in right as he was ready to call it a shift and head home. With a resigned sigh, he trotted to the back room and dug out all the equipment he had packed away, knowing full well he'd be working a solid hour late.

The man forcing him to do so wasn't much worth the effort, either. Some loafer who'd been lucky enough to live forty-odd years on a diet of wine and empty promises. As Argiey helped the threadbare excuse for a coat off of him, the man flopped around like a pig in the mud and stank like two of them.

First things first, once the customer was in place, Argicy set up the three-legged stand and attached the lightchamber to it, meticulously twisting all the screws to tilt it toward the haggard face. When he found the correct angle, he slid a clean plate into the slot and opened the lens cover. Afterward there was nothing to do but leave it for the next quarter of an hour while the picture developed, only making sure that both the box and the subject stayed completely motionless. At the very least, the latter was never a concern. If there was one thing the dead were good at, it was being still.

When Argiey first saw a lightchamber a few years earlier, he was convinced some form of thaumaturgy—if not necromancy—was involved in its mechanism. The fact that it worked with ordinary chemicals only made it more unnerving. It created a likeness hauntingly close to reality but drained of all color, as though the box somehow stole a piece of the subject's very life essence. Argiey had no qualms about operating the device, but it would be a dry day on the sea floor before he willingly stood in front of it himself.

Either way, his customers didn't have to trouble themselves with any of that. Their worries lay far in whatever distance their eyes stared into, blissfully unaware of the grief they left behind for their loved ones—and for the exhausted coroner they pressed into overtime.

While the lightchamber did its sinister job, Argiey went to the writing desk and pulled the flask out of the bottom drawer. He didn't stock caraway brandy at the office, so plain old pit bitters would have to do. His joints and the chair creaked in perfect unison as he lowered himself into the seat and scanned the papers before him.

Shortly after they were alerted to the dead body, the city guard also apprehended the man that the victim had been last seen with. The suspect admitted to having an "altercation" with the deceased, but denied so much as spitting on him, let alone causing him harm. According to his confession, the victim had stumbled back and fallen down a long flight of stairs, breaking his neck in the process.

Argiey tugged at the scruff of his sideburns and emptied his drink, waiting for the hourglass counting down the fifteen minutes to run out. Then he put away the lightchamber, took up his leather gloves, and returned to the corpse. It was time to hear the other side of the story.

If there was another thing the dead were good at, it was keeping secrets—some longer than others. At first, the victim seemed to corroborate the suspect's tale. His neck was definitely broken, and his face had a large, flat bruise on the side where it might have hit the ground at the bottom. But as Argiey's mentor had explained all those years before, sometimes the things that *weren't* there told the whole truth.

When someone rolled down a flight of stairs, they didn't only end up with one bruise. Forearms, elbows, hips, and sides all had plenty of sharp bones to knock against the steps and leave dark reminders of the impact. The victim's limbs, however, were as pristine as the day he'd been born, only a deal hairier.

Checking inside was nothing but a formality. All ribs were intact, and none of the organs showed any sign of injury. With well-honed motions, Argiey stitched up the body along the cut, washed his hands, and took a good few minutes to write his opinion with penmanship that wouldn't insult the judge who read it. All in all, short work. He might even have an hour or so to himself at home.

The thump from the back room was barely audible. Argiey tore himself away from the paper and glared at the door, half wondering if he had imagined it. In response to his doubt, a second thump came, accompanied by the faint rattle of metal.

He finished up his paperwork undisturbed, capping it off with the official seal of the South New Montres Deadhouse. He filed it away in his drawer, cleared all the nibs and inkwells away from the desk, and with the measured steps of someone who had done nothing wrong, proceeded into the back room.

It was pitch black, with Argiey's frame blocking most of the meager light that stretched in from the workroom. Sinking to his knees, he ran a hand along the floor toward the wall. Most of the deadhouse lay well below ground level, but some rooms—including this one—had the occasional window between the ceiling inside and the pavement outside. One of these windows was cracked open, and directly under it was a heap of rags. Argiey used these rags to wipe down slabs and stuff any crevices of bodies that needed stuffing. They also did an excellent job of muffling the sound of whatever was dropped through the window.

Grasping stiffly around in the blind cold, his fingers happened upon the satchel first. He ran his thumb over the coarse leather to feel out the coins inside. One, two, three. . . and four. All the right size. Argiey pocketed the money, then dug into the pile of cloth again.

The package was as small and nondescript as all the others. Slightly bigger than his fist, wrapped in cloth and tied with numerous thick strings. No label, no markings—nothing to indicate its contents, whatever those were. Argiey neither needed nor wanted to know. His part in the process had been settled years earlier, and he had no intention of broadening it.

Good thing he hadn't moved the body from the slab.

Not bothering with proper equipment, he used his knife to

rip up the stitches at the crotch end. He pulled apart the seam enough to make an opening, shoved the package inside, then sewed it back up. Finally, he left two inches of the thread to hang loose and tied a hoop on it—as per the agreed code.

He took a step back and surveyed the corpse. No one would ever suspect that anything was special about it, unless they knew what to look for.

A series of faint clicks echoed through the empty workroom as Argiey closed the quartz lights one by one, until darkness enveloped all but the smoky oil lamp he held. The front door locked with a resounding fall of the latch, putting a firm barrier between Argiey and his work. Clammy autumn rain splashed under his boot up the steps to the street, where the city of New Montres spread into the night.

Somewhere in that city, a man had died earlier, taking a hundred secrets to the grave. Argiey had made sure he would take one more with him. If only for a while.

# Chapter 2

Over eight years of service, Nel could have counted on one hand all the times she'd been late for work. Her personal life was another matter. At the Ilvior Island guardhouse, each day was precisely like the last, marching along to a rhythm as predictable and soothing as the ticking of a clock. It was a comfortable monotony that drew her in, and she had few interests outside of it. Her nerves had a habit of getting the better of her in unusual situations. Having some place to be that wasn't to do with her duties as an officer—*sergeant*, as she routinely had to correct herself—was unusual enough. Tonight's arrangement was nothing short of extraordinary.

The ticking of the clock did little to calm her down, either. It was less the noise itself that bothered her, and more the fact that it was only in her head. She couldn't possibly have heard it over the tumult that engulfed her. A dozen whistles blaring, a hundred voices talking, and a thousand boots clattering in all directions on the worn-out marble. No matter the time of day, the air in New Montres Central railway station always rang with noise, and this night was no exception.

"Train from Midorea arriving at platform six! Train arriving at seven-thirty on time and departing for Midorea at seven fifty-five! Passengers embarking to Midorea, please make your way to platform six!"

A uniformed station attendant nearly hit Nel in the face with his speaking trumpet, as he swung back and forth like a weathervane to be heard in all corners of the massive hall. As a comfort, he managed to reassure her that she was going the right way. Nel's eyes bounced frantically up and down the wrought-iron columns that towered above like a forest, with their canopy spread into the dizzying latticework of a paneled ceiling. Though the days grew shorter outside, the hall within was bright and clear. Dots of sharp quartz light were tempered with the warmth of natural flame and reflected a million times over in the elaborate glass chandeliers, illuminating the two-foot brass numbers that hung on the posts.

At last, there it was. Platform six.

Nel forced herself to slow down. The reddener she had hastily brushed on before leaving home had proven to be superfluous, as her cheeks were plenty flushed on their own. Stepping in the shade of a column, she fanned herself with both hands to catch her breath. Somehow, that only agitated her more, and on top of that, it made the ruffles on her sleeve twist up again.

She straightened them back and smoothed out the dress that had shifted around in her unladylike haste. Nel had nothing against dresses on principle—if she got to buy them on her own, to her preferred measurements. This one had been picked out by her mother, who insisted on a close fit and thin stripes to make it "flattering," particularly at the waist. Nel had long put off actually wearing it, as she suspected it would mostly turn her into a sausage, but seeing the results in the mirror, she had to give credit where it was due. All the lines curved the way they were supposed to, and breathing was much easier than she expected.

A whistle pierced the murmur of the hall, followed soon by the measured rumble of the engine pulling into the station. Brakes shrieked and whined as they ground away at its momentum, and with a final hiss of relief, the train came to a halt.

Clouds of steam, seemingly coming from the metal itself, flooded the platform. All carriage doors opened on a beat, and from behind each one came a conductor, who hurried to unlock the luggage holds. Passengers trickled out in single file to stretch their legs and wait for their things to be retrieved.

Standing at the end, not two yards from the engine, Nel clutched her hands and eyed the disembarking lot. Almost all those who got off first were Ardonnese, as if the train hadn't come from abroad. Gradually, flocks of blond heads began to speckle the crowd, as the visiting Midoreans patiently followed the notoriously pushy locals out into the hall.

Nel swallowed. Anyone coming next could be him.

Careful not to get washed away in the flow, she hiked up her dress anew and walked slowly beside the train, silently mouthing the line she had rehearsed the whole way from home. *Welcome back to the center of the world!* Hopefully, she'd be able to say it with enough conviction. Nel had never been one for theatrics, but this situation called for a bit of boldness.

After all, surprising Mainu at the station was a bold decision in and of itself. It had struck Nel as a good idea at first, but now that she was here, she also had to admit its shortcomings. Since she had not discussed any details with him, she didn't know which carriage he would be in. The two front ones had already emptied, as those were reserved for spacious compartments with few travelers. The more densely packed rear ones were still unloading, and so Nel continued toward them.

"Evening, young lady. And who might you be after?"

The stench of drink from the man's mouth hit Nel before his croaking reached her ears. It was one of the Ardonnese passengers, who had stumbled out of the third carriage, which housed the refreshment counter. Judging by the stains on his untucked and misbuttoned shirt, he had spent the whole six-hour trip there.

Nel drew back to get out of the miasma of his breath, but he only came closer.

"I'm meeting a friend," she said, trying to sidestep without treading on her dress.

Unsteady as he was, the man followed her quickly enough. "Friend, eh? Not a husband or a brother, then?" He leered at Nel with what he must have considered a winning smile.

"Sir, please cease at once." Nel put up a hand. As an officer, she'd had to deal with plenty of drunks, many of whom tried to charm their way out of trouble. "You are being inappropriate. Please, let me pass and be on your way."

The man snickered. "Oh, I should hope I'm inappropriate. Can't get far with a woman these days being all courteous." He walked backward to keep facing Nel, while she tried to reach the next carriage. "What's your name, sweetheart?"

"Sir, I'll have you know I'm an offi—" Nel bit off the end of the word as she nearly said the wrong title again. Then she realized how silly it was not to know her own rank, but there was no choice but to finish the sentence now. "I'm a sergeant of the city guard. I may not be on duty, but if you don't leave me, I will have you arrested for disorderly conduct."

She searched for any station guards or attendants that could help, but none were close enough to call over without causing a scene.

Her suitor did not share her fears and cackled out loud. "You'll need to make up your mind if you want to sell me on that story." He closed what little distance Nel had managed to keep between them and took her by the arm. "But I'd love to listen," he said in a low voice. "Why don't you and I go somewhere nice and quiet, Officer Sergeant Sweetheart?"

Nel had never been that good at thinking on her feet, but she was a creature of habit. Anything she made into a routine, she could repeat without so much as thinking about it. And when she was being trained, it had been thoroughly drilled into her what to do if there was an unwanted hand on her arm.

In one motion, she freed herself from the man's grip, latched onto his wrist, and twisted it around. Before he could do more than wince in pain, the heel of Nel's right hand shot forward and caught his nose with full force. There was an audible snap of cartilage, and the charmer sailed backward, tripping over someone's pulled luggage and crashing onto the floor in a whimpering heap.

A circle cleared around her, where the bystanders muttered between themselves before accepting that the spectacle was over and moving on. Two guards rushed over from the end of the hall, took one glance at Nel and one at the man, then drew enough conclusions to decide on their next step. While they dragged the drunk away between the two of them, Nel once again untwisted her ruffles and smoothed her dress, hoping Mainu had not walked past her amidst the kerfuffle.

He had not.

Nel jumped in place and narrowly avoided recoiling the same way her attacker had. Her back jerked into a stiff arch, her arms pinned themselves to her sides like a tied up roast, and the sudden clench of her stomach pressed a mouse-like squeal through her nose. All the while, she could do nothing but stare ahead with eyes so wide they threatened to pop out.

From a yard away, standing with the same posture of effortless discipline that Nel remembered, Mainu gave her an expression that was utterly indecipherable. The only hint was the crook of his eyebrows and a minimal tilt of the head, which could have meant anything from mild amusement to complete disdain. One of his hands kept a haversack slung over his shoulder, while the other one held a trunk by his leg.

After Nel failed to get a single word out, he nodded by way of greeting and said, "You look well."

Who it was that spoke with Nel's voice she had no way of knowing, but that person managed to reply with a coherent, "Thank you, so do you," and add, "It's good to see you again."

"It's good to see you, too."

"How was your trip?" Nel did her best to sound carefree.

Mainu held out with the answer. "Long and uninteresting. So far." His deep green eyes shifted to the spot where the drunkard had fallen, then back to her. "And a good deal exhausting."

"Right." Nel snapped out of her daze at last. "Of course. We shouldn't stand here." She motioned behind her. "You didn't mention if anyone was coming to pick you up, but if not, there are plenty of rent-coaches outside the entrance."

"Let's find one, then." Mainu adjusted the bag strap around his shoulder and set off, pausing only enough to let Nel fall in beside him.

Since they'd last seen each other, she had forgotten what a prime example Mainu was of the famously aloof Midorean temperament. But, in all fairness to herself, that wasn't entirely her fault.

It was already unexpected when Mainu suggested that he and Nel stay in touch after their brief time working together, but more so when she opened his first letters. On top of being four full pages long, notable portions were dedicated to the exploits of a certain Herringbone, Egg Thief, and The One Eyed Queen. Nel figured that these were perhaps individuals of such great confidence that Mainu couldn't mention them by name. As she read on, the trio turned out to be a clowder of cats that lived in the alley next to the High Court's office, and whom Mainu had made great efforts to befriend, often at his own injury.

His affection for animals wasn't the only hidden side of him that Nel had discovered. Later into their correspondence, after much deliberation, she decided to confide in him about the nightmares that refused to leave her. Months after that one evening, when they went to arrest the necromancer Lokenn Mar Enaë, visions of his gruesome death kept cropping up in her dreams, causing her to wake in a cold sweat. She hadn't dared tell anyone in person, and writing it down felt like an even greater challenge.

In his reply, Mainu shared his own experience with such dreams after witnessing the death of an innocent bystander during one of his first assignments, and he commended her on the effort it took to face the haunting memory. "If I cannot offer more than words on paper, then let me make them the words I would have wanted to hear: You are not alone in your struggle." And while they were indeed only words, the sentiment behind them meant the world to Nel.

After that, being met with Mainu's brisk nature felt like talking to a different person altogether.

He was different on the outside, too. When the two of them first met, Mainu's hair was tightly braided, and his beard trimmed in a meticulous pattern. Now, that beard was a mere strip along his jaw. The sides of his head were all but shaved clean, and the rest of his hair was tied back in a single band. Nel had never seen another man so impressively groomed, yet any impression of vanity that Mainu's hair gave was in stark conflict with his well-worn shirt and trousers. All in all, it was yet another paradox about him.

Nel was yanked out of her thoughts when, out of nowhere, Mainu's hand pulled her in by the shoulder to prevent her from walking into a closing door. She had been so caught up reminiscing that she didn't notice they'd reached the main entrance. The rest of her senses rushed on cue to remind her: the clamor of carts and carriages, the heavy smell of unending autumn rain, and the shivering glow of the gas lamps that struggled to penetrate its thick curtain. However busy the inside of New Montres Central station was, the street outside was always ready to compete.

"Are you uncomfortable?" Mainu asked as plainly as ever.

Nel followed his gaze to her hands, which were untwisting the ruffles of her sleeve yet again.

"Oh, no. A little." She stepped away and hurried to straighten the seams. "I don't wear this dress often."

"I don't think I've seen you in a dress at all."

"I prefer trousers outside of work as well. Even if they make me look"—Nel fished for a euphemism—"dowdy."

"'Dowdy'?" Mainu's brow furrowed.

"Out of fashion," Nel explained.

As fluent as Mainu was in Ardonnese, this likely wasn't the sort of word he used often.

"I don't fault you for it," he said. "I prefer comfort over fashion as well."

As if to prove a point, he walked out from under the awning and into the downpour to hail down an oncoming rent-coach. He waited for the driver to clamber down and help put all the luggage away, then held the door open for Nel, paying no mind to how much his hair got soaked. Once they were both inside and took their seats in opposing corners, he undid his band in an attempt to wring out his ponytail with a great amount of difficulty. Considering he was a lieutenant investigator of the Midorean High Court, he appeared so inept in this task that Nel couldn't resist the glibness that overcame her.

"Is this hair supposed to be fashionable or comfortable?"

Mainu gave no outward reaction, but his tone mirrored Nel's. "It's not comfortable at all, and it's not fashionable yet." His mouth twitched in annoyance as his fingers got caught in the tangled locks. "An old friend of mine works as a barber not far from the High Court's offices. He knows what's in style before anyone else, and he's agreed to give me free shaves and haircuts. His only demand was that he gets to practice on me before the paying customers of the season start coming in."

Well, that was one mystery solved.

"I think it suits you," Nel said. "Bit of a shame you don't like it."

A distant relative of a smile appeared on Mainu's face. "It's a shame, too, that you don't like dresses."

Once his hair was dry enough, or he simply gave up, Mainu threw his head back so he could tie his band again. While he did, the coach rolled past a street lamp, and the light fell on the remnants of a wide scar that ran from one side of his neck to the other.

"I forgot to mention your voice sounds much better," Nel said.

A year earlier, Mainu could hardly speak above a whisper. He was still a bit hoarse, but no longer straining to get the words out. As close as they had grown over their letters, he never mentioned when or how he got maimed like this, and Nel didn't press the matter.

"Are you still treating it with elm and licorice?" she asked.

"Yes." Mainu scowled. "And I still despise the taste."

There was something endearing in his rare display of emotion. It might as well have come from one of her own brothers back home, when they had to take castor oil as children because they hadn't eaten their oatmeal.

A few more blocks went by, with only the rain beating at the coach windows and the occasional call from the driver. Mainu had tidied himself and now leaned back in his seat, observing the carts and people outside. They were headed to an address in the Upper Court District, a decent way from the station in central Montres. Against her efforts to stay composed, Nel's eyes kept darting round and round, from Mainu to the window to her lap, so much that it threatened to make her dizzy.

"I'm sorry I'm not better company right now," he said at last. "I do appreciate you coming out to meet me."

"It's nothing, really. I'm sure you must be tired. I know I

would be. I get exhausted from patrolling Ilvior." Nel let out an awkward little laugh.

Why couldn't she pull herself together for once?

"And I was happy to hear you'll be in New Montres again," she went on. "Do you know how long you're staying?"

"As long as I need. Until I find the person I was sent to find or have enough reason not to try."

"Are you tracking down another necromancer?" Nel asked in what she meant as a lighthearted tone, to mask her dread.

Mainu shook his head. "A woman from Midorea has gone missing. Her husband was expecting her to return from New Montres a few weeks ago, but she never showed and didn't give notice. So he came to us."

"Does the High Court always send its investigators to find missing persons abroad?"

"Formally, no. But when the missing person's husband is the head of the national bank, exceptions are made."

In a way, that was reassuring to hear. Midorea had a fabled reputation among the Ardonnese as a land of idyllic perfection, where no one wanted for anything and nothing ever went wrong. The fact that the country was so difficult to enter—both physically and legally—only fanned the fires of this speculation against the sobering reality of life in New Montres. Some part of Nel took a sense of satisfaction in knowing that courts everywhere had their own strings ready to be pulled by the right hands.

"I expect you'll be busy, then," she said. "I was hoping we'd have more time together, but I don't want to hinder you in your work."

"I had the same hope as well. And I imagine you'd be anything but a hindrance." Mainu faced her with an odd intensity.

Was he... *nervous?*

"Tomorrow morning, I must report to your head office, so they can assign a local officer of the guard to supervise me during my time here. I was going to visit you at Ilvior beforehand, but since you're here—would you mind if I asked for you?"

Nel's ears had failed her. That couldn't possibly be what he had said. Not him. Not here. Not about something like this.

She wanted to blurt out a thousand protests, but the only thing she managed was, "Me?"

"We've worked together before and succeeded in our task. As far as the goal of finding our suspect, anyway. And I don't think you'll have to endure anything similar to what happened then."

"No, but. . . I barely helped that time, and—" Nel stammered.

Yes, the two of them had worked together, but only because she had refused to follow proper procedure, stumbled into a case she had no business meddling in, and didn't have the good sense to admit that. Besides, that was only supposed to be a petty local crime.

"This sounds important," she said.

Mainu's reply was as straightforward as ever. "It is. That's why I want to work with someone I can trust." He leaned forward on his knees. "You don't know her, but this woman isn't merely a rich man's wife. She's one of the most beloved and talked about figures in high society. Her disappearance must be handled with great discretion. And I hope you won't take it as an insult, but the Ardonnese aren't typically known for being discreet."

No, that certainly wasn't an insult. Most officers who gained insight into the lives of the upper crust were known to readily sell their stories to the highest bidder, be that a reputable biographer or a two-bit rag. Since Ilvior Island was decidedly lacking in the wealthy and influential, Nel had never faced this temptation, nor did the idea appeal to her. Then again, she had never figured she would end up in pursuit of a necromancer, either.

The coach came to a stop, and the driver pulled aside the panel to announce they had arrived. Mainu leapt out and gathered his belongings, then paid the driver for the trip, as well as to take Nel home. She thanked him for the gesture, relieved that she wouldn't have to trudge through the flooded streets of the suburb.

"I would appreciate it if you'd consider," Mainu said through the open door. "Can I meet you at the guardhouse to discuss?"

Nel mustered a hesitant "Yes."

"Thank you. Good night, Nel."

"Good night." She pulled back into the coach, only to remember the one thing she'd meant to say from the very beginning. "Oh! And"—she swung the door back open—"Welcome back to the center of the world!"

It had sounded much better in her head.

Out in the pouring rain, on the corner of two side streets, in a district that directly bordered the countryside, Mainu shifted the bag around his shoulder. "Thank you. I've been looking forward to it."

A bell rang inside the building as he entered, and then he was gone.

Nel wasn't sure what she waited for as she sat there for another minute, one hand on the coach door, staring at the spot where Mainu had stood.  Whatever it was, it didn't happen. The driver eventually asked her if they could head off, and she wordlessly agreed.  A whip cracked up on the perch, and the wheels set in motion, taking her home to Ilvior where nothing ever happened.

# Chapter 3

The head office of the Messengers' Guild was, without a doubt, one of the most hideous buildings Thessa had ever laid eyes upon. Not because it was decrepit, nor was there any one specific feature that spoiled the view. Rather, it gave the impression that it had been designed by five different architects who each had a different idea of good taste and competed to present as much of it as possible. The reliefs above the entrance clashed with the fresco under the roof, which in turn was at a two-front war with the carved window frames and the gilded lettering. The facade as a whole was a battlefield of garishness, its disparate parts vying for attention like so many spoiled children.

And much like a spoiled child, it all seemed to openly mock Thessa—as if to say, *"I am an eyesore, and you're still glad to see me."* Because when she turned the corner with her horse and ambled down the street toward that colorful abomination, it meant her day of work was nearly over.

Puddles as black as tar patched the cobblestone road and splashed loudly under Snake Eyes' hooves, while he marched along at an unbothered pace. The old gelding arguably knew the Lower Court District better than Thessa, and he turned into the service alley before she steered him. The pair of them rounded the office to its rear end, which, while not any prettier, at least wasn't exhausting to look at.

Exhausting. That was a feeling Thessa had become closely acquainted with over the past months. Working as a messenger was the job of her dreams when she got it, but it was, in the end, a job. The hours were long, the letters never ran out, and no matter how quickly she delivered them, it was never quick enough. That same afternoon, one recipient had spent minutes berating Thessa, claiming he'd been awaiting his delivery for a whole week, though the stamp on the envelope stated that it was sent the day before. When she pointed that out, he only got angrier and threatened to cite her to court for forgery.

Such things used to upset her at first, especially when her superiors began trusting her with deliveries to the more notable offices around New Montres. Every bureaucrat, regardless of standing, was wholly convinced that their work was the only one in Ardonne that mattered, and they all made sure Thessa knew that. Their puffed-up, indignant faces were a permanent etching in her memory—but as the weeks and months went by, they all washed together into a blur, as gray and formless as the slush that drenched the streets.

Snake Eyes rested his foot in a puddle, and Thessa's boots landed next to it as they reached the stables. She led him inside by the reins, which she then handed over to the aging stablehand.

"Good evening," Thessa greeted him wearily.

"Evening." The man patted Snake Eyes on the neck, right above the two black spots on his otherwise pure white coat that served as his namesake. "You two are last in today."

"The roads are all wet!" Thessa jerked the strings of her

cloak loose. "He could have broken an ankle in some of these potholes. It's not my fault this rain won't let up."

The stablehand removed one of the stirrups and shuffled around to get the other one. "Didn't say it was. And it isn't mine, either."

Regret stung Thessa over snapping at him. He was right. Neither of them was to blame for this miserable weather, and it wasn't going to get better anytime soon.

"I'm sorry. It's been a long day."

Above the old man's ashy mustache, the corner of his eye wrinkled. "Then stop dallying here and go do your papers so you can end it."

Thessa bade him and Snake Eyes good night, then hurried up the stairs that led to the office floors. Like the man said, everyone had finished up and gone home already. The rows of empty desks had an odd stillness to them that hovered between serene and eerie. Despite no one being around to hear, Thessa was compelled to soften her steps. She chose one of the corner spots, lit the oil lamp, and settled in.

Doing the books at the end of the day always took longer than she wanted. Growing up in her noble father's household, she had received many a painful rap on the knuckles if her penmanship wasn't up to scratch, and that wasn't the sort of instinct that went away in mere months. Try as she might, she couldn't bring herself to write any quicker than she had as a lady, and so she would routinely spend a half hour or more completing a simple ledger.

Once the last of her deliveries were accounted for, she dropped off the pages in the appropriate drawer, and at long last headed downstairs to the front door. In a rare mercy, the rain had relented, and the clouds deigned to allow an occasional glimpse of the fading sun behind them.

A bell rang faintly from the left, and in the distance, a railcar inched into view between the rows of apartment houses. The slippery rails forced the driver to move at more of a snail's pace than usual. If she stretched her stride a little, Thessa could make it to the next stop in time to catch it. She started briskly down the block, turning back over her shoulder every so often to check on the car's progress. The stop was on an island of pavement in the middle of the road, a dozen or so yards away. All she needed was a brief gap in the slog of traffic, and she could make it across.

Right as she turned back, another bell sounded. This one did not come from a railcar or any other vehicle. It rang much closer from the opposite direction, and it was followed by a jeering chorus of voices.

"Boo! Boo to the guilds! Boo to the traitors!"

In her fixation on the approaching car, Thessa had missed the small but loud company that occupied the corner. It was a motley crew of all ages and sizes; the youngest one a boy of ten at most, the oldest possibly his grandfather. All of them were equipped with some sort of noisemaker, except for one. The tallest of the bunch, his body was mostly covered by a sign that hung around his neck and read, *"Guilds are traitors to the republic!"* He stood directly behind the bell's owner: a massive woman whose red face glowed in sharp contrast with the blue scarf that covered her hair.

Upon the sight, Thessa scanned the rest of the group, and her fear was confirmed. Every one of them, including the boy, sported some sort of blue cloth around their neck.

*Oh, no. Not here.*

Before she could be spotted, Thessa spun around and

pressed herself against the wall. She tended to travel to and from work in her uniform as a matter of convenience, but it had become more and more of a hazard. She unfolded her cloak as innocuously as possible, so that it may hide her tan jacket—and more so the embroidery of the winged pen that adorned it.

The bluebells were known for collecting guild emblems like trophies. And there were other stories. Those of her colleagues who were in contact with the other guilds—the drivers, the freighters, or the millers—had come with secondhand accounts of being accosted on the street, dragged through the mud, or chased with clubs in broad daylight.

Thessa had heard enough gossip to recognize a tall tale, but some of those tales had made it into the town bulletin, and that made them much harder to ignore. Not to mention she had also encountered bluebells while delivering letters. Those times, she was on horseback in the midst of traffic, so they could do little other than shout at her from the corners. But she was on foot now.

Clutching the front of her cloak with both hands from the inside, Thessa peered out from behind her cover. It was one of the decorative pillars that lined the front of the guild office, carved into the majestic form of a messenger holding a scroll aloft. By the figure's heels was an eagerly alert hound, which had always struck Thessa as one of the most ostentatious details. Now she was huddled up next to it, directly at eye level with the animal that mocked her all the more. *"I am an eyesore, and you're still glad to see me."*

The railcar rang again. Unless she wanted to spend the next half hour waiting, Thessa had to go. She checked to make sure her uniform didn't show, then moved to pass the group.

She shouldn't be this afraid. They wouldn't dare hurt her. But if they tried—

Keeping her head down, she left the pillar and walked on as if the group wasn't there. Not an easy act, since they took up the entire pavement. The woman in particular was almost impossible to avoid, both with her size and the breadth of her movements as she flailed about. Thessa balanced on the curb, having to step off onto the road with one foot to squeeze by.

Could they shove her under a cart if they found her out? No, surely not. They couldn't go that far. Right. . . ?

"Girl! You there!"

The woman's voice struck her like lightning. Thessa's lungs seized up, and her muscles refused to move. Should she turn around? Should she run? She had to do *something*. If she turned around, she might expose herself. If she ran, they might follow.

She turned around. Most of the group stared at her with blank faces, except for their leader, who stepped closer.

"Mind your step, will you? You nearly threw yourself under a wheel right there." She waved her bell to indicate the line of wagons trundling by.

Like a little girl reprimanded by her teacher, Thessa pulled herself up on the pavement on instinct. The tall man and the boy sidled out of the way to make room for her.

"Sorry," Thessa said. "I'm trying to catch the railcar." She indicated the tracks with her chin, not daring to point while her fingers held on to the cloak.

"A sorry lot of good that'll do you if you get your brains trampled out." The woman reached into one of the many folds on her dress. "Here. If you're going up the line, then you have some time to read this."

Never had a single sheet of paper been such an open threat to Thessa. The woman extended it with a gesture of authority that she couldn't simply refuse. Pretending to shiver in the autumn chill, Thessa pulled her cloak as far to the right as she could, so that it covered her guild emblem, and she gingerly stuck her hand out to take the leaflet.

The crudely printed letters had smudged further in the damp air, but the words were legible. *"Guild prefects are lapdogs of the aristocracy!"*

"They voted against the republic, and you know damn well they'll vote against common rights, too!" The woman poked a swollen finger at the writing. "Boot-licking imperialists, the sorry lot of them. They'll kick the rest of us out in the cold, just to keep themselves close to the fire. Read it; it's all there."

Thessa withdrew her hand, looking from one face to another if any more of them had something to say. No one in the group paid her any mind. The woman told the boy to get his finger out of his nose, then took up her place at the center and resumed her ringing at a passing rent-coach.

As if nothing had happened.

Thessa turned on her heels and half-ran to the railcar stop, hands clutched before her chest, and the cheap paper rustling against her guild uniform with each step.

# Chapter 4

The autumn season put an end to much of the life on the streets of New Montres. Gone were the parasols that had sprouted outside the inns like glades of giant mushrooms. With them went the lutists who'd weave between the tables, crooning impassioned ballads to the couples there in hopes of an iron bit or two. The Ryonne was no longer dotted with colorful outing boats, nor did the avenues ring with the laughter of bright companies going by in open carriages. The city had shut its windows and barricaded itself in anticipation of the approaching winter.

All except for one street. On the Street of Canopies, summer lasted forever.

Ida loosened her shawl and let it fall off of her shoulders. Despite the chill that swept the rest of the city, her skin glistened with sweat. In the middle of the road stood a row of iron cages, each as tall as a grown man, their thick bars multiplying the heat of a roaring bonfire inside. The flames joined with the light pouring from the wide open doors, and together they turned night into day under the painted canvas sky that stretched between the buildings. The air was heavy with the damp breath of indulgence, as each salon and dance hall gaped with the promise of warm drinks and warmer hands.

Try as they might, Ida wouldn't yield to their temptation tonight. She too was headed to a place of revelry, but not one as open and welcoming. Her goal lay one step behind the colorful fronts—one turn off of the well-known road. And she had to make sure the young man beside her made it there safely.

Mendel had insisted on leaving the carriage behind at the crossroads and walking the rest of the way, so they could take in the sights of the street. Ida would have preferred to go as far as they could under cover, and only breach their privacy where they could vanish between the houses at once. However, the rules were clear: the needs of the customer came first. They were far from the Garden of Lilies, but Ida knew better than to risk the goodwill of her employer.

"Did you know every one of these was once the sail of a ship sunk by the Ardonnese fleet?" Mendel pointed to the canopies fifteen feet above. "When the sun's out, you can make out the coat of arms on some of them."

He spoke with such pride as if he had personally led that fleet into battle, although he was born half a decade after Ardonne had last been in a conflict. His outfit matched his demeanor, including a blue jacket trimmed with red string detail reminiscent of a captain's uniform—except his was made of finer materials than any naval officer could afford.

Ida humored him and followed his gaze, but only briefly. "I'd rather keep my eyes ahead, dear. We wouldn't want to knock into some unsavory types and spoil our evening with a brawl."

It was a passable excuse. The time of day never affected how many people milled about on the Street of Canopies, only how drunk they were. By now, there were more than enough louts out there angling for trouble, and Ida wanted them to find it elsewhere.

More than that, she had to be sure they weren't being followed or getting any other unwanted attention. Not an easy task, since the pair of them already attracted a fair amount of it simply by standing next to each other. Mendel took notice, too, once he had his fill of admiring the war trophies overhead.

"I wonder what some of them are thinking," he muttered to Ida, pulling her closer by their locked arms.

She patted his hand and leaned in. "They're thinking, 'Who is the dashing young man sweeping away that fabulously lucky girl?'"

It was, of course, a lie—and not merely because Mendel was as plain as they came. He had the light olive skin of the Ardonnese and was clad in a respectable velvet coat. Next to him, passersby only needed to notice Ida's dark brown complexion, the silken veil that covered the lower half of her face, or her deep-cut emerald dress, and they got plenty of ideas what the two of them were up to. Some of those ideas weren't wrong.

*Let them think what they want.* Ida kept her mind where it mattered. One block later, refuge found them at last.

Not only was the alley narrow and unremarkable, but closed off with a boarded gate, rendering it invisible save for those who knew it was there. Ida drew Mendel's attention to it and brought the two of them to a stop, waiting for an opportunity to disappear. A carriage approached from behind, making its way among the crowd one foot at a time. Once it fully blocked them from view, she tugged on Mendel's arm, and the two of them ducked between the buildings.

The noises of the street cut off like water from a shut tap. The darkness was so thick it pressed back against the palm of Ida's outstretched hand. She led Mendel behind her, as there was only enough room for one person to creep through. To his credit, the young noble showed no sign of regret or distaste, but instead followed diligently in her steps, turning where she instructed him through a silent pull or squeeze of the hand.

For a minute or so, they wound through the passages, until they emerged into a small open space. To call it a yard would have been overly generous; some ten-by-ten feet of unpaved ground, surrounded on all four sides by windowless walls. One of these belonged to a tower that rose to breakneck heights above its surroundings, stabbing the cloudy night sky like a dagger coated in ink.

"Is that The Belfry?" Mendel's whisper was hardly above a breath, but quivered with excitement.

"The one and only." Ida went up to the unmarked door at the tower's base, grabbed the heavy knocker, and gave the week's code: two knocks, then three, then one.

The echo of the final hit lingered between the walls, and only when it died out did a patch of light slide open in the wood before her. There was no face in the peephole, nor did a voice come from behind it.

"Good evening," Ida said. "Ida Nawoale with a guest. Approved."

A rustle of paper, followed by a terse, "Name?"

Ida stepped aside to make room for Mendel.

He leaned in close to the hole. "Mendel Scolsessi. *Lord* Mendel Scolsessi," he hastily added, while shifting side to side, as if trying to find the best angle for the doorkeeper to get a clear sight of him.

Ida smiled to herself, knowing full well that the person whose job it was to keep an eye on visitors had been watching them since before she touched the knocker. She waited for them to give the signal inside, upon which the door creaked open. Mendel jumped slightly at the sound and took Ida's arm, eager to enter the world he'd been aching to see since they first met.

He would have to wait a little longer, as their path first led them up flight after flight of stairs. They had to leave behind the bottom two stories, which housed the tavern that served as a public front. Above those came the attic space, which separated the guests of the lower floors from those they unwittingly covered for. The cramped stairwell seemed to stretch endlessly into the distance above, but after the sixth sharp turn, they reached a brightly lit landing with an arched doorway. Music seeped from behind the thick red curtain while they caught their breaths and straightened themselves out. Ida drew aside the heavy fabric, and at last, they stepped inside The Belfry.

A few of the patrons inside took note of them, not unlike those on the street below—but in here, most of the curious eyes fell on Mendel. It was only until they noticed Ida by his side, at which point they returned to their drinks and conversations unbothered. No one addressed them in any way, leaving Mendel plenty of time to take in the sight and come to the inevitable conclusion.

"It's. . . a tavern," he said with a confused laugh.

Ida laughed with him. "What did you expect?" She let go of his arm and wrapped the shawl around her shoulders again.

"Come, let's get you a drink."

They crossed the floor to the bar, passing between the tables and the companies huddled around them. In the flickering light of the lamps that hung from the low ceiling, Ida caught a handful of familiar faces and waved discreetly at those who noticed her. She rested on one of the vacant seats by the counter, close to the makeshift stage, where a plump Sallician man and his half-clad sons played a variety of flutes.

"Evening, Ida," the bartender greeted her. His voice was muffled by the folded-over scarf that covered his nose and mouth, similar to Ida's veil. "How's life treating you?"

"As good as I can hope," Ida replied. "How are you, Kolos?"

"Much the same. I was told you're bringing someone up tonight. Mendel, is it?" he directed the question at the young man, who had now caught up and positioned himself next to Ida at the bar.

"Yes, that's right. Mendel Scolsessi." Despite outranking everyone in the place, Mendel's answer was as timid as a schoolboy being called up to the front. It was hard to blame him. Kolos filled the entire height of the room, his tattooed head mere inches from grazing the beams. That head sat atop a pair of shoulders as wide as a barge, which continued in arms that could choke an ox on each side.

He rested ten leaden knuckles on the bar. "What'll it be, then?"

Mendel turned to Ida, who answered in his stead, "Cane brandy will do tonight, Kolos. Laerithian."

The barman sized up the young lord. "Can he handle it?"

"I'm sure he can. It's only for a short while."

Without further comment, Kolos took a wicker bottle from the second highest shelf and poured out two fingers of the rich amber liquid. From the color alone, Ida could tell it was laden with myriad spices. She had known that scent all too well. It was the scent of long summer sunsets under the manjack trees behind the old house, of young love, and her last days of innocence. That scent was a distant memory now, if not a dream altogether.

Mendel paid for the drink and wafted it under his nose, upon which he immediately burst into a cough. "It's potent; that's for certain," he said, with one hand over his mouth.

"I should hope so. I'd hate for your money to go to waste," Ida teased. "Shall we go find a seat upstairs?"

A wooden staircase stood in the far corner of the barroom, separate from the one that led them up here. It was covered in a thick rug, as was all the floor beyond, to absorb the noise of footsteps and keep the upper half of the establishment as quiet as possible. Instead of tables, this area had an arrangement of soft benches in the center, as well as a ring of booths around the perimeter. Each booth was fitted with its own curtain, much like the one that covered the entrance. Several of them were drawn.

Mendel's eyes went wide. This was clearly more in line with what he had pictured. He glanced cautiously at the stairs behind himself, then leaned into Ida's ear. "That barman—is he also one of the 'unlucky' ones?"

"Kolos?" Ida asked back, taking a seat in a booth. "No, he got better off than me. The scarf is there to protect his nose. All that wine and brandy he has to pour would knock him out in a minute."

The young man took the seat next to her and set down his drink. "He didn't lose his sense of smell like you?"

"He did. But what you can't smell can still affect you." Ida gestured at the liquor. "One sniff of that would make me dizzy, if not sick outright."

"Oh." Mendel put his hand over the glass. "I better keep this away from you, then."

"Or better yet—" Ida raised an eyebrow.

It took him a moment.

"Right!" Mendel chuckled off his embarrassment and toasted her. "To health!" He downed the spiced spirit in one gulp and made a valiant effort to contain himself this time. His eyes welled up, his forehead twisted into a dozen creases, and each corner of his mouth deepened into a stiff trench, but he did not cough.

Ida caressed his arm. "Give it a few minutes. You'll know when it's taken effect. Until then, we can have a nice talk like any couple out for a drink."

"Yes, certainly." He put one hand on her arm as well. "How's Forley?"

"I should be asking you that. Given how you likely see more of him than I do nowadays." Ida sighed with exaggerated jealousy, enough to make Mendel believe she meant it as a joke.

"Only in passing. I can't speak with everyone every time I'm at the tannery. But the foremen say he's nothing if not an exemplary worker."

"About time. I told him when he moved out, if he was going to play grown-up, he'd better start acting the part, too."

Ida had also played a number of parts over the years in her trade, and she had gotten very good at them. At the drop of a hat, she could be a wilting wallflower, a smoldering seductress, a mischievous minx, or whatever she had to be for whoever's pleasure. More recently, she had been forced to take on a role she was much less comfortable with: the unyielding parent.

Forley had been a handful his whole life, and worse yet, he was razor sharp. He knew that, while Ida would chastise him if he got into trouble, she could never truly blame him for any of it. It was nothing but a miraculous stroke of luck that the boy also had a heart of pure gold, otherwise he'd already be in prison, or worse. After what fate had put the two of them through, it was almost expected.

But he was alive, and so was Ida. And though fate had not been kind, it let them come safely to New Montres, where Ida found a good job at a good house—and a good client. Too good to lose over her son's misbehavior.

"Now, enough about me and my silly boy." She caressed Mendel's soft face. "How have you been keeping? You've only come to see me once this past week. I hope you're not getting bored with me."

The young man's cheeks glowed red, perhaps from the Laerithian spirit, perhaps from something else. "Bored? No, never. I—I could never get bored with you. It's just been terribly busy. That's why I can't speak to everyone as much as I'd like. I'm always being rushed to—to this supplier, or that reseller, or somewhere." His hand punctuated the sentence with broad movements. "I'm still learning how to do it all. Sometimes it gets overwhelming." He rolled his glass around and watched the few drops of brandy that had stuck to the bottom.

Ida weaved her fingers between his. "Then I'm all the more honored that you make time for me at the Garden, and that you'd come all the way here."

As if he'd only remembered where they were, Mendel's eyes swept over the room around them. Most of the booths had their curtains drawn, and the couples on the benches were locked in embraces.

His eyes briefly fluttered, and he let out an exhilarated breath. "It's hotter than I expected."

"I told you, you'll know when the drink takes effect." Ida stood from the cushioned seat and closed off their own booth.

The only light now came from the candle at the middle of the table. The dancing flame was tinted red by the glass dome over it, and it glistened in the beads of sweat that sprinkled Mendel's forehead.

"Should I loosen my collar?" His voice trembled, the way it always did when they closed the doors behind them.

Ida picked up his hand and slowly drew back the sleeve of the blue naval jacket. "Not tonight. What will they say of a respectable young man, showing up at this supplier or that reseller with a stain on his neck?"

He took her word, the way he always did. His face faded into darkness as he leaned back, leaving only two pinpricks of white where his eyes reflected the candle—until he closed them, and those were gone as well. His breathing smoothed out, and he licked his lips with a faint wet smack.

For a few heartbeats, Ida allowed herself to relish the throbbing of Mendel's wrist under her fingertips. Making sure none of the light fell on her face, she lifted her veil and gave his hand a series of slow kisses. The sinews in his forearm twitched in excitement, pressing his veins harder against her tongue.

After teasing both of them for so long, she bared her fangs and sunk them into that tender, olive skin. Ida's nose filled with the only scent she could smell for over fifteen years, and with each mouthful of Mendel's blood, she took in that spicy-sweet flavor of long sunsets and days of innocence.

# II

# Part Two

# Chapter 5

No matter how long she lived there, Nel would never be at home in New Montres. The crowds made the broad streets cramped and the narrow ones impenetrable. The high roofs blocked out the sky, the noise of traffic covered any vestige of natural sound, and the smell of soot and sewage permeated the very bricks of the tightly-packed houses. Ilvior Island was one of the precious few boroughs Nel could tolerate, with its sleepy pace much more in line with the village where she grew up. Now, as she made her way along the slope of Solluri Hill, she had to admit there was such a thing as too quiet.

After he settled into his accommodation, Mainu spent an entire day running back and forth between various offices, squaring away the approvals necessary for him to conduct his work. It was close to sundown when he showed up at Nel's guardhouse, armed with a stack of papers about the missing person. Taëminn Vei Ruola, aged forty-two, married to Yanne Vei Ruola, with whom she shared a house in the Midorean capital of Namahil. Regularly spent longer stretches of time in New Montres, to the extent that she had a permanent residence on the east side of Solluri Hill.

Considering her husband was the head of the Midorean

national bank, it was to be expected that Vei Ruola's home away from home would be in one of the most exclusive districts of the city. Of the four hills that rose north of the Ryonne, Solluri lay furthest upstream and thus enjoyed both the cleanest water and clearest view. A single paved road wound up toward the crest, lined with houses that grew in size and shrunk in frequency the further away from sea level they got. Big or small, all of them exuded an intimidating degree of wealth. Regardless of her city guard uniform, Nel couldn't shake the suspicion that the residents of the hill regarded her as an intruder.

Whether that was true she could only speculate, because not one of those residents was out on the street. To a degree, Nel understood that the weather urged most to stay inside, especially those who could afford not to leave their heated room for days at a time. But Solluri Hill was so mute, it might as well have been abandoned. Every so often, Nel ventured a glance at one of the spotless windows but saw only gray reflections of the sky, as if the houses knowingly shrouded their insides from her in contempt. Against all odds, Nel found herself missing the tumult of those crowded streets she had spent years staying away from.

After half an hour in this unwelcoming atmosphere, any human voice would have been a relief. To hear Mainu's soft "Good morning" as she reached her destination was an outright blessing.

Vei Ruola didn't have an estate all to herself; her residence was in one of the few apartment houses that were found here, halfway up the hill. Four stories tall, with a warm maroon facade and tasteful plaster accents. While the front garden was mostly bare in this season, it was nonetheless immaculately maintained and had a raked gravel pathway leading to the lacquered double doors.

Mainu stood at the street end of this path. Clad in his simple but flawlessly tailored green uniform, he fit in with the opulent surroundings better than Nel ever would. In one hand, he held a leather saddlebag, while the other one pulled out an ancient-looking watch.

"Good morning," Nel said back. "Sorry I'm late—I'm not familiar in this area."

"You're almost ten minutes early." Mainu tilted the face of the watch toward her.

It didn't sound like he was admonishing her, nor would it have made sense for him to do so. But when she was around Mainu, nothing Nel said or did felt adequate.

"Shall we?" She gestured toward the entrance in an attempt to gain some semblance of control.

They were there to question the caretaker and perhaps some neighbors about Vei Ruola and when they'd last seen her. Standard procedure for any missing persons investigation. Nel had done it dozens of times before and was eager to get back into routine. As long as she was in routine, nothing could rattle her.

"I haven't congratulated you on your promotion yet." Mainu pulled the bellstring and nodded at the additional bronze studs above Nel's badge.

"It's more of an honorary title than anything." Nel straightened her hair repeatedly. "Most of the time I just do whatever Captain Pomeno doesn't feel like doing."

"Hm." Mainu turned away from her to face the door, as a series of slow footsteps approached behind it. "Sounds more than honorary to me."

"What do you mean?"

"I don't know how these things work in Ardonne," Mainu told the door, "but where I'm from, that's usually how captains train up their successors."

Nel didn't grasp his meaning at first. When she did, her cheeks ran hot. "What do you—"

Her question was cut off by the loud clank of the brass handle. One half of the door opened by a foot to reveal the most elegantly dressed caretaker Nel had ever seen. His hair was combed and slicked with more care than most twenty-year-old heartthrobs, despite being as white as his perfectly starched shirt. The maroon trousers and tunic almost gave the impression that he was a part of the building itself.

Between the stark forehead and clean-shaven cheeks, a pair of bright blue eyes blinked at them, before he uttered a simple, "Yes?"

Thoroughly rattled from Mainu's words, Nel pulled herself to attention. "Good morning, sir. I'm Cap—I'm Sergeant Nella Dormanni from the city guard, and this is Lieutenant Investigator Mainu Eph Daëlin from the Midorean High Court."

The man sized up the two of them while she spoke, and his face changed before Nel finished her introduction. "Oh, dear. I take it this is about the lady Vei Ruola?"

"It is," Mainu replied. "May we come in?"

"Yes, please, by all means. This way. We can sit down in my day chamber if that suits you." The caretaker bowed and move away from the door. Across the marbled hall, he led them into the ground floor apartment. "Can I offer you some blackberry tea? I had one myself a minute ago, so the water should still be hot."

"That sounds lovely," Nel said, rubbing the autumn chill out of her fingers.

With another bow, the man bade them to take a seat, then set about to fetch the cups and kettle.

The interior was nothing like Nel had imagined from the outside—if anything, it reminded her of being back home. A circular fireplace stood where the walls of the kitchen, bath, and day chamber met, with sliding metal doors on the side so it could be accessed from each room. Instead of the more fashionable paper, the walls were painted with motifs of fruits and game, and various stuffed animal heads hung from trophy boards.

Across from Nel, Mainu also surveyed their surroundings, but it was hard to tell what impression they had on him. Neither of them spoke until their host emerged from the kitchen, carrying a tray laden with cups and jars.

"May I ask your name, sir?" Nel asked over the gentle rattle of the ceramics.

"Bornessi. Romer Bornessi," the man replied, while he arranged the jars of rock sugar, raisins, and honey.

Mainu took the latter and applied a generous amount to his own cup. "Are you the caretaker of this house?"

"Yes and no." Bornessi poured steaming hot water over the bed of dried fruits and herbs in their cups. "By title, I am the landlord. This house belonged to my late wife's family, you see. I myself am from common stock, you might say, but her parents were titled. We got the house as dowry when we got married, and when she passed some years ago, I became lord by inheritance. But I need to keep myself busy, so I live here and tend to our respected tenants."

He gestured around himself, then joined them at the table.

Mainu raised the tea to his lips. "You might say, then, that your lordship is more of an honorary title?"

The question took Bornessi off guard, but not by offense. "Yes, I suppose you might say that."

As usual, Mainu was hard to read. But when his eyes met Nel's over the rim of the cup, she was convinced he was hiding a grin.

"Well, Lord Bornessi"—Nel cleared her throat—"as you mentioned, we are here to ask about Taëminn Vei Ruola. Were you aware that she's been missing?"

The man clasped his hands over the table, as if to support himself against the burden of his thoughts. "I've had an inkling that something wasn't right. But I couldn't know for certain."

"Why, and why not?" Mainu asked.

"I'm not sure if you know about her living arrangements." Bornessi gestured again, this time above him. "Her husband is a high-ranking official in Midorea, but the lady likes to spend four to six months each year in Ardonne. She usually arrives in the first week of spring, right after the new year, then returns home in late summer or early fall."

"That's what she was supposed to do," Mainu said. "Her husband was expecting her to return weeks ago, but she never arrived in Midorea."

Nel asked, "If this is the time she'd normally leave, why did you think anything was wrong?"

Bornessi did not delay with the answer. "The lady has lived here for years, and I've come to know her as an exceptionally organized woman. She would give me several weeks' notice before she left, even if it was for a few days on a summer trip, so that if any guests came in her absence, I could let them know when to expect her back."

"And she gave no such notice now," Mainu concluded.

The man shook his head. "A pair of visitors came one day. I took them upstairs to the lady's apartment, but she wouldn't answer her door for minutes. I was forced to send them home with no explanation. Afterward, I talked to the drivers out back, and it turned out they hadn't seen her driver in two days." He motioned toward the back of the building, where the service wing and the stables stood.

Setting her cup aside, Nel produced a notebook and pencil. "When did this happen?"

Bornessi's eyebrows furrowed into a single white streak across his forehead. "On the third to the Full, I think. Maybe the fourth. Not later than Past Wax, because that was when the rain started, and this was a clear day."

It was a rare occasion when Mainu exhibited anything but collected confidence, but like most foreigners, the intricacies of the Ardonnese calendar seemed to have bested him. "How long ago was that?"

Nel and the landlord counted back to the dates mentioned, accounting for the varying lengths of weeks and the additional days of cardinal months, until they settled on a total of no more than seventeen days since the visit. Nel noted everything down, while Mainu proceeded with the questions.

"Did Vei Ruola get visitors often?"

"Oh, most certainly." Bornessi refilled their cups and took a raisin for himself. "Two, three times a week—more during the summer."

"What kinds of visitors did she get?"

For the first time since Nel and Mainu arrived, the landlord showed something akin to amusement. "I daresay it would be easier to ask what kind she *didn't* get."

"All right," Mainu said. "Then what kind of visitors didn't she get?"

Bornessi had evidently not expected to be taken up on his rhetorical suggestion, but to his credit, he accepted the challenge. "Ordinary ones, I suppose. The lady is something of a patron of the arts, you see. She would often invite some ambitious young painter or playwright, as well as one of her well-to-do friends, and convince the latter to patronize the former. So, as you can expect, there have been all sorts up and down here, from all walks of life and corners of the world."

Nel scraped away with her pencil. A woman of means, living alone and far away from her husband, entertaining a wide variety of guests. It didn't take much else for a theory to start forming in her head. "Did any one of these guests come more often than others? A younger man, perhaps?" she asked, in the hopes of jogging the landlord's memory.

He drummed on the side of his cup. "None that stood out to me. Some visitors were fairly regular, but those were her older friends."

"What about your other tenants?" Mainu chimed in. "When someone is as sociable as Vei Ruola, one would think some of her neighbors should notice her sudden absence."

The question put a damper on the landlord's talkativeness. His fingers curled back under his wrinkled palms, while he weighed his next words.

"The lady may be popular in artistic circles, but. . . perhaps less so with the rest of the house." He paused, seemingly waiting for Nel or Mainu to interject. When neither of them did, he reluctantly went on. "Two of the other tenants have voiced their displeasure with some of the company she's been keeping."

"Were the visitors unruly or threatening?" Nel asked.

"Not as such. But the tenants stressed that they don't wish to see any"—the landlord stiffened his lip—"blue scarves in the house."

Nel stopped writing. "Bluebells, you mean?"

Bornessi gave the faintest twitch of the head in confirmation, as if the mere act of acknowledging their existence would cause a horde of them to break down the door.

"I'm sorry—'bluebells?'" Once again, Mainu sought Nel's aid, but this time, she was much less prepared to give it.

"They're called that because they wear blue scarves as a sort of uniform, and they're often seen ringing bells on street corners. They preach for common rights and the abolition of nobility." While she didn't share the same level of discomfort as Bornessi, she also wasn't thrilled at the idea of the issue becoming a part of their investigation. "They've given us a lot of trouble recently. Disturbing the peace, harassing guild workers, starting fights—that sort of thing."

Mainu caught up. "I imagine they'd be unwelcome in a neighborhood like this."

The landlord raised his pointed chin. "They are. And I've said as much to the lady Vei Ruola as well. She has the right to pick her friends, naturally, but I made it clear to her that I will never allow such rabble in my house."

* * *

After the questioning, Bornessi led them up to Vei Ruola's apartment on the second floor. Having seen the difference between the building's elegant exterior and the landlord's old-fashioned home, Nel wasn't sure what to expect. Once the door opened and they stepped inside, she only knew she would have been wrong either way.

Vei Ruola, for all intents and purposes, lived in an art gallery. The walls had been turned into mosaics of paintings; some of them could fit in Nel's hand, while others were taller than her whole frame. A variety of instruments stood in graceful holders, and there even was something of a stage, complete with a velvet stool and a rack for sheet music. Most curiously, one corner of the room was decorated with over a dozen portraits of the same woman. As Bornessi explained, that woman was Vei Ruola herself, who would gladly model for any up-and-coming painter and show off the completed work to her affluent associates.

The one facet of the apartment Nel had correctly predicted was its unbridled and unabashed luxury. Everything her gaze fell on was gilded, polished, framed in ebony, or upholstered in velvet. Quartz lights glowed under iridescent stained glass domes, and the reddish glow of a two-foot crystal in the fireplace warmed the air.

"Did Vei Ruola have staff?" Mainu asked Bornessi as he showed them around. "Anyone we could talk to?"

"Like I mentioned, she had her own driver while she was here. I believe he spends the winters working in the country." The landlord dogged their every step around the apartment like they might try to steal something. "She had a maid come up daily to cook and clean for her, but no live-in servants."

Nel checked her notes as well. "You said that, by the time the visitors came, Vei Ruola's driver had supposedly been gone for two days. Didn't the maid come up during that time?"

"I didn't see her," Bornessi replied. "But most days she uses the back entrance, so she might easily have come by without me knowing."

"Can you tell us the maid's name or where we might find her?" Mainu asked.

"Yes, I should have it in my books downstairs."

"Excellent," Mainu said. "If you can copy it down, we'll pick it up from you on our way out."

The landlord picked up on the hint and shuffled out of the apartment, leaving Nel and Mainu to continue their search alone and uninterrupted. They divided up the rooms simply by which side of the day chamber they were on: Mainu took the kitchen, bath, and dining hall on the right, while Nel got the quarters and alcove on the left.

The first one she checked was the smaller of the two bedrooms, which must have been reserved for staying guests. There was a certain air to rooms that went unused for a long time, from the faintly musty smell of bedsheets to the uncannily perfect order of furnishings that no one had touched for months. If Nel hadn't known about Vei Ruola's sociable nature from the landlord, she would have imagined her a hermit from the guest room alone.

Across the narrow hall, the master bedroom painted a different picture. While it was as tidy as the other, it had much more of a lived-in quality—still, little in the way of clues about its owner's disappearance. The wardrobe beside the four-poster bed held an assortment of clothes, all of them fine, but nothing unusual. The book on the nightstand had a bookmark in it; the title was in Midorean, but the occasional illustrations on the inside hinted at a story of romance. A series of other volumes lined the shelf by the window, and the ones in Ardonnese confirmed the lady's passion for music and theater.

Nel was halfway through the chest of drawers when Mainu entered. "Did you find anything noteworthy?"

"Nothing that tells us anything we don't already know." She shut one drawer and opened the next. "How about you?"

"Only this. It was on the writing desk." He passed an envelope to Nel and went over to the wardrobe.

*"Dear Morna, Your service will no longer be needed this year. Please find the payment for the rest of the month inside,"* Nel read the message on the front out loud. "So she definitely left on her own accord, if she had the forethought to pay the maid."

"Seems like it. Did this strike you as odd?" Mainu pointed at the perfectly ordinary rail that held the row of perfectly ordinary clothes hangers.

"In what way?"

He pointed at the right half. "All the empty hangers are lined up here, but there are a few strewn in between the clothes. If she packed in a hurry, she might have grabbed some dresses without bothering to move the hangers to their place."

"Maybe it was Morna's job to keep the wardrobe in order."

"Maybe." Mainu continued his search by perusing the books on the shelf.

Meanwhile, Nel reached the top drawer. As was typical in a woman's bedroom, this one held Vei Ruola's stockings, laces, and other undergarments—nothing interesting, as expected. But before she pushed it back in, something struck her. Perhaps it was only Mainu's suspicion rubbing off on her, but her eyes were drawn to a conspicuously empty spot at the drawer's back corner.

"What is it?" Mainu asked.

"I don't know if it means anything." Nel indicated the array of rolled-up cotton strips, some of which were noticeably missing. "But it appears she took her sanitary cloths, too."

When Mainu responded with expectant silence, she elaborated, "Which might mean that she planned to be away for. . . a month or longer."

Much like when she sensed Mainu's hidden grin by Bornessi's table, Nel now picked up the slightest shadow of embarrassment, as the meaning of her words settled in his mind.

He turned to the window, arms crossed. "She packs for a month, but does so in a hurry. She remembers to pay the maid, but doesn't give the landlord notice. What does that all tell you?"

Nel ventured the answer that had been on her mind since they sat down to tea. "Captain Pomeno always tells us that if we hear hoofbeats, we should think of horses before zebras."

"A reasonable principle." Mainu scratched his chin. "What's your horse, then?"

"When someone's spouse disappears and does so willingly, there's usually a third person involved."

"The younger man you asked Bornessi about?"

"Given the life she led, it's the most obvious explanation."

"I suppose."

They walked back into the day chamber and continued to the writing desk. It was as spotless and orderly as the rest of the apartment, with all the pens neatly stacked in their holders and the inkwells corked. Mainu crouched beside the cabinet that made up the left half of the desk. After a brief examination of the lock, he took out a piece of wire, bent it in a few places, and two clicks later, the cabinet was wide open.

Nel leaned over, while Mainu pulled out a stack of letters from inside. They were all in the same handwriting, which was different from the message on the envelope, but beyond that, the foreign words meant nothing to her. As she turned her head to get a better angle, an enticing scent wafted into her nose. It came from Mainu's hair.

"Are these from our horse?" she asked, pretending to rub her face.

Mainu flipped through a few pages and shook his head. "They're from her husband. And if their content is to be believed, it sounds like their marriage was more than satisfying." He put the papers back inside. "Although that doesn't rule out anything."

Nel straightened herself with a twinge of disappointment and ambled to the middle of the room. If only it had been that easy. "Where to from here?"

Mainu joined her. "We can ask the neighbors and the maid once we get her address from Bornessi. Vei Ruola's husband also gave me a list of her friends who knew her better; perhaps they can offer some details. It's not a lot, but it's a start."

Nel followed along. Yes, that all sounded about right. Question the friends and neighbors, ask about new acquaintances the lady had made, and eventually track down the one person whom she told about her plan—as they always did.

The front door closed behind them, and Nel proceeded down the staircase with relieved steps. She really shouldn't have worried so much. Rich or poor, Midorean or Ardonnese, this would only be one more routine case.

# Chapter 6

Ida liked to believe that all curses had the seeds of a blessing. She would've had little hope of surviving the last seventeen years otherwise, after she made a mistake that led to her losing the second most important man in her life. But less than nine months later, in a windowless cabin aboard a ship from Laerithia to Ardonne, that same mistake allowed her to meet the most important man she would ever know. Ida couldn't imagine a greater fortune than that.

However, when blessings and curses were two sides of the same coin, they could easily flip the other way. As Ida took her son in her arms after seven hours of labor, she resolved not to let anything come between the two of them, and it was that resolve which led to her next great mistake. When the idea of losing her youth made her fear for her and Forley's livelihoods, she accepted what she believed to be the offer of a lifetime. She had been warned of the possible consequences, but she took the chance—and lost. And while the tides of time had worn away the regret over her infidelity, this misstep greeted her in the mirror each morning, until she put on the veil to cover the beastly rows of malformed teeth that resulted from her being turned.

Still, if she hadn't ended up so hideously disfigured, she

might never have been employed at the Garden of Lilies, whose owner was the only person willing to give her a job. Had she not worked at the Garden, she wouldn't have met Mendel, who in turn was willing to give her son a job. As long as Forley's future was safe, no price was too hard to pay.

And yet, in the end, the one to separate Ida from her son was Forley himself, when he waited until she wasn't looking and suddenly grew up. He moved out of the small room Ida had rented for him near the Garden, and he shacked up with some other young men of his age halfway across the city. Now, if Ida wanted to see him, she had to visit him at his place of work during the midday break, instead of dropping by whenever she wanted.

Winding her way along the wet and cramped streets of the Brewer District, Ida had to appreciate another one of her many disguised blessings. She never used to like the smell of either yeast or hops, both of which dominated the air around here—or so she was told. Being unable to smell or taste anything besides human blood had an occasional upside, especially as Ida neared her goal.

The low, flat building stood on the corner of two major streets. The longer side was almost entirely solid, while the shorter side featured the main entrance. Painted above it, under layers of dust that caked the formerly red bricks, was a curved banner emblazoned with the name of Scolsessi.

Ida walked past the gate and toward the service alley, where most of the double-shift workers spent their break milling about. One group was clumped around a table erected near one of the side doors. Four of them sat on stools that hobbled on the bumpy cobblestone pavement, while the rest of the men provided tips and encouragement in their game of cards.

"Excuse me, sirs!" Ida called out over the excited chatter.

All eyes turned to her, some with a hint of recognition. One of the players rose from his seat and removed his cap with a bow.

"I have come to seek audience with the young gentleman in the back," Ida went on. "If you could be so kind as to announce my presence, so that I may have a word with him?"

"*Maaa!*" Forley's embarrassed groan cut through the chuckles that filled the cramped alley, while he shoved a number of his fellow workers on his way over to Ida.

He may have insisted on living his own life as a man of age, but as a mother, it was still her prerogative to lovingly rub it in his face.

"How are you, dear?" she asked in their native tongue while pulling him into a hug.

Forley pretended to be reluctant in returning it, but his arms wrapped her far too tightly to be convincing.

"Have you been getting enough sleep?" Ida caressed his cheek. "Your eyes are so tired. Don't tell me you're already getting crow's feet at seventeen?"

"I'm fine." He shook off her hand.

"Good. Do you have some time to spare for a walk? Only a short one. I wouldn't want to tear you away from your grown-up responsibilities for too long."

He tutted at the remark, but he fell in beside her. Together, they went back out on the street and continued toward the main square a few blocks away. It was a rare mild day, which in this season only promised much worse to come soon, but it was worth taking advantage of while it lasted.

"You don't have to come out here, you know." Forley sunk his hands in the pockets of his stained uniform. "You can come to my home after hours. We can talk longer then."

He threw in the last sentence as a bargaining chip, but Ida had a full hand.

"My hours start when yours end. And with all due respect, young sir"—she hiked up her dress to curtsy mid-step—"I've seen the likes of men you live with, and I'd rather not spend too much time around them."

"They're decent folks, Ma. They wouldn't try anything. And if they did, you know I wouldn't let it happen."

"I trust you, dear. It's others I don't trust."

Forley pursed his lips, the way he always did when he held something back. Ida didn't need to ask or press the matter. Her son had never been the sort who could keep his thoughts bottled long enough to forget them. He made a show of trying nonetheless, keeping his sullen brown eyes on the pavement ahead, while his scowl scrunched up the wisps of a mustache that all but faded into his dark complexion.

This farce of indifference lasted all of two minutes, long enough for Ida to buy a bag of roasted nuts in sugar from a street vendor's cart. They waited for a railcar to pass before rounding the block and heading back toward the tannery.

"Did you take Scolsessi to the Belfry, then?"

There it was. The question so heavily loaded, it could have sunk a galleon to the cold depths.

"Yes." Ida picked a nut from the bag and slid it under her veil, careful not to lift the fabric, while doing her best to remember what the snack tasted like. "He got his first taste of Laerithian brandy. And his last, if his reaction was anything to go by."

Forley took a nut as well and rolled it between his fingers. "Did *you* get a taste of it?"

"After putting the poor man through that ordeal, it would've been rude not to."

"You've been seeing a lot of him."

"He's a customer, Forley. I have to see him."

"Do you?"

Ida stopped in her tracks, which forced him to face her at last. They stood locked eye to eye on the crowded sidewalk. Around them, some mumbled a mouthful of indignities as they shuffled past, but Forley's six-foot stature was enough to deter anything beyond that.

"I have no plans on landing you a stepfather," Ida said. "But as long as Mendel doesn't ask to be that, I can't say no to him. If I lose his patronage, I lose Beldora's goodwill. That's not something either of us can afford."

Forley scowled again. "I don't like it."

"You don't like what?"

"That you're in debt to Beldora, and I'm in debt to Scolsessi, and you're in debt to him because I am."

Ida sighed. He really was a silly, proud boy after all. *Her* silly, proud boy.

She grabbed his hand and pulled it out of his pocket. "Forley, love—those are called favors. Sometimes we do them for others, and sometimes they do them for us. And when favors are all we have, we must appreciate those who grant them to us."

He clasped his fingers around hers with as much feigned reluctance as before. "So now you trust others?"

She laughed and kissed his hand through the veil. "Do as I say, not as I do."

For the time being, that put an end to the story. Ida knew Forley wasn't going to turn his view around over a single conversation, but he dropped his sulking, which was a start.

Some things only came with time, and there was no choice but to wait them out. Hopefully, as the weeks and months passed, he would slowly make peace with their situation and learn to see the fortune in it.

She put her arm in his, and they resumed their walk along the busy street, finishing the bag of nuts between the two of them while they discussed some pleasant banalities. The dismal weather, goings-on at work, overbearing landlords—all the little reminders that some days, life could be merely ordinary.

Eventually, the tannery's flat roof came into view over the next corner.

"Break's almost over," Forley said, tossing the empty bag down a sewer grate. "I should get back."

"Right," Ida replied, but held on to his arm. As much as she relished small talk, there was one last thing she had to bring up. "If you hurry, you might get a quick game in with the others."

Forley picked up on the hint, as well as how intentionally obvious Ida had made it. "I was only watching. I told you I gave it up for good."

"I know you told me."

"You don't believe it?"

Ida caressed his arm. "I believe you now like I believed you all the other times."

Shame flickered in the sad, brown eyes. "It's different. I promise. I won't let you down again."

She wrapped her arms around him again. This time, he didn't hesitate to do the same.

"You never have," she whispered. "And you never will."

They said their goodbyes on the corner, and Forley jogged

back to the side entrance in the alley. Ida followed him with her gaze, until he gave one last wave, and the building swallowed him. She then hiked up her dress and went her own way, back toward the Upper Court District and the Garden of Lilies. A few hours of rest before they opened for the night would do her good. Mendel might come by again.

# Chapter 7

Thessa leaned back and let the autumn air flow through her nose, picking apart the hundred delicate scents one by one. The grass around her and the damp soil beneath it. The insects that crawled around in the foliage. The wind blowing from the west, bringing the soot of the city and the mist of the river beyond. Her eyes were closed, yet her awareness of the world around her was as sharp as ever. Some nights, it was as if she could smell the stars in the sky.

Keeping her body low to the ground, she stretched one of her front feet ahead and crept forward. At this time of fall, the grass was just tall enough to give her safe cover. Not that there was much risk of anyone seeing her out here. Beyond the railroad tracks that ran along the Wall District, the architects of the city had left a few acres untouched, so the less illustrious borough didn't quite reach the foot of the neighboring Escavol Hill. Over the past months, this strip of no-man's-land and its wild overgrowth had become one of Thessa's favorite places, where she could come out and be herself in a way she couldn't anywhere else.

And she was more of herself each time.

She sniffed the air again. There was something else in it

this time. The smell of fur. The warmth of a living creature. A badger. Thessa opened her eyes and continued her prowl, low and steady, so as not to make noise. Inch by inch, the distance between them closed. Her prey skittered here and there in its search for food, but it had not noticed her. And it wouldn't. Not until it was too late.

Catching them was never the hard part. Letting them go alive was.

When Thessa and Corlis went to Forterne province to visit his birth family, she repeatedly found herself overcome by her vicious urges at the faintest smell of blood. After they returned, Corlis offered to lock her in the cellar at The Lame Mare every so often, where she could safely transform without endangering anyone, until she learned how to control her condition. For a while, they stuck to that plan, and it seemed to work. Gradually, over the months of practice, the haze that descended on Thessa's mind became thinner, and her confidence grew stronger. She was no longer afraid to transform. Some days, she found herself longing for it.

By the end of the summer, the cellar wasn't enough. She wanted to get out and see the world through her newly opened eyes. After some convincing, Corlis suggested the fields between the Wall District and Escavol Hill, on the condition that Thessa would return to the inn afterward to make sure nothing got out of hand.

And so, week after week, Thessa left her clothes by the fence beside the tracks, and she spent an hour or so in the grass, safely hidden from any eyes that might raise an alarm. Week after week, she grew into a better and quieter hunter, stalking the wildlife that came out after sundown. She told herself she'd only catch them and let them go unharmed—but that was where her instincts held too much sway.

She fixed her gaze on the long, striped shape in front of her, then leapt forward. The badger heard the rustle and darted up the trunk of a nearby tree, but that was a dead end. Sinking her claws into the bark, Thessa shot up into the branches, and a moment later, her teeth were around the badger's neck. She held it down firmly, but otherwise made no motion.

Her prey squirmed and thrashed in its animal panic. As it wriggled, its shoulder got stuck on her fangs, breaking its skin. Hot, fresh blood oozed onto Thessa's lips. Her muscles tightened by themselves, and in a single snap, the creature was crushed between her jaws.

Thessa spat out the badger's limp remains and jumped down to the ground. This had to be enough for tonight.

She found the wormwood shrub by the fence where she had hidden her clothes and turned back to her human self to get dressed. Unlike the flowing skirts she preferred, the trousers and shirt of her work uniform didn't hinder her transformation—but, as Corlis had pointed out, any sort of clothing would make potential witnesses much less likely to mistake her for a dog if she kept it on.

He was still at The Lame Mare when Thessa got back, like he had been all the times before. The tavern was empty, and the entrance locked, so she came through the back to find Corlis behind the bar, scrubbing the inside of a wine tap with a thin brush. Thessa felt touched, and a little guilty. If Corlis was cleaning the taps on his own accord, that meant he was *really* bored.

"Sorry to keep you up for so long." She went up to the front side of the counter and sat before him. "Would you be terribly mad if I asked for a drink?"

Corlis fixed one of his greenish-gray eyes on her, while the other one looked off into the distance. Without a word, he got a cup from the shelf, filled the bottom third with wine, and topped off the rest with cold water, exactly as Thessa liked it.

"What taste do you need to wash out of your mouth this time?" he asked.

Thessa downed half of the cup before answering. "Badger."

"How does it compare to the snake from last week?"

"Anything's better than snake."

As soon as she finished the wine, he poured another, then resumed his cleaning. Thessa sipped away at her drink, now at a more measured pace, and watched him in the flickering light of the oil lamp. She enjoyed the nights she got to transform, but in truth, she might have enjoyed these minutes more. They never lasted long—Thessa had to get back to her home across town, and Corlis needed to close. But for a few minutes, the world came to a halt for the two of them, and everything outside the lamplight fell away.

Thessa adjusted the collar of her shirt, and something pressed against her chest. Reaching into her inside pocket, she pulled out a folded-up sheet of paper. It was the one from two days before.

"Where'd you get that?" Corlis asked offhand.

"Have you seen a flier like this?"

"Around here, it's hard not to."

"Really? Do you get a lot of bluebells in here?"

"Not any more." Corlis set down the brush and went to set the clean tap in its cask. "They tried to hold a few of their meetings at the tavern. Then I got raided by the city guard, so I told them that time was their last."

That explained why Thessa didn't recall seeing them around

Corlis's inn. It was also mostly in line with what the others at the Messengers' Guild had been telling her. None of it helped make her mind clearer.

"The bluebells have been harassing my colleagues for months, and I never understood why."

"And now you do?"

"I don't know." She smoothed out the paper beside the lamp and read out loud, "*The rights of both the nobility and the guilds are derived from the emperor. Without an emperor, those rights are forfeit. Neither nobility nor guilds belong in a republic.*" By this point, Thessa had read and re-read the words so many times, she could almost recite them. "Is that true?"

Corlis pulled out a rag and wiped down the bar. "I'm not a lawyer. But considering every seat in the senate has a noble's rear in it, my money says they found some way to lawfully keep those rights." He spat on a stain and rubbed it. "And if they didn't, what's anyone going to do?"

His reaction was fairly expected. Corlis never had any enthusiasm for things that didn't directly affect him—nor the ones that did, for that matter. By and large, the only sentiment he showed most of the world was varying levels of annoyance.

But regardless of his attitude, he had a lot more experience than Thessa, and right now she needed his advice.

"What about this one? That the guilds hold"—she squinted at the blotchy print—"*imperial monopolies?*"

Thessa's insistence was rewarded with a loud scoff. "That one I know too well. When the inn was ruined in the spring, I had four casks of wine in the cellar. I needed to get rid of them because I didn't know if I'd ever reopen." Corlis gestured in the direction of the basement door. "As it turned out, not just anyone is allowed to sell wine by the cask. I had to get someone from the Winers' Guild to make the deal in my name, and he helped himself to a nice commission from the price. Couple that with the fact that guilds pay barely any taxes, and you can start to see why some don't like them too much."

He put away the rag, then left the counter to go and put the chairs on top of the tables.

Atop her bar stool, Thessa listened to the monotone shuffle of Corlis's feet, alternating with the muffled thumps of wood hitting wood. She flicked at the dirty edges of the paper, while Corlis's words settled in her mind.

"Do you think I should leave my job?" she said, half out loud and half to herself.

Another thump, without so much as a heartbeat's pause. "When did I say that?"

"I work for a guild. If they truly are as corrupt and unjust as the bluebells say—doesn't that make me guilty as well?"

Silence. One breath, then another, then a third. Two more footsteps, two more chairs. Corlis rejoined Thessa, not behind the bar, but on the seat next to hers. His eyebrows knotted in thought.

"If no one sold wine or spirits anywhere, how many bar fights do you think there'd be?" he asked.

Thessa pondered. "Much fewer, if any."

"Does that mean I'm guilty of starting fights, and I should close the tavern?"

She hadn't phrased it like that, but a similar point had occurred to her. It was the whole reason she had so much doubt in the first place. "No." She shook her head. "But I don't know what to think about this whole matter."

Corlis drew a long, slow breath through his nose, folded up

the paper, and handed it to her. "Then do what the rest of us do: think about today's problems today and leave tomorrow for tomorrow."

# Chapter 8

The workroom door swung open so hard it slammed into the wall. Before Ida looked up from her work, she already expected the impatient voice that snapped, "Where's that garter, Teeth?"

Violet's slender frame loomed in the doorway, wrapped in an exquisite gown of her signature color and clutching a stocking in one gloved hand. Like all the women working at the Garden of Lilies, she was nicknamed after a flower and dressed accordingly. In her case, she had received the moniker because she was particularly good at being demure—when she wanted to. The rest of the time, when the men weren't around, it was a different matter. Ida preferred to keep herself out of gossip, but she had heard the words "heinous bitch" floating around, and she wasn't in any hurry to contest them.

She put aside the hook she was in the middle of sewing and picked up the delicately laced strip. Violet stomped over, snatched it from her hand, and inspected the seams in the lamplight. After tugging on it a few times, her heavily powdered face gave a begrudging grimace of approval.

"I guess it only needs to stay on for a few minutes. Move," she barked, and without waiting for Ida to do so, she set her foot on the bench to put on the stocking. Once it was at her thigh, she gathered up her skirt on the side and shot Ida an impatient glare. "Well? Are you going to help me or not?"

Setting her needle down again, Ida tied the garter and attached it to the straps dangling from Violet's undergarment to hold it in place. None of it was anything Violet couldn't have done for herself, but that would have interfered with her favorite pastime of treating everyone like a personal servant.

"How's the evening?" Ida asked while fastening the clasps.

"Busy," came the curt answer. "I've got a dance to put on in one minute, and I'm expecting two of my regulars later."

"Have you seen Mendel outside?"

Violet lifted her inky black hair above one ear. "Who? Speak up already. I can't hear you with that thing over your mouth."

"Lord Mendel Scolsessi," Ida repeated. "Have you seen him tonight?"

"What do I care? Go see for yourself. Now stop wasting my time." And without another word, she whirled out of the room, shutting the door as loudly as when she had come in.

Her comment was, naturally, nothing but another jab. Ida wasn't expressly *forbidden* to show herself in the front of the house, but she would have needed a good reason to do so. Along with a few others—such as Bramble and Thorn, the tattooed torturesses—Ida was reserved for clients who specifically asked for her brand of pleasure. The rest of the time, they were sent to make themselves useful in the back, so as not to put off the more conventionally inclined guests.

Ida had never fancied herself a seamstress, but her practice with a needle had proven enough to earn her that title within the Garden. Any given night, as the women tended to the scores of eager gentlemen, there was no end to the lost buttons and ripped seams. It gave Ida plenty to do as she manned the workroom, venturing outside only when called.

While she finished the last hook on the corset she was mending, Ida drifted back to the conversation she and Forley had earlier that day and the little white lie she told to assuage him.

*"I have no plans on landing you a stepfather."*

Word for word, it wasn't untrue. Ida had no plans with Mendel to speak of. Beldora, the owner of the Garden, had put it in no uncertain terms that love had no place in such a house, whether on the part of a guest or a worker. "Once a man walks out the door, he is as good as dead to you, and he must plainly understand this."

Ida had spent enough years in the profession not to be troubled by girlish infatuation, and she harbored nothing similar for Mendel. But she couldn't be sure that was true the other way around. The young lord was a mere four years older than her son, very much of the age when a man is prone to overvalue the attention of a woman. He had also recently lost both of his parents, leaving no one to give him guidance on matters of the heart. Entertaining him as a regular was a delicate line to walk, and for the most part, Ida had taken great care not to give him any misguided ideas.

For the most part.

"Hazel."

The door opened again. The person behind it this time was Beldora herself. She addressed Ida by her nickname—the official one, as opposed to the much less flattering "Teeth" that Violet delighted in using.

"Yes?" Ida asked.

"Your regular is here. Come, I'll walk you to the hall."

Ida packed away her things and exchanged her slippers for

a pair of strapped shoes in the same green as the rest of her outfit. The madam waited patiently for her to finish, and the two of them then proceeded side by side along the service corridor that ran the back half of the building.

"How was your outing the other night?" Beldora asked on the way.

"Good. I made sure he got his money's worth."

"You took him to that place? The one with—"

"With people of my kind?" Ida asked, making sure the smile was audible in her voice. "Yes, I did. He was most excited."

"You must trust him a great deal."

"The Belfry vet their guests thoroughly. If they trusted him enough to allow him inside, I don't see why I shouldn't."

Ida knew that was not what Beldora had meant, and that Beldora knew that she knew. But neither of them said anything else on the subject.

Before long, they reached the end of the corridor and landed in the main hall, with the sound of music and laughter filling their ears. What little light there was mostly fell on the stage, where Violet led three other women in a whirlwind dance, teasing the audience with momentary glimpses underneath their skirts. The rest of the floor was tightly packed with armchairs, recliners, and other invitingly cushioned furniture, as well as huge flower arrangements that doubled as both decoration and cover.

Beldora led the way, making sure not to block any of the guests' view as they passed, until they spotted the familiar face next to a table. "Thank you for your patience, Lord Scolsessi," she said.

Mendel tore his gaze from the stage and rose to his feet, almost ashamed. "Please, ladies. In here, I'm only Mendel," he said, with his best imitation of confident charm. He was clad in his favorite navy-inspired coat, to which he had added a red scarf.

Beldora answered by way of a polite bow of the head, then left him and Ida alone. As she turned to walk away, she gave Ida a brief glimpse as a reminder of their earlier discussion.

Ida shook it off and turned her attention to her guest. "Why, Mendel, I haven't seen you in *days*!" She slinked up to him and took his arm. "I was worried you had deserted me."

"You won't get rid of me that easily." Mendel chuckled and raised his hand to hers. The sleeve of his coat drew back in the motion, revealing a yellow silk ribbon around his wrist.

"I see you're prepared," Ida said, pinching the end of the ribbon with her finger. "Shall we head upstairs right away?"

A chorus of claps and cheers erupted behind them, as Violet and the women concluded their dance in the midst of the audience. In the dim light, Mendel's soft cheeks almost glowed. He might have been flustered, drunk, lustful, or any combination of the three.

"Yes—yes, we can go," he stuttered. "I just—"

Ida's fingers wandered from button to button up the velvet coat, all the way up under the red scarf. "You just what?"

Mendel swallowed and leaned into her ear. "I need to go and. . . shake hands with a friend first."

Ida couldn't help but throw her head back in laughter. "Is that how long you had to wait? Beldora was right to apologize." She leaned closer into his ear. "Tell your friend I hope to see him soon."

With a bashful smile, Mendel headed off to the privy, and Ida sat down at his table to wait. Across the hall, the musicians struck up a new song, and the dancers continued their act.

There were only three of them now, as Violet seemed to have caught the attention of one gentleman enough to take her off the stage. Poppy, Pepper, and Daffodil remained, twirling large feather fans and colorful veils, while their clothes vanished bit by bit amid the patrons' vocal encouragement.

They were down to their undergarments when Mendel got back, redder in the face than before.

"I'm so sorry," he said in a hushed mix of embarrassment and irritation. "I was waiting for my turn at the wash-basin, and this gentleman really wanted me to know what a deal he made on a fig orchard."

Ida let him help her up from her seat. "Lucky for you, I don't have anywhere else to be tonight."

Turning their backs on the stage, they walked leisurely through the arched doorway of the main hall, across the inner yard, and at last to the stairwell. The ground floor of the Garden held all the common areas, where the women and their guests could mingle freely with drinks and chatter. Those who wished for some intimacy would head up to the many bedrooms on the second floor—provided they showed proof of payment, that is.

Darno, one of the few male employees of the establishment, greeted them at the bottom of the stairs. Though his build wasn't nearly as formidable as men in his line of work tended to have, the white scar across his eye and the sizable blade on his belt more than made up for it. As Ida and Mendel approached, he drew himself to attention in his all-black uniform and blocked their way.

"Good evening, sir," he addressed the young lord and held out his hand. "May I?"

"Right away." Mendel pulled his arm out of Ida's, then drew

back his right sleeve, only to reveal a bare wrist. He frowned and pulled back the left one. Bare as well. He checked the right again, rolling the sleeve up to the elbow. No matter how many times he repeated, neither of his arms had a ribbon on it.

"I don't understand," he said. "I bought one, not half an hour ago. You can ask the teller."

"He's telling the truth," Ida told the guard. "I saw it. I can vouch for him."

"You know that's not the rule, Hazel." Darno's tone wasn't cold, but it left no room for debate, either. "Beldora will have my guts for garters if I let anyone up without proof."

"It was here a minute earlier. I had it before—" Mendel's eyes glazed over. "The washroom. I took it off to wash my hands because I didn't want the silk to get wet." Staring in front of himself, he mimed his movements as he narrated them. "I set it aside, and then—"

He and Ida came to the same realization at once.

"That man who talked to you," she said. "Did he take it? What did he look like?"

"About yea tall." Mendel hesitantly indicated a few inches above his head. "Fifty or so and bald as an egg. With the biggest mole I've ever seen on anyone, right under his nose."

"No one like that came this way," Darno replied. "If he has your ribbon, he'll be downstairs."

Ida patted Mendel's arm. "Maybe you simply left it there. Do you want to check? I can go with you."

"No, it's all right," the young main said. "I won't ask you to follow me into the men's washroom. I'll be quick."

With stiff and hurried steps, he strode off through the entryway toward the main hall. Darno moved to the side of the staircase and leaned against the wall, picking at his nails with utter indifference toward what had transpired. Ida couldn't blame him for adhering to the rules, but nonetheless, she felt a little betrayed. Did her word truly mean nothing to him?

Several minutes later, Mendel re-emerged. He had a ribbon in his hand, but neither his movements nor his face suggested that he was at all relieved.

"Did you find it?" Ida asked anyway.

"No, this is a new one. The ribbon I first bought was nowhere to be found, nor was the man who spoke to me." Mendel all but shoved the length of silk in the guard's hand. "Whoever got a free hour on my expense, I hope they show your colleague a good time."

Darno said nothing to that, only bowed his head and motioned for them to continue. Ida slid her arm in Mendel's once more and led him up to the second floor. The lights here were heavily dimmed behind tinted glass, bathing the narrow corridor in a sensual red glow. Hopefully, it would help placate the young lord.

He was visibly upset by this mishap and would be for a while. Over his numerous visits, Ida got to know him as somewhat prone to fixation. Once his mood turned sweet or sour, it stayed that way until something changed his mind. If they were going to spend an hour together, it would be wholly up to Ida to make it a pleasant one.

So she got to work. She caressed his hand and chest as they searched for a vacant room. She poured him a glass of wine and rubbed his shoulders while he sipped it. She unwound the scarf from around his neck and undid his buttons one by one. The blue coat landed on the back of a chair, followed closely by his shirt, vest, and belt. As she removed each piece, now and then he grabbed her hand and kissed it. It was a slow progress, but Ida's experience served her well, and Mendel's temper gradually softened.

When all he had on was his underwear, Ida lay him out spreadeagled on the bed, then told him to close his eyes and wait. That, at last, lured a smile out of him. She snuck behind the folding screen and began to undress, letting all the clasps and buckles of her garment rattle as much as they could, so Mendel could follow the process in his mind and let his fantasy fill in the blanks.

But as she was about to remove her second shoe, her efforts went up in smoke, when a loud banging shook the door.

"This room is occupied!" Mendel shouted from the bed.

An equally stern voice came from the other side. "City guard. Open up."

Ida was dumbstruck. *City guard?* In here, upstairs?

Behind the screen, she listened intently as Mendel pulled up his trousers and unlocked the door.

"What in the deep dark is going on?" he demanded.

The unseen figure paid no mind to either his ire or his status. "Sir, I must ask you to gather your belongings and follow me downstairs. Sergeant Vendriane has ordered all guests and staff to gather in the main hall presently."

"Guests? What are you on about?"

"There's been a murder, sir."

The guard's final word hung heavy in the silence that followed. The air was sucked out of Ida's lungs like she'd been struck in the chest.

Mendel's protests cut off. "A—a *murder*? Who?"

"The sergeant will relay all the necessary details. Right now,

I'd like you to come with me."

The young lord's noble indignity was gone without a trace. "Yes—yes, of course." He shuffled over to the chair where Ida had piled up his clothes and gathered them in a hurry.

Meanwhile, Ida's hands were frozen halfway in unstrapping her shoe. As far as she could tell, the guard was not aware she was in the room. Should she make herself known? Should she stay?

The answer came to her soon after.

"Am I. . ." Mendel stuttered. "Are we all suspects?"

"I can't say anything on that matter, sir," the guard said before his voice changed to a much less official tone. "But unless you're a bloodsucker, you shouldn't need to worry."

Another strike to Ida's chest. This one might as well have pierced her body outright.

"Bloodsucker?" Mendel asked.

"That's right," the guard said, misunderstanding Mendel's shock. "At least the freak should be easy enough to find if they're still around." The floorboards creaked softly as he put one foot over the threshold. "Is there someone else with you here, sir?"

Ida clasped both hands above her mouth and shut her eyes as tight as they went, as if she was trying to disappear from the world. Through her veil, the uneven ridges of her disfigured teeth pressed against her palm.

"No," Mendel replied. "Not any more, I mean. I was here with a woman, but we've been done for a while. She should be down already."

Then and there, all of Ida's playful condescension toward Mendel's military obsession went out the window, and he was her hero in shining armor.

"I see," said the guard. "Then, if you're ready, sir, we can join the others."

The knocking of boot heels on the wooden floor traced the men's steps toward the hallway, until they faded into nothing behind the closed door.

Ida couldn't open her eyes. If she did, she knew the world would spin around her so wildly she might be sick or faint. She couldn't faint. She couldn't be sick.

She had to get out of there right now.

The window was out of the question. Most upstairs rooms, including this one, faced the building's inner yard, precisely to avoid uninvited stares—or guests—from outside. Ida would have to take the hallway. If everyone had gathered downstairs, it should be empty.

Putting her shoe and dress back on, she crept to the keyhole and pressed one ear against it. Nothing came from the other side. She turned the knob a fraction of an inch at a time, then cracked the door open. The tinted red glass of the lamps that lined the ceiling turned the circles of light into pools of blood. Ida was no longer in the Garden of Lilies, but a slaughterhouse where she could be next on the hook.

The hallway had two exits. The first one was the main staircase that led to the entryway with Darno at the bottom. The second one was the service door, which the women and staff used to get up quickly from the basement. The basement, in turn, had its own exit into the alley. That was her only hope.

As she came to the treacherously narrow steps, her senses had returned enough to form coherent thoughts. Most of them were questions too absurd to answer.

How could a murder happen at the Garden of Lilies? Who could have done such a thing? Come to think of it, who was killed? Was it one of the women? Ida shuddered. None of them deserved such a horrid fate—not even Violet. But it didn't make sense the other way around, either. If the victim was a guest, the killer had to be one too, as there were no other bloodsuckers at the house. Could it have been someone from the Belfry? Ida almost never saw the main hall. For all she knew, it could have been.

The confusion made her all the dizzier as she rushed down the spiral staircase. She fumbled around in the pitch black darkness until at last she found the lamp and lit it. The flame flared up so brightly, for a heartbeat it was like a beacon alerting the whole world to Ida's presence. She turned it down until it was no more than an ember and continued into the kitchen. As she groped her way ahead from chair to chair and shelf to shelf, her concerns moved ahead from the past to the future.

What was going to happen? Was the guard after her? Did they know she was there? It boiled down to the same question: could she trust the others not to betray her? Mendel lied to the guard for her sake, but he was a nobleman. The guard had much less of a hold on him. Could the women be pressed into giving her up?

Each possibility was more terrifying than the last, but above all, there was one that Ida dared not entertain: *If she was caught, what would become of Forley?*

By the time she reached the steps that led up to street level, she was ready to collapse. Her trembling hand sent the lamp's glow into a mad dance against the backdrop of the dark basement, and her knees buckled under her own weight. With one final heave of effort, Ida threw the trap door open and emerged into the freezing cold autumn drizzle.

Dazzled from the lamplight, she didn't see anyone in the alley. She only felt the painful grip of one hand that twisted her arm behind her, while another one locked on her wrist. The lamp clattered on the alley floor and sputtered out, and a rough voice spoke next to her ear.

"Hazel, I presume? The sergeant's waiting for you."

# Chapter 9

It is a curious feeling to see a face that is entirely unfamiliar, and at the same time be equally certain who it must belong to. If anyone asked, Argiey would have been able to name two occasions when this happened to him. The first was during his training as coroner, when he accidentally splattered a pint of blood over the man he immediately guessed to be the New Montres prefect for criminal justice. The second was when the city guard brought him the dead body that was found outside the Garden of Lilies.

But nobody asked Argiey, and for that, he was immensely grateful. Because if the officers knew he recognized the woman lying between them, he would have had a lot of explaining to do. Thus, he stood and went through the motions, going over the initial examination with the men who brought her before he could sign off the paperwork.

"Midorean female. Five foot two, average build." Argiey noted the details on his sheet. "Age unknown, presumed between thirty and fifty."

"That's a generous margin you're giving her," one officer remarked from behind. After he and his colleague hauled the body from the guard's wagon to the deadhouse basement, he decided he'd seen enough of it and helped himself to Argiey's bitters.

"I can't ask her," Argiey replied while scraping away. "Until you figure out who she is, I can only write down what I see. Was there no one who knew her?" He pretended to add the last bit as an afterthought.

"Believe me, we asked everyone, and we took our sweet time doing so. Hours and hours of questioning all the guests and all the workers," the other city guard said through the piece of bark he was chewing. His freckles bunched up on each side as his mouth widened into a grin. "*Especially* the workers."

"Do you remember what any of them said?" Argiey asked. After his initial notes, he moved on to undressing the customer.

"Yeah, 'cause they all said the same thing," the officer behind him said, wiping spirit off of his enormous mustache. "A few people noticed her skulking around, but she never spoke to anyone. At some point, they lost sight of her." He poured himself a second glass. "Two hours later, she was dead. A passerby went to take a piss in the alley and found her lying there, bone dry." He shuddered loudly at that part.

Midoreans were already light-skinned while alive. A dead one, drained of all blood, might as well have been made of plaster. Argiey gently tilted the woman's head to the side and examined the bite mark. It was eerily unassuming. No finger marks, blunt bruises, or any signs that might linger after a strangling or a lethal blow. Nothing but two dots on the otherwise pristine neck. Then again, with near two decades of experience under his belt, Argiey had seen plenty of sudden deaths with fewer clues. Life was much easier to slip away than most realized.

"If no one saw her inside, how do you know that's where she died?" he asked.

"From that." The freckled guard took the bark out of his mouth and used it to point at the Midorean's wrist, which had a yellow silk ribbon tied around it. "Guests at the house have to buy one of those, pick a woman in the main hall, then hand it back to the guard on the way upstairs. They use a different color every day to make sure people don't cheat them by buying ten yards of ribbons at the market. So she must have gotten this today, though the woman in charge of selling them swore she didn't."

"She was covering herself like all the others," the officer behind grunted into his glass.

His colleague's grin stretched wider. "Well, all except one." He crossed his arms and drew himself up to fill the coat of his uniform. Clearly, this whole time he'd waited for the conversation to reach this part.

"We'd been there for over an hour, shaking down all the guests and all the staff, when I notice one of them making eyes at me from across the room. I take her aside and sit her down in an alcove, the two of us, nice and cozy. The shy little thing—Violet, they call her—she can barely look me in the face, let alone get a word out. So I spend a minute to make her at ease, until at last she opens up and gives me everything we needed to hear." The young guard spread his hands in humility. "What can I say? I have a certain effect on women."

"No doubt." The older officer finished his drink.

Argiey listened patiently to the play that unfolded before him, while cutting open the woman's dress lengthwise with a knife. Seeing how it had spent hours soaking in the city's filth, there wasn't much reason to try to salvage it. He tipped the nearly weightless body to one side so he could pull the remaining fabric out from underneath. More rags for the pile in the back room. Not that he'd be receiving any packages for the time being.

The freckled charmer prattled on. "Once I got her talking, Violet spilled everything. She told me there was a bloodsucker working at the house. A Laerithian who went by Hazel. Being turned did a number on her face, so she never showed herself with the rest of the women. Only a few guests knew she existed at all. But she was there all night—working in the back, out of sight."

"And your little friend warned us she might try to sneak out." The officer behind pushed himself out of the chair. "Which she did. The sergeant sent me to wait by the service door to the basement, and I caught her twenty minutes later." He joined the other two by the table, throwing a brief expression of disgust at the now naked, pale body.

"Sounds pretty cut-and-dried," Argiey muttered. He ended his outside check of the body, stamped the papers, then handed them over to the guards. As a formality, he asked if they wanted to be present for the internal examination, which they both politely and emphatically declined.

"There is one more thing," the freckled one said. "You've got one of those lightchambers here, right? Sergeant said you'll have to take a picture of her to the guardhouses first thing tomorrow, so they can try to identify her."

"Will do."

Argiey escorted the pair up to the street, where the wagon awaited to take them home. He stood there, coat drawn tight around the shoulders to protect him from the rain, until the night swallowed them in the distance.  Once he could be sure they wouldn't turn around, he rushed back down to his workroom.

There was a lot that needed to be done, and opening up the body wasn't close to being the most important. Letters had to be written, plans had to be rethought, and a *lot* of questions had to be asked.

But those were concerns for others. The first thing Argiey had to do was get out that lightchamber.

III

# Part Three

# Chapter 10

Some days, there was no escaping the truth of finality. Summer would turn to fall, however bright. Childhood would turn to adulthood, however carefree. Friendships and loves could fade, however strong. If a good thing had a beginning, then it had to have an end.

Nel closed her eyes and swallowed the last mouthful of the best porridge she'd ever tasted. Had she been twenty years younger or home by herself as an adult, she would have picked up the bowl and licked it clean—alas, such a display would likely have been frowned upon at the Midorean consulate. Mustering the best of her manners, she took a sip of her hot honeyed wine and distracted herself with the view outside the window.

The consulate lay on the so-called "Golden Circle," which was the popular nickname for the road that ran the perimeter of Crescent Bay at the heart of the city. The street was home to the most important and illustrious offices of Ardonne, second only to the ones in the former imperial palace. While each building sought to outdo the next in their craftsmanship, all of them shared the same splendid panorama of the river Ryonne, as well as the hundreds of colorful boats that made up the famous Crescent Bay Market. Like Solluri Hill, it was not the sort of place Nel would have imagined setting foot in, let alone having a leisurely breakfast among high-ranking officials.

The only thing more remarkable was how little it intimidated her. For that, Nel would much rather credit her surroundings than her own nerves. The whole building had an atmosphere of peace that was rare to find in New Montres. The lavish decorations, crystal chandeliers, and mock-gold finishes that characterized the "more is not enough" philosophy of Ardonnese taste were completely absent here. Anywhere Nel looked, she was met with bare walls, clean surfaces, and pale colors in some shade of green or brown. What little there was, however, was of a quality that the emperor himself wouldn't have questioned. Mainu told her once that Midoreans prefer to make more of less, and after tasting what they could make out of milk, oats, and almonds, Nel couldn't have argued if she wanted to.

Across the table, he was cleaning up his meal as well. He had ordered some sort of Midorean specialty, which resembled flat, round pieces of bread, only thicker and softer. It came with a small heap of whisked butter, fruit preserves, and—at the lieutenant investigator's explicit request—a copious drizzle of honey.

As he mopped up the last precious drops of sweetness, a glob of fruit ended up sticking to his wrist. He pulled back the sleeve to wipe it off, revealing a row of thin scratch marks. Judging by their bright red color, they couldn't have been more than a day old.

"Have you been making new friends?" Nel asked, gesturing at the scars.

"Not quite friends yet." Mainu straightened his shirt.

"Anchovies clearly aren't the way to go."

"Did you name any of them?"

"I'd need to know them a little better first. Two-Face might be a good fit for one."

Nel laughed. To imagine a thirty-three year old man in the Midorean High Court's uniform, crouched in an alley behind an inn and trying to bribe a ragged street cat with a piece of fish—that certainly was something. "I wish I could've seen you do it."

"You're welcome to, if you want. I should think they'll be there this evening."

"Perhaps I will. To be honest, I've never gotten along with cats much. We had one back home, and she wasn't really *our* cat to speak of. She holed up in our grain shed and stayed to hunt the mice. My parents named her Hissy because that was all she'd do if anyone got close."

"That sounds about right." Mainu nodded. "How are your parents, by the way? Has your mother's ankle gotten any better?"

"Yes, somewhat. Last time Father wrote, the physician had ordered her not to walk more than ten steps at a time, so he's been waiting on her hand and foot." She added, "He said she's taking every advantage of the situation while it lasts."

There was something strange to Nel about how naturally she and Mainu talked between themselves. Exchanging well over a dozen letters the past year, they both learned a great deal about the other one's past and present. Nel read about Mainu's time growing up in the Midorean capital; his sister, who studied medicine abroad in Pasmany; or the summers he had spent with his twin cousins, who inspired him to take up service. She, in turn, told him about her family's farm in Astercium; her two brothers, one of whom had gone to work on an overseas freighter; her own trials when she moved to New Montres; and, most recently, her mother's twisted ankle. Now that they were face to face, they could pick up the conversation where they left off, as if they'd known one another this whole time.

But had they?

Nel remembered other friends and colleagues and how their familiarity had grown over one year after meeting. Compared to that, sitting at the table with Mainu was almost the same as it had been last fall. It took her a few minutes to put her finger on it: that knowing things *about* someone was not quite the same as knowing them. The letters Nel and Mainu exchanged greatly outnumbered the days they had spent together, and they only contained what each of them considered worthwhile to mention. Nel had known about Mainu's family and childhood from his writing, but only when they sat down to breakfast did she learn that he was a messy eater with a sweet tooth.

And yet, this one detail felt more significant than pages upon pages of his life story.

A serving woman—one of the few staff members of Ardonnese descent—came by to clear away the plates, then returned a minute later with two cups and a pot of coffee. Nel had not considered herself a great lover of the drink, as she'd only had it a few times before, and none of those times were especially memorable. After a cautious initial sip, she was once more reminded that whatever Midoreans did, they did well.

As pleasant as the meal was, sooner or later they had to get back to work.

"What's our plan for today, then?" she asked.

Mainu stirred a lump of rock sugar in his cup. "The maid and the neighbors weren't of much use yesterday, but they didn't contradict anything the landlord said. We can continue with Vei Ruola's other friends. Before I left, her husband was able to give me a list of names and addresses."

"How long is it? Maybe we could divide it between us to save time."

"It's not that long. Even if it was, I'm supposed to be supervised at all times. I'd rather not risk bringing the case to a halt over a formality."

"Right—I forgot about that." Nel swirled her coffee. "And what are we asking them about? Same as before?"

"Same as before. Usual habits, changes in behavior, and"—Mainu tilted his head—"new acquaintances."

Nel smiled. "So we'll be professional gossips."

Captain Pomeno liked to use that phrase whenever the guards had to scrounge up every little detail of someone's private life during an investigation. Thinking back to it made Nel remember another tidbit of the captain's wisdom she had recently quoted.

"Do you have a zebra?" she asked. Upon Mainu's puzzled expression, she continued, "As opposed to my horse, I mean. I've been trained to think of the most boring answer to every question. I'm curious how an investigator of the High Court thinks. If you don't mind me asking, that is."

Mainu set down his drink. "Your reasoning about Vei Ruola having run off with a younger man makes perfect sense. If I'm being honest, I hope the solution will be that simple. But I've seen cases where it wasn't, and because of that, I need to consider all options."

"Such as?"

"She could have been afraid. Of what, I'm not sure. Like I mentioned before, she was beloved in Midorea for her support of the arts and charitable efforts. It wouldn't lead you to think many had a reason to hurt her."

"No, I suppose it wouldn't."

Nel pondered Mainu's angle, trying to see what might have frightened Vei Ruola. Whatever it was, it must have been something she couldn't reveal to anyone. Otherwise, she might have asked the city guard for help or simply fled home to her husband. Nothing of the sort sounded likely.

"Bornessi did mention she'd been keeping some undesirable company," Mainu said.

"The bluebells, you mean? You think it might have been them?"

"I'm asking, rather. Are they dangerous?"

Nel weighed her answer. "I wouldn't call them that. They do cause a lot of trouble—loitering, harassment, destruction of property, and such. And a fair number of them are violent. Anywhere they show up regularly, there's bound to be a brawl sooner or later. But it's all petty. I don't see what they'd have against her. She's not nobility, is she?"

"No, she's not."

"Then I shouldn't think she had a reason to worry about them. At least, not as an organization. One of them might have had a grudge against her personally, but that's not closer than any other guess."

Their deliberation was interrupted by a young Midorean wearing a simple green jacket with the consulate's emblem on it. He bowed courteously to Nel, then addressed Mainu. "*Eph Daëlin taiskedett.*" His tone rang with a sense of urgency, further underpinned by the sharp movement with which he handed a folded-up copy of the New Montres bulletin to the lieutenant.

Nel had not seen the morning's paper yet, so she didn't know what article Mainu was reading. She did, on the other hand, recognize the page. It was the same one where she had posted an announcement one year ago when she needed to report a dead person of unknown identity.

Mainu asked something in Midorean, to which the aide shook his head and gave an equally terse response. Finally, he dismissed the boy, but he kept the paper and passed it over the table. It wasn't difficult for Nel to recognize which section had grabbed his interest.

> *Last night, on the Second to the High of Fall, an unidentified woman of Midorean heritage was found dead near the corner of Upper Court Road and Keymaker's Lane. The Upper Court District branch of the New Montres City Guard requests all citizens aware of a missing person that fits the below description to report either to the South New Montres Deadhouse by the Broken Bridge or to any district guardhouse, where lightpaper pictures of the victim will be posted.*

Following that was a description which, as far as Nel was concerned, could have fit any of the staff around her.

"Has the consulate received one of these pictures yet?" she asked.

"No," came the expected answer. "He said it should be arriving later."

"Do you want to wait for it here?"

The answer to that one was no surprise, either.

* * *

The Broken Bridge was at the southern tip of Crescent Bay, a short walk from the Midorean consulate. All Nel and Mainu had to do was follow the Golden Circle around the market and then the riverbank for a few minutes. On another day—and another occasion—it would have been an idyllic way to spend a few minutes in the city. As it was, the two of them marched at a tense pace along the busy road, dodging potholes and puddles while the rain beat down all around them.

Neither of them said anything the whole way to the undistinguished building of the deadhouse. Nel pushed the entrance open and led the way downstairs, several yards below sea level, where it was shivering cold regardless of season. At this time of year, the modest light of the wall lamps showed Nel's breath hanging thick in the air before her. The office at the front was empty, but the cracked-open door at the back allowed the sound of carefree whistling to echo forth from the work area.

Mainu stepped up to the unmanned desk and rang the bell.

"One minute," the coroner called and, true to his word, took a while before emerging.

Nel had paid him a handful of visits since the incident with Ollie, and each time, he greeted her with the same lukewarm affability as a tailor might greet a returning customer. The only thing that differed was the length of his sideburns, which he apparently thought a good idea to grow out.

"Morning to you, officers." He stood behind the desk. One of his hands rested on the handle of a knife in his spattered leather apron. "How can I be of use?"

"We're here to see the Midorean you found last night,"

Mainu answered.

The coroner casually gestured inside. "Right this way."

Sharp, white quartz light flooded the back room and illuminated the row of tables that held the bodies waiting to be dissected, identified, or transported. Most of them were covered under sheets, except for the one whose examination Nel and Mainu had interrupted. Nel kept her eyes on the floor, though the blackish red rivulets that ran toward the drain left little to the imagination.

"How did she die?" Mainu asked on the way.

"Well," the coroner began with something of an arc in his voice, "the direct cause of death is bleeding out. As you'll see, it's quite in the literal sense in this case."

In the corner of the room, he opened the light above the table, then pulled back the canvas to reveal a body so pale Nel could hardly believe it had ever been alive. Corpses were never particularly frightening to her, but when she realized what the coroner meant by his odd choice of words, she had to cover her mouth.

"A bloodsucker?" she blurted out.

"Too right." The man nodded. "After twenty years, I thought I'd seen everything in this profession. Goes to show you can never get too comfortable, you know."

Comfort was the furthest thing from Nel's mind. Exactly *what* was on her mind was up in the air. For one, there was the abject horror of a dead body completely drained of blood. For another, there was bewilderment over the very fact that something like this was possible. But above all, there was a sudden and profound sense of confusion—one that reflected in Mainu's eyes as their gazes met above the table.

"This isn't her."

He was the one who spoke, but the words may as well have come from Nel. Having studied the dozens of portraits in Vei Ruola's day chamber, she would have recognized that face better than some of her own relatives.

"I'm sorry—this isn't who?" the coroner asked.

"We're searching for a missing person," Nel replied. "Taëminn Vei Ruola. She disappeared about three weeks ago from her home on Solluri Hill."

"Ah."

"Where did you find her?" Mainu asked.

"I'm told she was in an alley behind the Garden of Lilies." The coroner emphasized the last words as if they were meant to be self-evident. After a brief, expectant silence, he clarified, "A plush cathouse in the Upper Court District."

"A cathouse?" Nel blinked. "Was she killed in there?"

"Can't say for certain, but a few things are for sure. Several people saw her inside. She was wearing one of the ribbons given to guests there. And there is a known bloodsucker working at the Garden." The coroner counted off on his fingers. "Or *was*, rather. The guard arrested her shortly after the body was found, when she tried to sneak out the back."

Mainu received the explanation with a plain, "I see."

Chewing off a bit of his fingernail, the coroner asked, "You don't know who this is, then?"

"No. Someone at the consulate might. I understand you took pictures of her?"

"I did, yeah. They went to the guardhouses right away. I can send one over to you tomorrow. Or if you don't mind coming back later in the evening, I should have it by then."

"I don't mind," Mainu said.

With that settled, Nel figured they had no reason to linger.

The coroner thanked them for their company and escorted them to the office, after which he ducked back into the room, resuming both his work and the jaunty tune where he left off.

Nel and Mainu climbed the rugged stone steps to the street and walked out into the slightly less chilly air. They headed back toward the consulate with markedly slower steps as they pondered the significance of this revelation.

"Do you think they're connected?" she asked once they were at the bay, and the constant rattle of coach wheels filled their ears again.

"I don't know. It doesn't make sense either way. I don't see what this would have to do with Vei Ruola, but it's too much of a coincidence."

That it was. Over eight years, Nel had never heard of a Midorean getting murdered in New Montres, or being involved with a serious crime in any capacity, for that matter. Now one had disappeared, and another one was killed. It beggared belief that two such extraordinary events would simply happen within a few weeks.

"Could this—" Nel began tentatively. "Could this perhaps be what Vei Ruola was afraid of?"

For the first time since they left, Mainu turned to her. "That's quite the zebra to consider."

She gave an awkward shrug by way of response. "When you're faced with the victim of a bloodsucker, the boring answers aren't of much use anymore."

"I suppose not. For the time being, I think we should focus on our own investigation and leave this one to your colleagues. If there is a connection, maybe Vei Ruola's friends and acquaintances can tell us about the other woman."

Nel hemmed in uncertain agreement. On the one hand, she

was never sorry to fall back on routine. Routine was familiar and safe. Spending the rest of their day as professional gossips promised a chance to get back in her element and regain confidence. Hopefully, it would also yield some bit of information to lead them to the next step.

On the other hand, given the new set of circumstances, Nel had serious doubts about how routine that next step would be.

# Chapter 11

How long she'd been awake when she heard the door creak, Ida couldn't tell. It might have been a minute. It might have been hours. Her body was as good as frozen to the cot, with her back against the wall and her knees pulled up to save every precious drop of warmth. The autumn light that trickled into her holding cell was so uniformly weak, she could only guess at the time of day. If her mind was to be trusted, it was early morning.

She stretched out one stiffened leg, which immediately cramped from the cold. Ida rubbed her calf through the coarse fabric of her trousers. The guards had given her a set of clothes upon her arrival, so she wasn't forced to spend the night in her nothing of a gown. Their hospitality had not extended to a pair of shoes, leaving Ida to massage the life back into her toes one by one. Whether she'd need them to walk anywhere was a question for later.

The door that opened was well out of her of view at the top of a staircase. It was the same one she'd been ushered down the previous night, after being shackled and humiliated—not in the confines of the Garden, but out on the open street. They didn't allow her back inside; they didn't so much as show her the person she'd supposedly killed. They simply tore off her veil, threw her into a wagon, and led her here to await trial.

But Ida wasn't content with waiting.

She had faced hopelessness before, seventeen years ago, when she was forced to leave her home country in shame. That time, it was her own fault—both for being unfaithful to her husband and for believing he might forgive her if she confessed. The other man refused to take her in, despite Ida being over seven months along with his child. He only threw enough money at her that she could buy passage across the Gray Sea and disappear from his life. The despair drove Ida into early labor aboard the vessel, and it was nothing short of a miracle that an ancient midwife was among her travel companions. Had it not been for her skill, neither Ida nor Forley would have made it to the shores of Ardonne.

Yet, against all odds, they did. Over seventeen years, Ida clawed out her hope ounce by ounce from the grasp of misfortune. Each day she saw, she had earned through strife and hardship. They wouldn't be taking that away from her so easily.

A series of unhurried footsteps rang between the peeling walls of the guardhouse basement. Ida stood up to greet her visitor: a lanky, freckled young man of no more than twenty, loudly chewing on a piece of entwood bark. He stopped before her cell and turned to face her, revealing the deep metal tray he carried at his side.

"Arm's length from the bars," he drawled, holding the bark fast between his reddened teeth.

Ida obliged and put her hands behind her back for good measure. The guard slid the tray through a horizontal opening in the middle, which was fitted with a wooden plank on the inner side to serve as a table. Once he stepped back, he motioned permission for Ida to take her breakfast. It included two pieces of stale brown bread, a generous thimble of olive oil, and half a cup of wine.

She offered the latter to the guard. "I won't be needing this, Officer—" she trailed off, inviting him to finish the sentence. As she'd been stripped of her veil, she had to fashion a new one by tearing a strip of cloth from her unused gown. Coupled with the unflattering sack cloth outfit, she wasn't quite the picture of seduction. Nonetheless, she kept her poise.

The young man returned a grin that was too lazy to be called smug. "'Officer' works fine." He accepted the cup and took a swig. "You don't drink wine?"

"I'm enough of a burden on you already. I wouldn't want to make it worse by getting sick all over your floor."

"Oh, you needn't trouble yourself about that." The officer downed another mouthful, but he didn't walk away. He slid one hand into his trouser pocket and leaned against the bars, comfortably swirling the wine that was already half gone.

"Is there something you need from me?" Ida asked.

"I'm going to need that back." The man nodded toward the tray. "And I don't like to make two trips."

On the surface, there was nothing more to his words than simple sloth, but Ida was keenly aware of their real meaning. Like the exotic beasts on display at the imperial menagerie, Ida existed to him as a curiosity, a plaything to ogle and throw scraps of food at for entertainment.

Biting her lip under her makeshift veil, she sat back down and began chipping away at her meal. The thick, leathery crust on the bread made it especially difficult to break off pieces that she could slip into her mouth beneath the fabric. Had she been alone, she would have lifted it altogether and torn straight into the slice with her teeth. No doubt the officer was expecting something similar, but Ida wouldn't give him that satisfaction yet.

"You do eat human food, huh?" he said, while Ida forced down the third spongy bite.

"What else do you imagine a human would eat?"

"Your kind must be called bloodsuckers for *some* reason."

"Blood is something I need to survive. But not everything."

Ida picked her tone carefully to be soft-spoken and humble, with the slightest hint of inviting defiance. She recognized the officer as one of those who arrested her the night before—and, more importantly, the one she overheard bragging about how he'd "sweet-talked" Violet into telling him about the kitchen exit. That alone was enough to tell Ida what had happened after the guards arrived. It also told her what kind of man the officer was, if Violet's charms worked so easily on him.

"So how's it feel?" he asked after another minute.

Ida said nothing. It was abundantly clear what he meant, and that he'd been dying to ask it since they met.

He shifted his shoulder to prop himself higher up against the bars, so he looked further down at her. His tongue flicked at the soggy end of the bark between his chapped lips, while he tapped the side of the wine cup.

"I once heard it's better for the one being sucked than the one sucking. Though I guess that's true of more than one thing," he said and chuckled. "You should have plenty of experience in either case."

Ida responded after a measured pause. "I've only ever been on the one side, so I can't say how it is for the other. But I've never had any complaints. . . in either case."

"With those teeth, I have a hard time believing that for one of them."

While he rolled the bark over to the other corner of his mouth, Ida's fingertips ran along the edge of the tray.

"Is that a challenge, Officer?"

He emptied his wine and grinned wider. "Maybe."

* * *

The rest of the morning dragged by in numb emptiness. Ida had fully expended her strength being upset and worried the previous night, leaving herself with nothing but to wait and wonder. What would happen next? How soon would the guard put her on trial? Was anyone from the Garden trying to find her? Would she be allowed visitors at all—and if yes, who would show up?

Out of all questions, the last one was answered first, and it was the answer she had dreaded the most.

The frantic sound of Forley's footsteps gave him away in a heartbeat, as he nearly sent himself tumbling down the stairs in his blind haste. Ida barely had the time to straighten herself before he skidded to a halt in front of her cell. He wasn't wearing his uniform, which meant he had not been to work at all.

"Ma!" he wheezed in between gasping breaths. "Ma, what happened? Are you all right? The paper said someone was killed at the Garden, and when I went there, it was closed down. They said the guard thinks you're the killer!" His eyes were the size of saucers. "You didn't kill anyone, right?"

"Of course I didn't!" Ida wrapped her hands around his, which clutched the bars so tightly his knuckles threatened to snap.

"But it was a bloodsucker that did it," he rattled on. "Was it someone from the Belfry? Do you know them?"

"Shhh!" Ida pressed a finger on his lips. "Keep your voice down." She couldn't see the officer or any other guard behind Forley, but she wouldn't risk being eavesdropped upon.

Forley strained himself into a whisper. "It must have been one of the others. They did it at the Garden because they knew you work there, and you'd be suspected. You've got to tell the guard about them."

"No one at the Belfry had any reason to do such a thing," Ida spoke slowly but firmly over his rambling. "And I'll need their help if I'm released. Until I'm certain one of them turned on me, I won't rat them out to save my own hide. For now, I don't know anything and neither does the guard. That's how we need to keep it. Anything I tell them, they'll use against me."

She caressed his hand and tried her best to soothe his nerves. Unfortunately, as was his nature when upset, Forley proved impervious to reason.

"Then what? I can't sit around and wait for them to hang you! I have to get you out of here!"

Any other day, Ida might have been moved by his affection. Knowing what she was about to tell him next, however, only made her more concerned about his reaction. "You need to find Mendel."

The mention of the name doused a good portion of Forley's passion at once.

Ida continued, "He was with me when the murder happened. They didn't let me talk to him last night, but he can vouch for my innocence. If you want to help me, get him down here."

She could tell her words had reached the boy's mind, but

outwardly, he only said, "So you do trust him."

"Don't start this. Not now."

"If he can vouch for you, why didn't he do that already?" he asked, accusing both Mendel and her at the same time. "He should know you're here."

The question hadn't escaped Ida, either. All she could answer was the truth. "I don't know why. Maybe he tried, and they didn't listen. That's what I need you to find out from him."

"Why can't *I* do something for you?"

"Like what?"

Forley chewed his lip. "I heard upstairs there might be a release bond."

At first, Ida didn't understand what he meant—not because the concept was unknown to her, but because she didn't want to believe he was serious. "Darling, even if there is one, that'll be thousands of silvers."

He lowered his head in sullen resignation. "Right. That's the kind of money Lord Mendel has."

Ida reached out of the cell and cupped his cheeks. He pursed his lips and avoided her gaze, before at last giving in to sense. Between the bars, she touched her forehead against his. Some days, he really was only a silly little boy.

"Forley, please. You have nothing to prove to me. This is a matter of life and death, and I need you to listen now more than ever. Go back to the tannery, speak to Mendel, and apologize to the foreman for missing work. You'll still need to have a job when I get out of here."

He nodded without a word and wiped his eyes, then hugged her one last time and took off. Ida lay back down to await his eventual return. She could only hope Mendel would be with him, and that he wouldn't try to do anything foolish.

# Chapter 12

Thessa banged on the door five times. The brass knocker, cast in the shape of a flower crown, was ice-cold under her fingers and slick with rain. It was heavy too, as it hit the lacquered green wood with a resounding force that must have been heard all throughout the house. But no answer came.

She took a step back and surveyed the building. Every window on every side was shuttered, even the ones on the attic floor. Sidling up to them, Thessa believed to hear voices or some other sign of life from within, but nothing distinct enough to give her confidence. She knocked again and kept waiting. Behind her, Snake Eyes snorted in irritation at the downpour and shook the reins tying him to the post, as if chiding Thessa for wasting time when they had work to do.

Right when she was about to heed him and turn around, a panel on the door slid open to reveal a stern face with a prominent white scar across one eye.

"Darno," Thessa almost shouted the greeting in her relief.

"How are you, Thessa?" he answered warmly. "What are you doing, standing around in this rain? You'll catch a monster of a cold."

As the main guard, one of Darno's duties was to appear

as intimidating as possible, and from the stories Thessa heard from the women, he had no trouble living up to that appearance. Once she had talked to him in person, he revealed himself to be one of the gentlest souls she had ever met.

"It's true, then?" Thessa asked. "It happened here?"

"If you can believe it." Darno nodded. "It happened out the back, and that was close enough for the guard to lock us down."

"Can you let me in?"

"I'm under strict orders not to allow any visitors." While the guard shook his head in regret, a twinkle flashed in his eye. "But if you have a delivery, I don't think there's anyone watching the side door."

On that hint, Thessa drew up her hood again, made sure none of the passersby paid attention to her, then snuck into the service alley behind the house. According to the town bulletin, as well as Darno's comment, this was where the Midorean woman's body had been found the previous night. Whatever trace there had been of her, the rain had washed it all away by this point, leaving only the rough stones streaked with caked-on mud and grime.

The side entrance was indeed unlocked. Thessa only opened it enough to slip through, then hurriedly closed it behind her right away. She continued along the service corridor until she reached the door to the main hall, where at last the low murmur of voices confirmed the suspicions she had on the outside. Raised as a seasoned eavesdropper in her father's court, Thessa held out to discern the atmosphere inside the other room. Once she was certain she wouldn't be interrupting at a bad time, she turned the knob.

The shuttered windows made the hall considerably darker

than usual, but nonetheless, Thessa recognized all eight faces huddled in the middle. Ever since she shared a coach to New Montres with the Garden's owner, and the women showed her so much kindness in her hour of need, Thessa had made sure to drop by every once in a while. Over time, she became fast friends with a number of them. Chief among those was the sprightly young Ivy, who sprang to her feet and threw herself into Thessa's arms as soon as she crossed the threshold.

"Thistle!" Ivy yelped in delight and threatened to squeeze the very breath out of her.

Thessa had never worked at the Garden, despite Beldora making that offer to her before she got hired as a messenger. As much as she appreciated the gesture, Thessa had more than her share of sweet-talking men, both during her time at home and on the road as a grifter, so she had turned it down. Still, Ivy and some other girls insisted on giving her an honorary title, eventually settling on Thistle as both a play on her name and a reflection of her staunch nature.

Once relieved from Ivy's embrace, Thessa went to the rest of the group to make her round of greetings. The women sat in a haphazard circle, where they each busied themselves with darning tights, patching shifts, or some other form of needlework. Apart from the chairs they occupied, all others in the hall lay upturned on the tables. Thessa removed one for herself to join them.

"What's going on with you?" she asked.

Poppy, the red-headed Mountain girl, was first to answer. "We're being forced to keep closed, but Beldora wants to make the most of it." She waved her needle at the ceiling. "The others are cleaning the house from cellar to attic, while we do all the sewing and mending we've been putting off."

"But what happened? Darno said someone died outside. Is that true?"

At that, eight voices gave eight different answers.

"Yes."

"No."

"They said she did."

"It wasn't really here."

"Here's what happened for sure," Poppy spoke up again when the commotion died down. "We were having a night like any other. The men came, we served them, danced for them, bedded them as always. All of a sudden, the city guard barges through the door and says there's been a murder, and that no one is to go anywhere. They start rounding up the guests, both downstairs and up, half of them with their trousers undone. Everyone's asking what in the deep dark's going on, and at last, the sergeant spits out there was a Midorean woman dead in the alley with our ribbon on her wrist."

"Your ribbon?" Thessa repeated. "Was she a guest here?"

Yet again, eight different answers came from eight directions.

"Yes."

"No."

"They said she was."

"She wasn't really here."

Ivy picked up the thread this time. "She came in not an hour after we opened. Darno remembered her, and a few of us saw her too."

"Me and Daffie did," said Poppy. "And Ebony as well."

Daffodil, the straw-haired Werrish girl in the corner, chimed in, "But she didn't talk to anyone."

"And she sure as day didn't buy a ribbon," said the black-haired Ebony, who usually tended to the counter where guests paid for the Garden's services. "Or a drink or anything."

"Right." Daffodil pointed at Ebony with her spool. "All she did was wander around for a while, and then she was gone."

Thessa did her best to follow along with the group's chaotic retelling and piece together the events. "The Midorean left before she was found dead?"

By this point, she should have seen the result coming.

"Yes."

"No."

"They said she did."

"We don't really know."

Poppy wrestled back the reins of the discussion, much to Thessa's gratitude. Her down-to-earth temperament was a great help in untangling the situation. "None of us are sure, truth be told. The night got going in earnest, and we weren't getting any business from her, so no one paid any mind whether she was around."

"But Darno didn't see her leave," Ivy piped up.

"Could she have used the side exit?" Thessa ventured, hoping the question was straightforward enough not to elicit another wave of contradictions.

Poppy shrugged. "None of us showed her where that is, and someone would've noticed her snooping around."

"Unless Hazel told her," Daffodil said, "or took her through it."

Ivy's curled locks flew in all directions as she snapped at her. "Daffie!"

The blonde girl's tone hinted at much more than simple guessing, as did the group's reactions. The chatter of voices died in a heartbeat, and a chill swept over the room. It wasn't so much the meaning of Daffodil's words that appeared to shock the other women, but rather the fact she said them out loud.

"What?" Daffodil asked back impatiently. "We're all thinking it."

"No, we aren't!"

"Speak for yourself."

In between the retorts, Thessa nabbed the opening to get a question in. "Why would you think that? You said none of you spoke to her."

"None of us *here* did," Daffodil answered before anyone else could. She made another gesture with the spool in her hand. "But what these two are dancing around"—she pointed in succession at Poppy and Ivy—"is that the Midorean wasn't simply found dead. She was sucked dry."

If her words had sent a chill across the hall before, now she might as well have thrown open the windows and conjured the coming winter itself. Most of the women shushed and hissed at her. Poppy pressed her lips in disapproval, while Ivy and Ebony watched Thessa's face with concern.

Thessa, meanwhile, was stunned speechless.

The name of Hazel was not unfamiliar to her. She had some faint memories of meeting her a few times in the past, but they rarely spoke. For the most part, Hazel gave the impression that she preferred to keep to herself. It was Ivy and her friends who confided in Thessa the truth behind the Laerithian's aloof demeanor—and the veil she never took off.

Could this woman truly have murdered someone in this very house? Thessa's skin bristled at the idea. Then again, she knew all too well that no one could be discounted as a killer.

As the commotion in the room was about to erupt anew, a

ninth voice commanded from the archway to the entrance, "That's enough of that."

Beldora marched into the main hall with Darno close behind. He had her fur-trimmed autumn coat on one arm, while he extended the other in anticipation of taking the madam's finely embroidered shawl. As Beldora unwound it from around her head, she revealed her graying hair tied up in a bun with not a single strand out of place. Her dark eyes, marked with the deep lines of age, scanned the hall and landed on Daffodil.

"Unless you're in a rush to follow Violet out the door," she said, "you will stop that kind of talk. Am I understood?"

Thessa rose to her feet on instinct. "I'm so sorry, Beldora. It's not her fault. I was the one who asked." She tried to soothe the madam, only to remember that she herself wasn't supposed to have been allowed in to begin with.

Beldora's expression remained stern. "Her words are her responsibility. I won't have any more backstabbing in this house, and especially not from another Werrish. We don't need to play into Vendriane's schemes, wittingly or not."

She turned back to the group, where a contrite Daffodil hung her head and muttered an apology from behind her straw-colored locks. Beldora acknowledged it, then asked Thessa to accompany her to the office, while she instructed the rest of the women to resume their work.

Walking behind the madam reminded Thessa of all the times she had to follow a teacher or governess to the day chamber, so her parents could punish her for misbehaving. Her apprehension was eased by Darno who, after opening the room and hanging Beldora's garments, helped Thessa into a chair and gave her a brief smile on his way out.

Thessa spared a moment to take a second glance at Beldora. She had known her to be poised and strong of character from the day they'd met, but it was always with a hint of playfulness. Their journey to New Montres was a vivid memory in Thessa's mind—how kindly Beldora greeted her in the coach, or how little reservation she had about referring to herself as a whore. Thessa had never seen her this strict and intense, but given the circumstances, she couldn't fault her for it.

"I shouldn't have pried so much," Thessa said. "Please don't punish Daffodil because of me."

As a welcome sign of her usual personality, Beldora swigged her hip flask before answering. "I won't, don't worry. But we can't go pointing fingers at each other in a time like this."

She lowered herself into a cushioned seat next to Thessa. Her room, situated in the furthest corner of the house, didn't give the impression of a regular office so much as a day chamber. Soft, inviting chairs stood in a loose arrangement, mixed with tables of varying sizes, and plants loomed in enormous copper pots polished to a fine sheen.

"All right, then." Beldora heaved a resigned sigh and passed Thessa a glass of wine from one of the various drink trays scattered about. "How much have my girls babbled to you?"

"Only that a Midorean woman came in here, and she was later killed by. . . a bloodsucker."

"That's right. *Some* bloodsucker. Any one in the city, for all we or the guard know."

"You're quite sure it wasn't Hazel, then? I knew her very little, but I can't imagine her a killer."

"No, never. She's been in her state for fifteen years, and she's been getting by perfectly well. Not to mention she has a son—a grown man, mind, but Hazel thinks of him as a babe in arms. There's no reason she'd do something this senseless."

"Where is she now?" Thessa asked.

"At the guardhouse in a holding cell. They caught her after Violet cozied up to one of them and told him about the kitchen exit. Then she had the gall to tell me the guard had threatened her into speaking. Ha!" She let out a bitter laugh. "As if I didn't know what a smooth little minx she was. It was the whole reason I gave her a job. After that, I told her straight up to pack her things and be out within the hour."

She swigged her hip flask again, and Thessa sipped politely at her wine.

"And what will become of Hazel?"

"I don't know. I've been fighting all morning to visit her, but the guards refused. They didn't want to give me a chance to *collude* with her."

"Collude?"

"That's right. One of the local officers, a sergeant named Vendriane, has it in for us badly." Beldora tipped her flask. "In for me, rather. He's convinced that every Werrish person of any standing in New Montres works for the Werrish syndicate. Have you ever heard of them?"

"In passing, yes," Thessa afforded herself a white lie.

In truth, she had gotten intimately acquainted with one of the syndicate's members, a man named Rasser, when she and Corlis unwound his efforts to steal smuggled quartz. Luckily, as no one saw her in human form at the time, she had managed to escape their attention since.

"Vendriane thinks I'm running some sort of hideout," Beldora went on. "He and his men have raided us more than once over the years, but they found nothing. I would bet decent money he'll take advantage of this incident to try to put me away for good."

She picked a piece of lint from the sleeve of her tailored dress. "So you see, that's why I don't want the girls turning on each other. It was a rash enough decision on my part to kick out Violet last night. I have no doubt Vendriane will use her against me. But that's my mistake and my responsibility. For now, I have to make sure everyone stays safe."

Thessa fiddled with her glass as she listened. Knowing how Beldora cared for those in her employ, there was no doubt this situation burdened her in more ways than one. It was deeply unfair.

"I could try to visit Hazel for you," she said. "I know enough about her to claim to be a friend. I don't work here, and the guards have no reason to think I'm involved. They should let me talk to her. I can give her a message or ask questions for you."

Beldora frowned at the suggestion. "I appreciate the offer, dear, but I can't expect you to get caught up in this mess."

"I won't get caught up. I'll only be a messenger. That's my job, anyway," Thessa added. "I can come back later this evening or talk to more people for you. I have every excuse to go wherever in the city."

The madam's long fingers drummed on the polished wood of the table while she considered the proposition. It wasn't much longer until she relented. She explained where Thessa would find Hazel and who she must talk to in order to be allowed in. As for questions, all Beldora wished to know was what she'd been doing at the time of the murder and if she had any knowledge of the dead Midorean.

Thessa noted down the important details for later. Following that, she passed through the main hall to give her goodbyes to the women, and at last hurried out into the rain, where Snake Eyes awaited her with eager stomps of his hooves.

The district's local guardhouse wasn't far from the Garden of Lilies, a quarter of an hour on horseback. But Thessa didn't direct her horse that way. Instead, she turned onto the wide road that led to the bridges and would eventually wind toward the northern outskirts of the city.

Inwardly, she apologized to Beldora for telling another white lie, because Thessa had every intention of getting caught up in the situation. She only needed to make a detour to the Wall District first.

* * *

Corlis dropped his rag on the counter and took a long, slow breath through his nose.

"Really, Thessa? For once, someone dies without either of us being a suspect, and you *volunteer* to investigate?"

Around them, The Lame Mare was packed wall-to-wall with neighborhood workers who required some encouragement in the middle of their shifts. In the middle of this rush, Thessa managed to snatch her friend for a few minutes to recount what she'd heard at the Garden of Lilies. The cuff of her uniform sleeve stuck in a puddle of wine as she leaned forward to raise her voice above the racket.

"I'm not going to investigate. I just. . . want to help them figure out what happened."

Corlis didn't dignify that with any response beyond a stare from beneath his thick black eyebrows.

Thessa pushed on. "These women were kind to me when I

had nowhere to go. I owe them this much."

"How much is that?"

"I'll go down to the guardhouse and speak with Hazel. Get her side of the story to see if she knew the victim. Whatever she tells me, I tell Beldora, and then we're done."

"Mm-hm." Behind the bar, Corlis grabbed three tankards with one hand and filled them with ale. "Which guardhouse was it again?"

"The one in the Upper Court District."

"That's a fair trip." The innkeeper sucked his tooth. "The lunch rush should be over in a half hour. I can leave things over to Addie then, but not before." He cocked his head toward the barmaid waiting next to him.

"Oh, no." Thessa pulled away from the counter in defense. "I wasn't asking you to come. I only needed your advice."

"I know that. My advice is you should take me with you."

"What? Why?"

Corlis passed the tankards to Addie, who spun on her heels and plunged herself into the crowd, her tray full of ale held high for safety. Afterward, Corlis flung the counter open and walked past Thessa with his trusty rag in hand.

"Because everything about this murder reeks of a frame-up," he said. "Whether it's the guard or not, someone has it in for your friends. Which means you'll want to help them more, and you'll inevitably get yourself into some sort of trouble, and I won't have it on my conscience to let you do that alone."

# Chapter 13

If anyone asked, Ida would have imagined many things to be the worst about being jailed. The biting cold, the hard cot, the pittance of food, or the abuse of the guards might have come to mind amongst a myriad of other guesses. What would not have occurred to her first was boredom.

But nobody asked Ida. Not about that, nor about anything else, as there was nobody there to do so. She would have expected some day-drinkers or loiterers to be taken in at some point, but as the officer helpfully explained when he brought her lunch, those were in a separate area upstairs. Ida's cell was specifically meant for those waiting to be put on trial or transported to a more permanent arrangement.

"We wouldn't want to mix hardened criminals like yourself with some ordinary folk who had one too many," he said, with his usual bit of bark poking out from between his teeth.

It was sometime after midday when the door at the top of the stairs opened again. Ida all but leapt to the bars when she heard two pairs of feet shuffling down the steps, hoping Forley had already returned with Mendel. Her spirits, however, were quickly brought closer to the ground. As the visitors approached, they muttered indistinctly between themselves, and neither of the voices sounded familiar. With a mixture of disappointment and uneasy curiosity, Ida pulled back and waited for the mysterious couple to come into view.

When she saw the one in the brown messenger's uniform, Ida first assumed she was about to be handed official news of her trial—or sentence. Only upon closer inspection did she recognize the tan cheeks and almond eyes of the Sallician girl who had occasionally turned up at the Garden.

"Hazel," she said. "Are you all right?"

"Yes, I am," Ida replied, trying to remember the Sallician's name. "Thistle, was it?"

The girl gave her an awkward smile. "That's what Ivy and the others named me. My real name is Thessa. And this is my friend, Corlis."

At the mention of his name, the unknown figure fell in beside her. A scrawny, pale young man with sharp features, coarse black hair, and a pair of greenish-gray eyes that pointed in two different directions with equal amounts of distrust. His clothes gave no hint of his profession, which in and of itself hinted that it was nothing worth notice.

"Good to meet you, Corlis," Ida greeted him, unsure what to make of his presence.

"I was at the Garden earlier," Thessa said. "I spoke to Beldora. She wanted to come see you, but the guards didn't allow her. She's doing everything she can to help you from the outside and to get you a lawyer for your trial."

"I see." Ida's mood cooled further. If all the girl brought were empty promises, she might as well have saved herself a trip. "Thank you for telling me that. If there's nothing else—"

"There is," Thessa cut her off eagerly. "Corlis and I want to help, too."

Ida studied the pair of them warily. "How?"

"Thessa wants to find the real killer," Corlis said in a tone that rang with little enthusiasm. "I'm here to keep an eye on her."

*Find the real killer?*

Ida made no effort to hide her doubt as she looked them up and down. Corlis couldn't have been much older than twenty-five, the same age Ida had been when Forley was born. She certainly wouldn't have considered herself mature enough to investigate a murder at that age, to say nothing of this Thessa girl, who could barely call herself an adult. If the situation hadn't been so dire, Ida would have found the whole thing a farce. As it stood, it was more of an insult. Her life was on the line, and these two wanted to treat it like a riddle.

She mustered her good graces. "I'm grateful for your offer, but it's not needed. My son should be here any minute with the man who can vouch for my innocence. Once he does, I'm sure the guard will release me."

Thessa blinked meekly at Corlis upon the rebuttal. He, in turn, crossed his arms and leaned sideways against the bars, not unlike the officer.

"Was this man with you at the Garden last night?"

"Yes. That's how he knows I'm innocent."

"Then the guards have already questioned him and decided they don't care for his story." He chewed at his fingernails. "Thessa says the local sergeant has a bone to pick with your employer. You'd think he'd want a quick sentence in that case, but I'm not convinced. As long as you're under suspicion, it's an excuse to keep the Garden locked down. Likely that's half the reason they're willing to post a release bond—they might be outright counting on you to run off. The sergeant's got all the time in the world to find whatever evidence he needs, while your friends starve and slowly turn on each other."

Ida listened to his disaffected monotone with mounting frustration. The arguments he laid out were, for the most part, precisely in line with what she had managed to coax out of the officer over the course of the day.

Corlis concluded, "I don't have a dog in your fight, so do what you want. All I'm saying is, it doesn't seem like you're in a place to turn down help."

"He's right, Hazel," Thessa said. "Corlis is one of the sharpest minds I know. He solved another murder this summer, and last year, he uncovered a whole conspiracy among the paladins!"

"Neither of those of my own accord." Corlis spat out a bit of nail. "With your case, we're running three for three. But I'm here if you need me."

It was a bitter pill to swallow, but Ida had no choice. Reluctantly, she told them everything she could recall from the evening before, including the part about Mendel's disappearing ribbon. To their credit, Thessa and Corlis let her speak without interrupting or getting ahead of her. Their silence was so profound, Ida couldn't resist lowering her own voice, despite the three of them having the cellar to themselves.

"Let's start with the obvious," Corlis said when she was done. "Did you know the Midorean?"

"I've never known any Midoreans," Ida replied.

"No one else knew her, either," Thessa added. "They only saw her walk about without talking to anyone."

"She must have been waiting for someone," Corlis said. "The question is whether that person showed up in the end—and if yes, what their intentions were." He kept his head down and his eye fixed intently on one point, like he was reading an invisible sheet of paper. "What does Violet have against you?"

"Nothing she didn't have against the rest of the world," Ida said. "She always was a chore to be around. Wouldn't shut up about what a great dancer she used to be and how much she traveled."

"Was any of it true?" Corlis asked.

"The girls said men would sometimes recognize her, so there must have been something to it."

Thessa chimed in, "Did she ever say why she gave up dancing?"

"She didn't need to say. It's because she turned twenty-six. In the cruel world of dancing, that's as good as ancient." Ida shook her head. "It's rather sad how desperately she clung to her glory days. Beldora had to take her down a peg once or twice. After that, she'd usually take out her tantrums on me, ordering me around and calling me 'Teeth.' I didn't pay it much mind, which only annoyed her more. But I never thought she'd go as far as to frame me."

Rivalry had not been unknown within the Garden. As much as Beldora strove to foster fairness and understanding within the house, any group that spent all their time together would fight sooner or later. Petty tiffs, name-calling, or the occasional practical joke occurred regularly. But when push came to shove, the women would stand up for one another without fail.

"People have done more awful things out of nothing but spite," Corlis replied.

"Maybe she wanted to direct attention away from herself," Thessa wondered aloud. "Could Violet be a bloodsucker?"

Ida shook her head again. "If she is, she's either the first one who can drink, or she found a way to fool everyone. All of us at the Garden have seen her guzzle like a sailor."

"What about the man who stole that ribbon?" Corlis asked. "Any idea who he was?"

"None. I only heard he's middle-aged and completely bald, with a large mole under his nose," Ida recounted Mendel's description.

"I assume that's not someone you recognize. But if he is one of your kind, do you know how we could find him?"

"Many of us in New Montres go to the Belfry in the Riverside District. I don't think he's a member, but someone there might have met him."

Thessa brightened up. "We can go there and ask if you tell us where it is."

"It's not that simple," Ida said. "They don't allow in anyone off the street. A member has to ask permission beforehand and take responsibility for you." She stressed the second half of the sentence to emphasize why she'd be unwilling to do that even if she was free as a bird. "It's not against the law to be a bloodsucker, but it can attract a lot of unwanted attention."

"Murdering someone behind one of the city's most well-known brothels doesn't help much with that," Corlis noted.

The Sallician girl fell quiet, squinting in thought. "What if that was the idea? Someone got on bad terms with those at the Belfry and decided to get revenge by sending the guard after them." She turned to Corlis. "Like you said, people have done awful things out of nothing but spite."

Strangely enough, that did make a certain appalling sense. To Ida's knowledge, the guard had not yet officially announced the Midorean's cause of death. Unofficially, it was impossible to keep such a secret. The rumor rags of

New Montres would happily slip a fistful of coppers to any guardsman who came with the latest, most dreadful bit of news. Whether or not Ida got hanged, her story would put bloodsuckers in the public eye, and the city guard would be pressed to show their strength in protecting citizens.

"If that's true, you'll never find him." Ida faltered. "If someone did this to frame the Belfry, I can't imagine he'd stay in the city after the guard found out. He may as well be a hundred miles away by now."

All at once, her limbs grew heavy and tired. The bloodsucker's curse might have kept her appearance youthful, but it did nothing for her inside. Her bones, her mind, and especially her heart held plenty of reminders of the four decades she'd lived through, and right now, it felt more like eight. Surrendering to the weight of uncertainty, Ida lowered herself back on the cot.

On the other side of the bars, Thessa and Corlis weren't faring much better. The latter pinched the bridge of his nose while drawing a long, slow breath.

"There are too many blind spots." He rubbed his eyes. "We need to get started somewhere, and the only lead we have is Violet. Even if it's only to rule her out."

"How do you plan on finding her?" Ida asked.

"I know someone at the dockyards who can ask around," Corlis said. "When a woman of her profession needs quick work, that's the surest place to get it."

"I'll try to dig up more about the victim," Thessa added. "My colleagues at the guild might know something about her. And I'll find some reason to visit as many guardhouses as I can to see if I overhear anything interesting."

For lack of a better option, Ida thanked them for their

effort before they went on their way. If those two had truly accomplished what Thessa boasted about, then who knew? They might turn out to be useful to her, too. As with Forley, she could only trust them to be dependable. As with Forley, she had great difficulty doing it.

# Chapter 14

*"On my count, men! One—two—THREE!"*

*There was a deafening CRACK! as the combined weight of the three guardsmen lunging against the rickety door tore it clean off its rusty hinges and sent it collapsing to the floor in a cloud of dust and splinters. But while the men succeeded in their effort to break into the wretched abode, the sight that greeted them upon entering took the very breath out of their lungs and threatened to drive them mad where they stood, for at once they found the answer to all the questions that had pained them throughout their search. Half a dozen women had disappeared over as many months. All of them had been seen on the street later, but none of them returned to their homes or spoke to those who'd known them. Most curiously, all witnesses had reported seeing one of the missing women in a long, brown coat that was torn at the elbow, as though all six of them had been the same person.*

*There, in the sole room of the cottage where the suspected kidnapper had fled, tied to the main beam by the ankle like slaughtered cattle, hung six human bodies with their faces cut off.*

As always, the bell rang at the best part.

Argiey folded up the issue of *Bloodcurdling Tales for The Fearless* and dropped it on the end table, next to the oil lamp and his mostly empty tumbler. Leaning forward, he tossed aside the blanket from his lap, while his feet emerged from the pail of hot water on the floor. He toweled them off at a leisurely pace, stretching his toes and massaging his soles in the process. If someone was going to interrupt his evening time, they could very well spare him this one minute.

His stockings were already back on when the bell rang again. Hands still on the boot he had half a foot in, Argiey hop-shuffled over to the window to see who was in such a hurry. The coroner's quarters were directly above the deadhouse, and the drawing room gave a decent view of the main entrance below. At least, that was the case on clear days. When the cold months rolled in, the riverside streets disappeared under a thick fog after dark, which at this time revealed only that the visitor was alone.

Once he was presentable enough, Argiey swigged the last of his caraway brandy, grabbed the lamp from the table, bid a heartfelt goodbye to the masonry stove he'd been warming himself by, and braced himself for the chill.

The entrance opened onto an outdoor staircase, which in turn led down to the yard where hearses and guard wagons could unload incoming customers at basement level. From there, he opened the gate and walked out onto the mist-coated pavement, toward a figure that was little more than a shadow in the scattered light of the gas lamps. At the sound of gravel under Argiey's heel, the visitor turned toward him and pulled back his hood, uncovering a head of bright platinum hair.

"Good evening, coroner," the Midorean said.

"Good evening"—Argiey paused to remind himself of the man's title—"Lieutenant." He didn't bother trying to guess his name.

"I apologize for calling on you at such a late hour."

"That makes you the first to do so. You're here for the picture, I assume?"

"That's right."

"I've got it downstairs." Argiey waved the lamp at the door, then swept it around in an arc while he cast a meaningful glance behind the lieutenant. "Is your colleague from the guard not joining us?"

The man stepped closer. "No. It's only me."

The front of his cloak parted to reveal his forearms, clad in the same immaculate green uniform as earlier that morning. One of his gloved hands reached into the other sleeve, not unlike those streetside entertainers who conjured live birds, playing cards, or endless ropes of handkerchiefs. The young lieutenant performed no such act—he merely pulled out the end of a plain blue scarf.

"We'd better get inside." Argiey loosened the keyring from his belt. "Hope you like pit bitters because that's all I can offer."

Few things demonstrate as much trust in a stranger as going before them into a dark stairwell. The way the lieutenant did so without a flicker of hesitation spoke a great deal about him. For better or worse.

The basement was exactly as Argiey had left it, which meant spotless and perfectly organized. His mentor had an obsession with cleanliness, and besides training up Argiey in his profession, he made sure to instill the same habits in him. As Argiey opened the cover on one of the quartz lamps, the cold, white light fell on a marble slab that may as well have been newly installed.

The lieutenant stood next to the table. "I won't ask more than what I need to know."

"I can't say more than what I do know," Argiey replied.

The bottom drawer rolled out with a deep echo across the room, and the decanter rattled against the glasses pressed up against it. He set them on the desk and poured the drink.

"Is she safe?" the Midorean asked.

"To my knowledge, yes. For now."

"When can I take her home?"

"Not anytime soon." Argiey stuffed the cork back in. "I'm told she insists on finding the killer first."

He carried the drinks over and slid one across the slab. After a few tentative sniffs at the pungent spirit, the lieutenant judged it safe enough to take a mouthful—maybe a little too much so. As valiantly as he fought the urge, not even his rigorous discipline was enough to keep him from flinching. Solidarity demanded that Argiey sip some along with him.

"What else were you told?" the lieutenant—*Mainu*, it came to Argiey at last—asked once his stifled coughs subsided.

"Not a lot. Her name was Kalevi—the dead woman, I mean. A friend from back home, apparently."

"That much I know as well. I saw their letters in Vei Ruola's apartment." Mainu bit his lip. "A bad price to pay for friendship."

"You reckon that's why she was killed?"

"Do you know any other reason someone would want her dead?"

"I pointedly try not to know such things." Argiey drank again. "The less I know, the safer I am. I'm happy to play my part for a better tomorrow, but I'd prefer to see it as well."

The reasoning clearly didn't sit well with the lieutenant. Or maybe that was still the bitters. "Can you arrange a meeting for me?"

"I can try. In the meantime, I'd say your efforts are best spent on the murder."

The corner of the Midorean's mouth gave a twitch of frustration. "That will be a challenge, after I told Nel this morning we should leave it to her colleagues. Not to mention I can't officially know who the victim is." He took a chance on a second gulp of bitters and put up a much better fight this time.

Argiey allowed him a few moments, then asked, "'Nel?'"

Mainu met his gaze. "Sergeant Dormanni."

The clarification was wholly unnecessary. Argiey was well aware whom the lieutenant had referred to, and more so the significance of *how* he referred to her.

"Sounds like you're on good terms."

By and large, bluebells and the city guard got along like water and a grease fire. Sergeant Dormanni had not struck Argiey as a bloodthirsty scourge of the cause—she hadn't struck him as much of anything at all. Besides that, if Vei Ruola's people saw fit to send Mainu to retrieve her, they must have counted on him to have a good head on his shoulders. But his connection to the guard could pose a risk, regardless of his or the sergeant's intentions.

"I tried this morning to get a feel for her attitude," Mainu said. "She doesn't think highly of your organization, but she's not intent on hunting you, either. I don't think she'll be a problem."

"*She* doesn't have to be the problem. Words are like marbles, you know—once you let them slip by accident, there's no telling how far they scatter."

"I trust her."

"Why?"

"Because she's a good person."

The sentiment was simple and touching, but the matter was too important for Argiey not to prod further. "Would that make you feel bad for lying to her?"

Mainu raised his glass to his mouth. "I've lied for worse reasons."

*Fair enough.*

Argiey promised to set up that meeting as soon as he could and to have the details later the next day. The lieutenant, in turn, agreed to stall his pretend investigation and concentrate on the murderous bloodsucker. They walked back up the stairs and out onto the misty streets. Mainu headed off toward his accommodation, while Argiey went to finish his bloodcurdling tales in peace and safety. As much as he took pleasure in reading them, he had no desire for his life to become one.

# IV

# Part Four

# Chapter 15

The door clicked behind Nel with a faint echo across the empty floor, which was followed immediately by the captain's voice from the opposite side. "Dormanni!"

As per usual, the two of them were first at the Ilvior Island guardhouse. Nel headed directly toward the office, straightened out her uniform jacket, and cautiously pushed on the half-open door. Captain Vidore Pomeno's office was a marvel of nature in its own way, as it was impossible to predict what state of disarray it would be in. Since Nel got promoted, it wasn't uncommon for her to run in and out of that room a dozen times within an hour, and she could have sworn the mess inside was different each time she entered. The only constant was the mystery of what kept the captain so busy at the most uneventful guardhouse in all of New Montres—and the fact that his mouth was never not full.

On this particular occasion, Pomeno's lanky figure was surrounded by three stacks of papers that teetered precariously at the edge of his desk. In the middle was half a loaf of emmer bread, some strips of dried meat, and a loose heap of capers. He swept a handful of crumbs on the floor before running a hand through his hair, which had been stuck in a constant state of thinning for the past decade.

"What's the news on that missing Midorean?" he asked. "Has she shown herself already or is the High Court determined to waste more of my officer's time?"

"We have a few theories," Nel began, hands behind her back. "And we've been questioning the friends and acquaintances to confirm if any of them might be valid."

"That's a lot of words to say you have nothing. You and that decorated dandy keep running around the city all day, while I'm drowning in work without you!" Pomeno waved theatrically around the office which, as far as anyone could tell, was in no worse shape than normal. "What good was your promotion if you can't be of use to me here?"

"It's true, sir, we don't have any concrete leads right now. But I assure you, Mai—Lieutenant Eph Daëlin and I are doing our best to solve this case, so I can return to assist you."

She had hastily corrected herself, but her slip of the tongue did not escape the captain's attention. He rose from his chair and leaned forward, squinting with more accusation than he'd give a suspected burglar.

"I know what's going on here." He pointed one finger repeatedly at Nel. "You two—you're in this together, aren't you?"

Nel could only ask back, "Sir?"

Without taking his eyes off of her, Pomeno bit off half a strip of dried meat. "I've been wondering why he asked for you. You met last year when you ran off investigating that murder—without my permission, might I add!" The mouthful of beef sucked all moisture from his tongue, making his words all the harder to make out, but the captain was undeterred. "Suddenly, he's back in New Montres on some alleged kidnapping, and he wants *you* to help him? Out of everyone in the city guard? I wasn't born yesterday, Dormanni. Don't think you can pull the wool over my eyes."

"Sir, I—"

"What are you really doing out there all day? Fooling around on the riverbank while you pretend to be questioning people? Cavorting on the Street of Canopies? Is he teaching you Midorean already, for when you hop aboard a train out of Ardonne?"

"Train?" Nel resorted to single words in the hopes of getting one in edgewise.

Her attempt proved fruitless, as Pomeno threw his hands up in exasperation. "I should have seen this coming. A vivacious young woman like you can get a man on each finger." He turned his back to Nel and was thus unable to see the sheer bewilderment on her face. "No wonder you'd set your sights high. I'd have expected you to be wiser, Dormanni, but it seems you're still a girl at heart. And now, you're about to discard a splendid career at the Ilvior Island guardhouse to run away with that pale-faced pansy." He shook his head. "You're making a big mistake, *Sergeant*. Don't say I didn't warn you."

In all her life, Nel had never spoken as sincerely as when she said, "I don't know what to say, Captain."

Pomeno lowered himself back into his chair and stroked his patchy beard. "You can say I was right when you slink back here two months from now with your tail between your legs. Can't promise I'll forgive you right away. . . but I'll try."

"Thank you, sir," Nel said for lack of a better option, then added, "Am I dismissed?"

The captain grunted an affirmative and attacked his meal

anew.

Nel exited the office, leaving the door halfway open as it was before. She fetched the bag from her desk and decided it would be better to wait for Mainu at the main entrance instead. He arrived right as she reached the doorstep.

"Good morning, Nel." He sized her up. "Is something the matter?"

"Oh, no, nothing." Nel fidgeted under her shoulder strap. "I had a brief talk with the captain."

"Did you? What did he want?" Mainu asked as they crossed the island's main square.

Nel stared straight ahead. "Truthfully, I have no idea."

* * *

Mainu suggested they visit the Upper Court District guardhouse first to see if there was any progress in the Garden murder before the two of them got on with the day's work. While Nel readily agreed it was a sensible choice, it was not without apprehension. Walking into other guardhouses always gave her the uncanny feeling of being in a place that was supposed to be familiar and yet completely strange. It was like coming home one evening to find that all her furniture had been moved around, and there was an unknown person in her kitchen.

On the ground floor, behind a long desk, a middle-aged woman greeted Nel and Mainu with little semblance of collegiality. She surveyed them through her greasy spectacles while Nel explained their purpose.

"Sergeant Vendriane handles all murders," the woman rasped, "but he's out for the morning. His deputy can fill you in. Two flights up, to the right." She pointed the way with a long nail at the end of her knobbly finger, then ignored them to yell at some men for being too loud while they waited to be taken to a holding cell.

Following the instructions, Nel and Mainu proceeded down the hall toward the stairwell. Along the way, they passed some of the questioning rooms, most of which were unoccupied. They were about to reach the last one when the porter's voice stopped echoing between the walls.

"Do you hear that?" Nel asked.

The last door was closed, but now that silence had returned, a few scraps of sound made it through the crack underneath. A muffled thump, some indistinct grunting, and the scrape of wood on the floor. Nel motioned for Mainu to wait, then inched closer and turned the handle. Familiar or not, if there was a scuffle inside, she had to see if she needed to call for help.

Through the opening, the first thing she saw was a face wincing in pain. It belonged to a young man—a boy, rather, of no more than seventeen years. His clenched teeth were smeared with blood from the cut on his lower lip. He appeared oddly short at first, until Nel realized he was doubled over, while one guard twisted his arms behind his back, and another one bent down to level with him.

"I'm not asking again." The second man yanked repeatedly at the boy's ear. "Where are the others, you little sh—"

"What are you doing?" Nel stepped in, hand on the doorknob.

Caught off guard, the two men pulled back from the boy, but not enough to let him stand up. After some confused blinking, the one further back answered.

"Questioning a suspect in a violent crime." His thin brown mustache twitched as he spoke, and his stiff tone suggested that, although he recognized Nel's rank, he did not appreciate the intrusion—either in the room, or in the guardhouse.

"Violent?" Nel asked back. "He's only a boy!"

"He was man enough when he and his pals tried to rob a carriage this morning," said the guard who had been threatening him. He too regarded Nel with the thinnest veil of respect, stroking his salt and pepper stubble as he spoke.

"What pals?" Nel asked.

"That's what we're trying to find out."

"Not like this you won't." She gestured at the boy. "Let him go."

By this time, both men had shaken off their initial surprise. They may have been outranked, but Nel was both outnumbered and out of place.

The stubbled one crossed his arms. "Who are you again?"

Nel drew herself to full height, which was a good four inches below either of them. "Sergeant Nella Dormanni from Ilvior Island."

The mustached one let out a cackle. "The place where boredom dies of old age? What's one of you doing here? Are you out of chicken thieves to chase?"

Whatever pretense of authority Nel could claim was gone. And while the men now directed their bile at her instead of the boy between them, that was only temporary. She had to come up with something more convincing.

"I'm investigating by order of the Midorean High Court," she said, "and the person you're manhandling happens to be a key witness."

What rush of boldness made her tell that lie, she had no

idea. How she was going to follow through on it, she had less of an idea. Nonetheless, it was enough to wrest away some of the guards' confidence.

"Him?" The stubbled one frowned. "What would he have to do with it?"

The stone floor beneath Nel's boots had turned into a swamp and threatened to sink her. She stood rooted to the spot, like an actor who had made their grand entrance and immediately forgot all their lines.

Luckily for her, someone else picked up on her cue.

"Sergeant Dormanni? Are you in here?" Mainu strode into the room with brisk steps and a face of total unawareness. He bowed to the guards. "Apologies, gentlemen. I was trying to catch up to the sergeant. Is this our witness?" He directed the last question to Nel.

"I believe so," she replied as flatly as she could, while fighting the urge to kiss her savior's hand. "If you're ready, we can take a few minutes with him in private."

The sudden appearance of an actual Midorean, coupled with the exchange between him and Nel proved enough to intimidate the guards into compliance. They sidled out of the room amidst curious glances at all of them, but especially the boy. Nel ushered them through, then closed and latched the door.

"I hope I judged your intentions correctly," Mainu said.

"It was perfect, thank you."

Nel turned to the youth, who now stood at full height, easily as tall as the lieutenant. The chain between his iron cuffs rattled as he rolled his shoulder and rubbed specks of dried blood from his lip. The sleeves of his shirt were dusty, but his clothes were otherwise in decent shape, and he was not unkempt. Overall, he didn't give the impression of a delinquent who knew a guardhouse better than his own home.

"Are you all right?" Nel asked.

"I don't know anything about any Midorean," he said sullenly. Though his dark complexion didn't imply that either of his parents were Ardonnese, he spoke without an accent. He picked up the chair that lay toppled on the floor and sat down with his back against the wall.

"I know," Nel said. "I only made that up to get rid of them."

"Why?"

"So they'd stop hurting you."

The boy made an irritated tut. "They're going to come back."

That was undeniable indeed, and it wasn't likely that the guards would develop a more patient nature during the time they were away.

"Were you really trying to rob a carriage?" Nel asked.

"I'm not telling you anything."

"You don't have to," Mainu chimed in from the room's single narrow window. "The sergeant and I only need to keep you company for a short while to make sure our lies don't get exposed. I'd rather not risk getting on Vendriane's bad side this early."

The last sentence was directed at Nel, but it had a much stronger effect on the boy. He unfolded his arms and stared up at Mainu. "You're going to talk to Vendriane?"

Mainu raised his eyebrows at this sudden interest, but didn't reply.

"We're investigating a disappearance," Nel said. "We think it might be related to a recent murder."

"The one at the Garden of Lilies?" the boy asked.

"Yes! Would you know something about it?"

His eyes had flashed with recognition at the mention of both Vendriane's name and the Garden murder. Upon Nel's question, he seemed to realize he'd given too much away, and he drew back again with a curt, "No."

"I hope you don't gamble, young man," Mainu remarked.

Nel, however, got the perfect idea. "If you speak to us, I can make you an official witness in our case and have you moved to the Ilvior Island guardhouse instead. It won't erase your charges, and you'll remain in a holding cell, but no one will treat you like this there. You heard the men: it's the place where boredom goes to die." As bitter as it was to repeat the insult, Nel had to use whatever worked.

The young man's aloof demeanor showed a few cracks. "Can you do that?"

"I can get it done right now," Nel said at first, but wavered when she turned to Mainu. "That is, if it's all right with you as well. I know this is taking time away from our own investigation, and we haven't properly started work for the day, but I promise it'll only be one or two hours—"

She had half a dozen more apologies lined up, but the lieutenant waved them away. "Do what you think is best. I can wait." He then excused himself and left the room, so the newly appointed witness could speak more comfortably with Nel.

Before she asked the first question, the boy got to his feet with an intense glare. Nel stumbled back on instinct, but he didn't move closer.

"What I'm about to tell you, you have to promise it stays between us."

Nel wasn't sure what to make of the demand. "Well, if it's

pertinent to the investigation, I have to take down—"

"I'll say whatever you want me to say," the boy cut her off. "But first, promise me you won't tell anyone what I tell you now."

Despite the forced hush of his voice, it wasn't a threat. There was fear in his eyes, of something he dreaded far more than anything the guardsmen could do to him.

Nel nodded. "All right. You have my word."

He deliberated for a few more breaths, then began in a whisper. "My name is Forley Nawoale. My mother works at the Garden of Lilies—or used to work there, until two nights ago. When that Midorean was killed there, she was arrested."

"Arrested?" Nel couldn't help whispering back. "The killer was a bloodsucker. Does that mean—"

"She is one, yes. But she's innocent. I know she is. She would never do something like that, not to anyone. She's being framed. I had to get her out.

"Yesterday evening, the guard posted a release bond. Two thousand silvers. I talked some of my friends into helping me rob and steal that carriage so I could get the money. When everything went sideways, I told them to get away from there. It was my idea. They shouldn't have to take the fall for it.

"The guard brought me in here, and they've been beating me for however long because I won't tell them anything, not even my name. I can't. My mother's being held in the cellar in this building. If she finds out I'm here, and that it's because of her"—he sat back down and put his head between his hands—"she'll never forgive me. She's always telling me how stupid I am, and that I can't do anything on my own, and now she's right."

Tears of frustration streamed down his cheeks, and he

wiped them away with such anger as if they were strictly responsible for his troubles.

Nel was distinctly unfit to handle the outburst. By the time either of her brothers were Forley's age, she had already moved to New Montres and was surrounded by men five or ten years her senior. She made her best effort to console him in whatever way felt appropriate for a seventeen-year-old boy and hastily tried to regain footing by diverting the topic back to the administrative side of the situation.

She had never fancied herself a lawyer to any degree, but she knew the guard's regulations inside and out. Though she had denied Mainu's suggestion about Pomeno training her to be captain, deep down Nel was keenly aware of what an asset she was to the Ilvior Island guardhouse. Official documents had a secret language, impenetrable to those who lacked the dedication to study them. With the right choice of words, almost anything within the city guard's considerable power could be attained. Turning one district's nameless robbery suspect into another one's key witness was practically trivial.

The letter took less than half an hour to draft and sign, including Captain Pomeno's stamp, which Nel had in her bag at all times. With it, she, Forley, and Mainu proceeded back to the front desk and handed it to the same woman who had greeted them. The clerk wiped her spectacles with a handkerchief that was arguably greasier than the lenses, pursed her lips all the way up to her eagle-like nose, and studied each line of writing for a solid minute. Unable to find any point of debate, she put her own stamp on the bottom and went off to get a formal signature.

The entrance hall had rows of chairs by the wall for visitors and detainees to wait in. Forley sat down on one of these and stared blankly at the floor, while Nel and Mainu remained at the desk to await their document.

"It's an admirable gesture on your part." Mainu lowered his head and his voice. "But do you really think he'll be useful?"

"His mother is the main suspect in the Garden murder. He could have valuable insight."

"Ida Nawoale is his mother?" The lieutenant frowned, then added, "I spoke to Sergeant Vendriane's men while you wrote the letter."

"Yes, that's right," Nel whispered, careful that Forley wouldn't overhear. "He tried to rob a carriage so he could pay her release bond."

Mainu shook his head. "That's unfortunate."

"It is. But I have to admit, it's a very devoted thing for a son to do."

"That's not what I meant." He motioned over to the waiting area, where the boy scraped restlessly at the chips of rust on his chain. "It's unfortunate because Ida Nawoale's bond was paid this morning. They released her not two hours ago."

# Chapter 16

*Ida,*

*I trust that when you read this, you are already a free woman, as much as the circumstances allow. I am deeply sorry I could not deliver this message to you in person, but I have no doubt my presence at the guardhouse would have put you under more suspicion. For the same reason, I cannot show myself near the Garden, but for the time being, I am content knowing you are safe. Please take care of yourself, and I will write to you as soon as possible, in whatever manner I am able.*

*Your friend,*
 *M.*

One short paragraph. Laerithian words, unfamiliar hand. No name at the top and no signet in the plain wax seal that was blatantly broken when the officer passed the folded-up paper to Ida. Mendel must have anticipated the guard's disregard for privacy and enlisted one of the many scribes who worked around the Crescent Bay market. For a few coppers, they would translate any letter to any language; for a few more, they would keep quiet about its contents.

Ida was free, as much as the circumstances allowed. She was still accused of murder. She was still unable to work. But she was allowed to walk under the open sky again, and compared to the harrowing prospect of dying a prisoner, that was a vast improvement.

Once the guardsmen unceremoniously led her outside, the first place she headed was the Garden. She had no illusions of a warm welcome, but she needed a change of clothes and some of her own money. The other women kept their distance, only asking the briefest questions about what had happened to her and how she got out. Beyond that, they left her alone—either as a gesture of respect or to retreat and gossip. Ida knew which one she thought more plausible.

Let them gab all they want. Ida had any number of other concerns, and the slightest of them was a hundred times more important. After she put on a proper dress and her own veil again, she hailed down a coach on the street and took to the Brewer District. It wouldn't have been a terribly long walk, even in the rain that had picked up again, but Ida needed the time to think.

Mendel saved her again. First, he had lied to the guard for her sake. Then, he had paid two thousand silvers out of his own money to let her walk free. No one did that sort of thing out of pure generosity. Most wouldn't do that for a relative, and certainly not for a whore.

The truth was as clear as it was frightening. He loved her. He *wanted* her, at least. He wanted her affections, and he made sure she knew how much.

Was that so terrible?

For the past seventeen years since she left her home, Ida's love had always come at a price. She had never entertained the thought of letting another man have it for free, and she never tried to convince the men otherwise. Mendel was no exception. But perhaps that was the reason. Perhaps he wanted to show he was prepared to pay the price—any price. And as that young man Corlis had pointed out the day before, Ida was not in a position to turn down help.

The cramped space of the coach was suffocating her. She called for it to stop, paid the driver, and covered the remaining distance on foot.

The morning shift at the tannery was close to over, but the workers had not come out yet. There were only two of them huddled under the foot and a half of overhanging roof, pressing their backs against the wall to stay dry and passing a hip flask back and forth. The smell that oozed from the building kept away all but those who had business nearby, so they spotted Ida from the next block over and muttered something between themselves.

"Excuse me," she said when she got within earshot. "I need to talk to my son Forley."

The one on the left had the answer ready. "Haven't seen him in two days, I'm afraid."

"He's not here?"

Forley had come to see her at the guardhouse the day before, but he should have returned to work after speaking to Mendel like she told him to. And right when it seemed he'd gotten some sense in him at last. What was he doing? What was he *thinking*?

"Will he get into trouble for that?" she asked.

"The foreman sure ain't happy about it. If you wanna know

more, ask him. Just make sure that cloth is on real tight." The man motioned at Ida's veil, then toward the massive double doors that opened onto the street.

She thanked them and followed his guidance, gingerly moving one boot over the threshold.

Whether or not she had her sense of smell, the inside of the tannery was nauseating. Raw animal hides stood in piles five feet tall, slick with blood and lymph, the undersides covered in offal. A dozen vats stood in various corners of the room, each of them big enough to drown an ox, and filled to the brim with brown-yellow slop or some other unidentifiable liquid. The very air around the tubs attacked Ida's unfeeling nose with an acrid burn that pierced down to her throat. At one station, a group of women stood with an array of slanted racks between them, pounding sheets of skin with what could only have been a mixture of various dungs.

No one questioned, or indeed acknowledged, Ida's presence. No sane person would set foot in this building without a good reason.

The foreman—tall and round in the belly, with eyebrows thicker than most men's mustaches—stood in the middle of an elevated gallery, from where he shouted instructions over the din of the workshop. He was the only one who noticed Ida at all, and he followed her path along the floor with a heavy frown of disapproval. Once Ida had clambered up the steps and explained her purpose, his brow only knotted deeper.

"What kind of man sends his mother to speak on his behalf?" he grunted.

"He didn't send me. I'm looking for him."

"Well, you're looking in the wrong place. I'd tell you to try again tomorrow, but—*You two!*" He bellowed at one of the vats. *"Enough with the lime, we'll need that for the rest of the year, too!"*

Ida waited impatiently for him to tear his gaze away from the workers below. "Whatever he did, he was only trying to help me." She strained to make herself heard from behind her veil. "You can't think to dismiss him because he missed two days?"

"You'd be amazed what I can think." The foreman dug out a bit of entwood bark from his pocket and clamped it between his teeth. "Anyway, it's not up to me. The young lord makes all decisions himself. He's already saved your boy's hide once—question is whether he'll do it again."

"Saved his hide?" Ida echoed. "When?"

"Two months ago. Didn't he tell you?" The hefty man's belly shook in his mirthful chuckle. "He was caught stealing."

The noise from below was unbearable. That must have been the reason she misheard him. He couldn't have said that.

*"Stealing?"*

"Right from the money box in the office." The foreman pointed his bark toward the door at the far end of the gallery. "I'd have turned him in to the guard then and there, but Lord Soft Scolsessi thought otherwise. He said that, because the apple of your eye was caught before he could take anything, there was no real damage done."

He scoffed at the ridiculousness of his own words. Ida wanted to do the same.

There was nothing else to be said. Ida turned on her heels and marched off. He paid her no mind, instead barking at some workers to hang the finished leather up to dry. Amidst the splashing and yelling that filled the workshop, Ida made her way back to where she'd come in.

Nothing made sense.

The foreman was lying, plain and simple. Forley wouldn't steal. He had gotten himself into trouble before, snatching up unconsidered trifles or pilfering from a market stand, but he'd never do something this brazen. He must have been framed, or tricked, or maybe threatened into it. Most likely by those other young men he shared a roof with. Ida had known it was far too early for him to be on his own. He always tried to prove what a man he was, and they could easily have goaded him into something foolish.

But this foolish? And *two months ago*! That meant it happened mere weeks after he was hired. This whole time, he'd hid this from her, lying to her face that everything was all right, meanwhile he'd narrowly escaped not only being dismissed, but jailed.

Narrowly escaped, thanks to Mendel, who had been lying along with him.

At that, all of Ida's lingering guilt and sense of debt toward Lord Soft Scolsessi evaporated. Did he truly think she was that gullible? That she would fall for him if he deceived her?

Ida stomped into a puddle, shattering the colorless reflection of the buildings above. The midday crowd slowly filled the sidewalks, as hundreds and thousands flocked to the streets in search of a meal before the afternoon shift. Only then did Ida's own pangs of hunger claw their way through her clouded mind.

One corner further down, a milkman stood by his cart and hoisted a series of empty cans onto the back. Ida begged his pardon for the interruption and asked his advice for the shortest route to the Wall District.

# Chapter 17

Commissioned by the third Calesses emperor, the Broken Bridge was one of the oldest in New Montres. With salt blowing on its arches from the winds of the Gray Sea and its cobblestones worn to a shine by feet, hooves, and wheels, the many centuries of its age were readily apparent. It was a relic of a bygone era, when rulers routinely erected monuments to commemorate whatever accomplishment they deemed great enough, whether it was fighting off an invasion or being able to reproduce.

While the age of the bridge was undeniable, its length was somewhat a matter of debate—or rather, whether it was one bridge or two. It was meant to stretch from the western tip of Crescent Bay to the east end of Ilvior Island, relying on a small islet halfway through for added support. For the sake of efficiency, construction started both at the bay and on the island at the same time, with the intention to meet up and join at the islet. It was at this point the engineers realized that the two halves of what should have been a straight bridge were, in fact, at an angle.

The mishap left the emperor in something of a predicament. Demanding the bridge to be torn down and started anew was as good as admitting failure, not to mention he might not have lived to inaugurate the completed work. And so, it was through this quandary that the Broken Bridge became a symbol not only of the emperor's successful war campaign, but also the importance of settling for as-is.

Since that day, millions had walked over the bridge in utter ignorance of its history and significance.

Argiey was one of them. He crossed the bridge twice a day and never once thought of any long dead emperors. It wasn't out of any particular resentment toward them—Argiey crossed the bridge with the express intent of not thinking.

The same mentor who had instilled in him a rigorous attention to cleanliness in the deadhouse possessed a similar obsession with cleanliness of the mind. In his view, being surrounded by death at all hours of the day had a poisonous effect on the spirit, which could best be combated with what he called "thought fasting." To this end, he dedicated one hour each day to a solitary walk around the area. He ordered Argiey to do the same, on a different path from his to avoid any temptation of talking.

Since his mentor chose to stroll around the bay, Argiey picked the opposite direction, across the bridge. Regardless of season or weather, they set out at midday, returned precisely an hour later, and continued their work as though they'd never left.

Like the Calesses emperor, Argiey's mentor was long dead. But much like the bridge that survived the emperor, the habits he'd ingrained in his former apprentice lasted far past his own expiration. Hands stuffed deep into his pockets for warmth, hood turned up to shelter his face from the pounding rain, Argiey walked with steps of practiced monotony and decidedly did not think.

And on that day, he had a lot to not think about.

He had to not think about how long Vei Ruola had been in hiding and why she'd chosen to do so.

He had to not think about what her absence meant for himself or his accomplices, who depended on her in more ways than one.

He had to not think about Kalevi's murder, where she might have met a bloodsucker, or what she'd been doing at the Garden of Lilies.

Because if Argiey were to think, that might have brought on the disastrous consequence of knowing things. Things in which other people had a vested interest—either to learn for themselves, or to make sure no one else learned of them.

He plodded morosely along the chipped stones, watching the passersby with a sense of envy. How many of them were burdened with such concerns? Then again, how could he tell? For all he knew, the dozens of faces around him could each be concealing a hundred thoughts more troubling than his. . . or a hundred plans for cold-blooded murder.

Having done a lousy job on his thought fasting, Argiey was desperate for an afternoon of mundane distraction by the time he got back to the deadhouse. The door opened and closed behind him with a reassuring *thunk*, and the dry cold of the cellar welcomed him home to safety. Better yet, an envelope waited in the basket next to the entrance, the yellow of its paper practically glowing in the dark entryway. If the city guard had to deliver a customer while the deadhouse was unmanned, the agreement was to leave it in the back room and drop the paperwork through the letter slot by the door, so the returning coroner noticed it at once.

Argiey snatched up the envelope with renewed vigor and

leafed through its contents on the way to the back, opening all the quartz lamps to brighten the workroom with that familiar white light. He left the papers on his desk and unlocked the back area where, as promised, a fresh body lay on the slab, wrapped in a sheet and ready for examination.

Exactly what drew his attention to the pile of rags, Argiey couldn't have said. It might have been instinct. It might have been routine. It might have been some mystical sense yet undiscovered by physicians. Whatever it was, it was like a fishhook had been stuck in the bridge of his nose, and it pulled his gaze toward that specific corner with violent force. Argiey lowered himself to all fours and proceeded to dig through the cloth heap, emerging after a minute with the fruits of his search: a scrap of burlap, fashioned into a makeshift pouch and tied with string.

There were only two things inside. One of them was a pebble, meant to weigh down the package, so it was easier to drop through the crack of the window. The other one was a rolled-up strip of paper which, when unfurled, revealed two words that shattered any faith Argiey had in a peaceful end to the day.

*"SHE'S GONE."*

Argiey scratched the brush of his sideburns. No details, no instructions. The wordless way of saying, "I have no idea what happened; figure it out yourself." Argiey definitely did not want to figure it out. And if he had no choice, at the very least he did not want to figure it out alone.

He rushed to the cabinet and yanked open the middle drawer, filled with the files of the most recently deceased before they were taken to the public archives. With nimble fingers, he rifled through them until he happened across one that gave him adequate pretense to visit the Ilvior Island guardhouse. It wasn't perfect, but if an emperor could settle for as-is, then so could he. After that, all that remained was to trust Mainu would be there.

*  *  *

Mainu wasn't there.

Argiey scanned the upper floor of the building from the stairwell to no avail. The blonde ponytail among the dozen Ardonnese heads would have struck him on the first pass. Furthest across, however, there was someone else he recognized. He tucked the papers under his arm and marched to the desk right outside the captain's office.

Sergeant "Nel" Dormanni didn't notice his approach, as her focus was on the document she sat hunched over. The one who did notice Argiey was a lanky Laerithian boy, sitting opposite from her with a sour look and a pair of iron cuffs. He followed Argiey's path the whole way, but he said nothing. The sergeant only saw Argiey when he was directly beside her.

"Coroner!" She capped her pen. "I didn't expect to see you here. Is something the matter?"

"No, not really," Argiey lied. "I was hoping I might run into your colleague—the lieutenant. I have some paperwork about the deceased woman, but half of it is in Midorean, and I meant to ask if he could double-check them for me. I reckoned it's quicker to cross the bridge than to wait at the consulate."

The sergeant gave him a sympathetic smile. "I'm afraid you'll have to do that anyway. Lieutenant Eph Daëlin headed out there a short while ago to send his reports to the Midorean authorities. If it's not terribly urgent, I can hold on to this for you and ask him to go over it once he's back."

She extended a hand toward the file. Argiey jerked it back, perhaps a little too suddenly.

"I'd rather be done with it before the shift's out. Maybe I can ask for him personally and hand it in while I'm there. Two birds, one stone."

"That sounds reasonable." The sergeant gave a supportive nod. "He left about a quarter of an hour ago, so you might catch up to him if you hurry."

Argiey thanked her for the encouragement and, using this perfect excuse, bade her goodbye. Dormanni waved and continued scraping away, while the Laerithian continued to glare up at him.

A clump of patrolmen blocked the way to the stairwell as they filed out of the office floor to resume their sworn duty to protect the streets of New Montres. By the time the last one sleepwalked through the door, Argiey could have run across the bridge and back. He followed them down the steps, but not before turning to catch one more glimpse of Dormanni's desk to see if the boy was still staring at him.

He was not—but Sergeant Dormanni was.

# Chapter 18

The railcar operator rang the bell. Thessa counted the remaining stops on her hand, mouthing along the street names before their destination. Her discretion was largely unnecessary, as the car was fully packed like always. She and Ida were lucky to claim two seats at the very back, while Corlis stood next to them, clutching a pole for support during the bumpy ride.

Whether standing or seated, none of them were comfortable. Although it had been a relief to see Ida walk into The Lame Mare on her own, the news she'd brought with her did little to put Corlis and Thessa's minds at ease. After she explained what she'd found out from the foreman, Corlis suggested the three of them head back to the Garden of Lilies. They didn't know where Forley had gone or what he was up to, but it should only be a matter of time before he learned about Ida's release and tried to find her there.

"Does he get into a lot of trouble?" Corlis raised his voice above the squabbling elderly couple behind him. He had whiled away the trip across town by questioning Ida about whatever could be helpful to shed light on the events.

While Ida had agreed to answer, it was evident she didn't always care for the subject. This one elicited a particularly stiff pause, followed by a reluctant sigh. Thessa did her best to pat her arm in a comforting manner, as much as the frequent and violent shaking of the car allowed.

"He's never had a chance to make friends," Ida said. "Not the good kind. Any time we moved to a new town, the local children were already close-knit, and they weren't looking to invite him in—especially not someone as visibly foreign. He often ended up with the outcasts and loafers, who'd lure him into all sorts of misdoings. It was harmless enough when he was little, but as time went on, it got more and more serious.

"I tried to keep him safe. Talk some sense into him. Sometimes he listened; other times he said I meant to cut him off from the only company he had. What was I to do?

"Last year, we had a terrible fight. He played dice with some roughnecks, and they got into a quarrel about the winnings. In the end, he lost his temper and pulled a knife. If the guard hadn't been patrolling nearby, he could have died or killed someone. When I found out, I was furious. I called him a disgrace and threatened to abandon him. But I didn't mean a word of it. I was only distraught that I nearly lost him over some stupid game."

She wiped her cheeks before the tears trickled into the fabric of her veil.

"At last, that seemed to get through to him. He pulled himself together, enough so I dared to ask Mendel if he might have a job for him. I warned Forley that this was his last chance. That if he really was the grown man he insisted on being, then he'd have to start acting like it. For a few months, I truly believed he had changed."

Thessa patted down the numerous pockets of her uniform in search of a handkerchief, which she passed to Ida. During the minutes she took to dab her eyes and clean herself up, Corlis gazed off into the distance. Thessa knew his eyes saw nothing of the buildings that rolled past the grimy windows of the railcar. He was locked deep in his thoughts, so she left him to it and mulled over her own reflections.

Having never met Forley, it was hard to tell how much of Ida's recount was truth and how much of it was colored by her feelings as a mother. She loved her son deeply regardless of his flaws; that much was beyond a doubt. And it did sound like Forley loved her back. If he didn't, he could have simply run off at any time, not unlike Thessa running away from her parents. The only reason it had taken her almost twenty years was her unwillingness to give up the luxury of living in a Sallician greatlord's court. Forley had no such reason to stay with his mother over years of hardship.

The brakes screeched on the car, and the operator called out. "General Astercio's Square! Alight for General Astercio's Square!"

Thessa rose from the wooden seat and helped Ida up, while Corlis shoved his way between the passengers toward the exit. The Garden of Lilies was only a few more blocks away. They landed on the slick pavement and proceeded along the edge of the square, passing the life-sized marble statue of a man in a cape and breastplate. In the fountain around him, a gaggle of children had their sleeves rolled up to the shoulder, arms bright red from the cold water as they fished for wishing coins.

"Is Forley good at picking locks?" Corlis asked out of nowhere.

Again, Ida made no secret of her displeasure at the question. "One of his friends might have taught him. I certainly never wished to know."

"Why do you ask?" Thessa addressed Corlis, knowing he wouldn't do so without a reason.

"I'm wondering why Mendel let him off so easy. The boy breaks into the office barely a month after he's hired, and he walks away without so much as a slap on the wrist. I believe Mendel would keep you in the dark out of. . . let's say sympathy"—he gestured at Ida—"but to shake the whole thing off like nothing happened? That's practically inviting all the other workers to have a go at that money box."

"I'm sure they're taking more precautions now," Thessa said. "But what does this have to do with how good Forley is with locks?"

"Even before the attempt, a money box is bound to have a decent lock. Forley would have known that, so he wouldn't have dared if he didn't think he could break it. Besides, he would have made sure no one was around when he went in. But, according to the foreman, he was caught before he could steal anything. Either he wasn't as good with thieves' tools as he thought—or he got distracted."

"Distracted? By what?"

"There's more in that office than money. Mendel could have had all sorts of things lying around, under the assumption that no one would see them."

Above the trim of the veil, Ida's eyes went wide in livid disbelief. "What are you trying to say?" she asked. "That Forley's blackmailing his employer?"

"I'm not saying that's what happened," Corlis replied. "I'm trying to figure out *if* that's what happened. Because if it is, then he's in a lot more trouble than we imagined. Blackmail is a dangerous game and an all too quick way to make an enemy."

Over the past year of knowing him, Thessa had plenty of time to get accustomed to Corlis's habit of thinking out loud and his matter-of-factness in discussing any subject. Ida, however, did not take it so well.

"This is ridiculous. You know nothing about either of them, and you're suggesting Mendel could be plotting to—to *kill* my son, who's blackmailing him?" She took no notice of the many furrowed brows that passed her as she spoke. "What does any of this have to do with the murder at the Garden? I thought you wanted to help us with that! Or is this how you amuse yourself? By throwing out accusations?"

Thessa moved closer in an effort to placate her. "I promise he meant no ill will, Ida. Corlis is very thorough, that's all. And I can say from experience, you can never truly know another person."

"Experience?" Ida snapped at her. "What experience? Do either of you have a child? Do either of you have someone you're so scared to lose that you'd sooner die than see that happen?"

Thessa shook her head in response.

Ida composed herself. "If the two of you want to speculate about what horrible crimes my son might have committed, you can do so between yourselves. And if you have proof for any of it, then I'll make sure he takes responsibility. Until then, I won't tolerate this kind of talk when I'm around."

The three of them stood in a circle, halfway across the square, amidst dozens that walked by in utter disinterest of their predicament. The scene reminded Thessa of a similar situation that had occurred a year earlier. Back when she, Corlis, and Lokenn were forced to work together on an investigation, they got off on very much the wrong foot. Thessa and Corlis in particular had a number of heated arguments out in an open street like this one. At that time, Corlis had reacted to their clashes by threatening to walk away and leave Thessa to fend for herself.

"I'm sorry," he now said to Ida. "I'll try to be more considerate."

And though Thessa suspected it was little more than a gesture to keep the peace between them, she was immensely proud of him.

* * *

Within minutes, the Garden's facade appeared at the next crossroads, its characteristic green shutters all closed, still giving no hint of any life within. It was strange how dire this one change made the whole building appear—or maybe it was only the knowledge of the reason behind it. Thessa had hoped the sight of this familiar haven might ease the tension between the three of them, but to no avail. Ida gathered up her dress and hurried on ahead, leaving her and Corlis a whole block behind.

As they approached, Thessa kept her eye out in case Forley was nearby. She'd never seen his face before, but a Laerithian was fairly easy to spot in most New Montres crowds. Wherever she turned, though, it was only the usual blend of Ardonnese and occasional Werrish faces.

But not for long.

A short distance away from the Garden, a carriage came to a halt right in front of Ida. The door opened, and a massive pair of legs flung out from inside. The legs were then followed by

168

a pair of similarly enormous hands, and a giant of a Sallician unfolded himself from the passenger space.

On most occasions, Thessa would have been happy to greet a fellow countryman in the Ardonnese capital, but this wasn't one of them. With a single stride, the man blocked Ida's way on the pavement, while his tattooed head turned downward.

"Ida," he greeted her.

"Kolos," Ida replied. "What are you doing here?"

"Braselius wants to speak to you. In private." His voice was as deep as rolling thunder, loud enough to reach Thessa over the surrounding noise without being raised above a plain speaking tone. It rang with no threat or aggression, sounding almost concerned instead. At the same time, the way he said "in private" left nothing to the imagination about what might follow if Ida refused to accompany him.

Thus, Thessa had no choice but to watch Ida oblige without another word. The carriage sagged with a desperate creak when Kolos climbed back in, and the wheels slowly began to turn anew as they pulled away from the side of the road.

It was all done in less than a minute, yet Thessa felt like she was emerging from a dream. She whipped her head around to speak to Corlis, but he too had vanished—for one moment. A sharp whistle came from the road, and a rent-coach rolled up next to Thessa, with Corlis standing in the open door while he held on to the inside.

With only a hint of urgency behind his usual matter-of-factness, he said, "I can only assume you want to follow them."

# Chapter 19

The carriage rocked to a halt as gentle as a newborn's cradle. The driver knocked on the panel to signal their arrival, and the vehicle tilted steeply as all three hundred of Kolos's pounds shifted to the side to climb out.

Throughout their short journey, Ida had kept her head down and didn't bother to see what path they took across the city. Out of sheer routine, she had expected to find herself at the side alley on the Street of Canopies when they stopped, but instead it was the wide open front door of the decoy tavern that greeted her. Ordinary members like Ida could never access the real Belfry through here, but someone like Kolos was an exception. He might have picked this entrance in case anyone tried to tail him, so they'd walk into a dead end. Although it could as easily have been because he simply wouldn't fit through the narrow gap of the alley.

Kolos stepped out onto the pavement and reached back to help Ida down the steps. His fingers wrapped delicately around hers, while his support was as steady as the thousand-year-old rocks along the shore. The softness of his touch almost seemed to say, "It's nothing personal." But only almost.

Ever since she was accepted into the Belfry, it had been a safe place to Ida. Now it was hostile territory. The sturdy walls that hid her from prying eyes were instead a prison. The many security measures that kept her safe were a trap, keeping out anyone who might come to help her. If anyone did come.

Together, Ida and Kolos made their way inside the dimly lit and miserably dirty fake tavern. Anyone who wandered in from the street would be met with dreadful wine at extortionate prices from a barkeep who'd all but openly spit into the guest's cup. Everything about this place, from the grubby tables to the grubbier guests, was meant to deter those who didn't come here knowing exactly what they were after.

That same barkeep drew himself to attention when Kolos's frame filled the seven-foot doorway, as did all the pretend patrons at their tables, turning their gazes to Ida. Kolos nodded his unspoken acknowledgment and directed his steps toward the bar. The man behind the counter hastily unlatched and lifted it to let him and Ida through, then folded it back and continued to mind his own business.

Kolos had always been a friendly face to Ida, but not a friend. At the end of the day, he answered only to Braselius. Whatever the Belfry's enigmatic owner decided, he would carry out without question. There were plenty of local folk tales about the lengths he would go to serve his employer, and the ruthless efficacy with which he did so.

Though the area behind the bar was unlit, Ida soon found herself in a familiar place again: the same stairs that she took on her regular visits. It was a trivial detail, but it went a long way to ease her distress. Moreover, it helped steer her thoughts toward how she might gain some benefit from this turn of events.

The prospect of meeting Braselius in these circumstances

wasn't a promising one, but regardless of his intentions, it was Ida's one chance to speak with him. That by itself was a rare opportunity given to anyone inside or outside the secretive circle of bloodsuckers. Braselius had been at the center of that circle for over half a century, and the depths of his knowledge were unmatched. Provided that age hadn't gotten the best of him.

The Sallician's giant feet rattled the stone of the stairs as he led the way up, past the curtained archway where guests entered the Belfry proper. Beyond the next corner, their progress was barred by a door so thick that the wood was barely visible under the dozens of iron braces. Kolos unlocked it, waited for Ida to squeeze past, then locked it again. After that, he crossed his arms and leaned against the frame.

"It's at the end of these stairs." He motioned in the only possible direction.

"Are you not coming?" Ida asked.

"I wasn't invited."

"I thought you were his right-hand man."

"Doesn't mean I follow him into the privy. When it's his business, it's his business alone. And yours, in this case."

Ida took the remaining dozen steps that curved gently away from the outer wall and toward the middle of the tower. By her estimate, this room was right under where the bells had been when this building fulfilled its original purpose. In the fading light of the afternoon, she could make out the windows that had been fitted into the openings under the roof. If anyone fell out of there, it would easily be a thirty-foot drop to the nearest neighboring house.

There was no way but forward. Carefully parting the many strings of beads that hung before the entrance, Ida crossed the threshold into Braselius's private world.

If the air in the tavern was palpably stale, up here it was suffocating. That was because most of it wasn't air, but rather a choking mix of what she could only guess to be incenses. Whatever they were, they penetrated Ida's veil and left a chalky coating on her tongue with each labored breath. While there were dozens of candles all over the floor, each one two feet tall and half a foot wide, the swirling haze dimmed their light like the evening fog in the bay. Coupled with her watering eyes, Ida had to rely on her hearing for guidance, tracing the origins of soft, sluggish laughter to the furthest corner.

The laughter didn't come from Braselius, but rather from the three women splayed around him in varying degrees of undress. He lay on an old-fashioned recliner covered in a mound of fine pillows and drapes, his frail body glistening head to toe with oil. All he wore was a gilded wreath, sitting precipitously atop his head as he buried his face in one of the women's necks. His lips smacked with each lazy sip of her blood, while she in turn held a long ebony pipe over a burner and let a white ribbon of smoke unfurl from her chapped lips.

Ida waited dutifully for him to indulge in his depravity, and he took full advantage of her patience. It wasn't until several minutes later that he leaned back and brushed aside his shaggy brown hair to reveal a visage younger than Forley's.

"Ah, Ida." He squinted vaguely in her direction. "Our little lost black sheep. Don't lurk around there, my dear—pull up a cushion."

As he waited for her to do so, the other two women slithered closer and weaved their hands around him.

"You've been through a dreadful lot these past days, haven't you?" he asked without a smidge of interest. "Had a murder at your place of work. Arrested and dragged off in front of everyone, in a manner most unbecoming of a lady. Thrown into a filthy cell like some common criminal. Why, if I had to endure such misfortune, I'm not altogether certain I'd have the wherewithal to so much as breathe."

Despite his complexion, he sounded old enough to be Ida's grandfather. There was a strained, wheezy quality to his voice that hinted much more strongly at his true age than his flowery speech. Ida had heard third-hand tales about how he was turned as a boy, then hid away from prying eyes, and clouded his mind with whatever he could suck from the veins of his concubines. A natural body would have mercifully given out before he turned thirty, but the bloodsucker's physiology kept him healthy enough into his eighties.

He slid one hand blindly toward the back and rested it on whatever part of whichever woman it reached first. "But life's not all bad. You're free now."

"Free within the city," Ida said.

"A great many would kill to have that freedom." Braselius pushed himself up on one elbow. "Do tell, then—what are your intentions?"

"I want to prove I'm innocent."

"And. . . ?"

"Is there something else to it?"

"Very much so. Do you endeavor to find the true killer, or are you content to wash your own hands?"

Ida knew which answer Braselius expected to hear and which one was true. She straightened her back and replied, "I'll do whichever I can first."

From underneath the mess of hair tangled in his gilded wreath, the boy-man's shimmering eyes rested on Ida. All that moved in the room was the smoke, swirling and billowing in the faint drafts of wind that dwindled through the gaps of the high window.

"You understand, I have a. . . complicated relationship with the city guard," Braseilus said.

"Being a bloodsucker isn't a crime."

"No, but murder is, whether or not one is a bloodsucker. All that fuss around your place of work is drawing a lot of eyes toward us."

At long last, he was getting to the point. Ida had figured as much when Kolos showed up. The question was where Braselius stood on the issue. It would have been easy to discount him as a vacant cloud chaser upon first sight, but anyone who made it to his age without losing the last of his senses had to have an iron will.

"I didn't commit that murder," Ida said flatly.

"But of course you didn't. No one ever *commits* murder. It simply happens, like rain." Braselius twiddled a woman's hair between his fingers. "But the guard will want to blame someone. When it comes to a culprit as elusive as a bloodsucker, it's only expected that they start in the places they know first."

"Have they come here?"

"Not yet. Not while they had you for a scapegoat. But when you wash your hands clean, that dirt has to trickle somewhere else."

"What are you trying to say?"

"What I'm saying, my dear, is that right now, the guard needs to either find evidence that you indeed are the killer—or they need to apprehend another bloodsucker. And if the latter option means they'll come knocking here, then we'll gladly oblige in helping them with the former."

So, that was that. Braselius confirmed Ida's suspicion: he would readily serve her up to Sergeant Vendriane on a silver platter to save his own hide. Never mind how long she had been a respectable member, nor the hefty fee she paid each month on the dot. When it came down to a matter of survival, camaraderie held as much weight as the tufts of smoke that poisoned the air of his room.

* * *

With the discussion ended, Ida sought her way back to the beaded entrance and down the stairs to Kolos, who escorted her to the landing outside the Belfry's real tavern. There, he turned to part the heavy curtains in the archway.

"Aren't you going to see me all the way out?" Ida asked.

"My orders were to take you up to Braselius."

Through the opening that Kolos's massive hand created between the drapes of fabric, Ida heard the tavern's usual sounds of music and chatter, though the latter noticeably more faint than usual.

She nodded toward the door. "Does that mean I can come in?"

"No one told me not to let you."

He bent his head to fit under the arch and walked in, the boards quivering under his boots with each step. After some brief deliberation, Ida braced herself and joined him.

The news of the Garden murder had spooked a fair number of the regular patrons. Less than a third of the tables were occupied, and the few groups that were present regarded

Ida with both suspicion and apprehension. It was more insulting than embarrassing—as if they thought her some kind of animal that might abandon all judgment and jump at their throats on the spot.

Keeping her chin up, she crossed the tavern floor at a measured pace, glancing side to side in search of someone with a hint of reason who'd be willing to tolerate her company. The few faces she recognized turned away as soon as their eyes met, retreating into their huddled whispers of half-baked rumors. One by one, each group closed off to her, until she came to the bar.

As on any other evening, the far right corner of the tavern featured some twelve square feet of slightly raised flooring to serve as a stage. Upon that stage stood the same trio as before: a stocky, middle-aged Sallician man and his significantly more appealing pair of sons, as far as Ida assumed their relation. All three of them blew some variation of a flute in well-honed harmony, playing whatever song patrons asked for, provided it was accompanied by a copper.

Ida waited for them to end their song, then approached the stage with her purse at the ready. The younger men reacted with wary looks at their leader. He, in turn, proved to be a seasoned entertainer and kept his attention where it mattered: the coins between Ida's outstretched fingers.

"Would the lady care to request a song?" he asked in a played-up accent.

"Not quite," she replied. "I'd like to request your company at a table. For, let's say, the next three songs' time? Drinks are my treat."

The pudgy man's thick eyebrows rose impressively close to his receding hairline, but his expression of polite interest remained.

"We have a whole room full of witnesses," Ida said in a slightly raised voice, then lowered it again to add, "Or maybe not full, but enough to raise the alarm so that two of you may survive."

At that, the bandleader broke out in laughter. "Well, it does get tiring to play for an empty tavern. Come along, boys." He waved at the other two. "Let's not be rude in the face of a generous offer."

While they all set down their instruments and took a seat at the closest table, Ida ordered a pitcher of wine for them and some water for herself. Kolos had not yet taken up his post behind the counter, but the moon-faced woman who replaced him seemed to be one of the few in the Belfry who were unaffected in Ida's reputation. Upon receiving the payment, she promptly set about to fill some jugs.

The drinks helped lighten the mood around the table, especially for the eldest of the three men, who went on to present himself as Papa Lappadelis.

"This handsome young man is my son in blood," he said, patting the bare shoulder of the one next to him. "And come spring, the one on his arm will be my son-in-law."

He beamed at the couple, who had no doubt been hearing this introduction for months. On cue, they bowed with bashful smiles and showed off the silver engagement bracelets on their wrists.

Ida raised her glass in a traditional toast. "A thousand well-wishes upon the newlyweds, then!"

Lappadelis added some words in Sallician, and the three men downed their first wine in one go. It didn't take long for the second to follow, and then some. While they drank, the father regaled Ida with story after story of their family escapades, and as his face became ever more colorful, so did the tales. The three songs' time stretched into nearly an hour, during which life slowly trickled back into the Belfry. The crowd and the noise grew steadily, with several voices calling for music.

"Seems the pace is slowly picking up." Lappadelis wiped his mouth. "I'm afraid after this round we'll have to get back to work. But I do thank you for your hospitality, my lady." He took Ida's hand and planted a kiss on the back.

"And I thank you for your kind words," Ida said, resisting the urge to yank her fingers from the man's sweaty grasp. If she had any hope of getting her money's worth, this was her last chance. "I haven't been hearing a lot of those lately—as you might imagine."

Lappadelis's enormous brows lowered into a sorrowful frown. "Nasty business, that whole thing." He shook his balding head. "Must have been dreadful for you."

"It's not an experience I'd like to have again."

The son-in-law-to-be piped up. "And you're released now? Does that mean the guard found who really did it?" He sounded as eager to bring up the point as Ida. As he spoke, his eyes darted around the crowd, as though he might spot the murderer.

"They released me, but they haven't found the killer yet," she replied, leaving out the part that she remained under suspicion.

"Were you the only one they took in?"

Ida spread her hands. "They didn't have any other candidates. I'm the only bloodsucker at the house."

"You are?" the young man asked. "I thought there was

someone else, too."

At that, the crowded tavern, the Belfry, and the whole world may as well have gotten swallowed up in darkness. In Ida's mind, there was nothing but the table and the man across from her.

She raised her glass under her veil. "Well, that's news to me."

The younger Lappadelis playfully shoved his future husband's shoulder. "How would you know?"

"Kolos mentioned it a few weeks ago."

"Kolos? Since when does he tell you things like that?"

"He didn't tell me. I only overheard him. He was vetting someone on the list."

*Vetting?* The Belfry was famously selective about its members, whether they were bloodsuckers or not. Anyone who wished to set foot inside had to have their name put on the list, after which Kolos and the other staff would rigorously investigate them to make sure they were trustworthy. Getting Mendel approved for a single visit had taken three weeks. Had someone from the Garden applied?

Ida sipped her water again. "Who was it?"

"She had some sort of flower name. Something—" The son-in-law screwed up his face before turning to the other two. "What's *ainobhe* in Ardonnese?"

"Lilac?" the father asked back. "No, no. Violet."

"That's right." The young man snapped his fingers in relief. "Violet. She wanted in, but Kolos said they turned her down."

Ida had to grab on to the table with one hand to keep herself from falling. *Violet?* At the Belfry? That couldn't have been right. He must have misheard or remembered the wrong flower. If she—or really, anyone from the Garden—was being vetted, how come Ida never heard of it, either from Kolos, or from anyone else?

The room spun around as if she'd been the one drinking instead of the three Sallicians. They, in turn, set down their cups and pushed their chairs back, ready to take their place in the corner again. They couldn't go. She had to make them stay. She had to make them talk more. She had to find out something that would make this ridiculous story make sense.

And that was when Kolos screamed, "GET HER!"

# Chapter 20

Thessa peered out from behind the corner of the decrepit apartment-house. Kolos's carriage was stationed some fifteen yards down, outside the entrance of a bell tower that rose several stories above its surroundings. The giant and Ida must have already gone in, but the driver didn't move.

"Is he waiting for them to return?" Thessa whispered.

"I think he's only waiting for a sign that they made it in," Corlis replied next to her.

He was right. Moments later, the driver cracked his whip and pulled away, disappearing into the darkening streets ahead.

Thessa tightened her jacket against the evening cold as she and Corlis crossed the bumpy road. The tower's entrance cast a faint pool of yellowish light onto the muddy pavement, illuminating the battered old shingle that read, *"The Belfry."*

"A tavern?" Thessa asked.

"We'll see." Corlis eyed the signage with suspicion. "Stay here. I won't be long."

Before she could react, he turned up his collar and climbed the low steps to the door. Thessa wavered between keeping away from the light and remaining close by in case he needed her help. Thankfully, he soon reemerged in once piece, albeit in a sour mood.

"Well," he began, rolling his shoulder, "I spent a whole copper on a cup of pure vinegar and got called a lizard-faced scum-sucker when I pointed that out."

"I'm sorry," Thessa said.

"Don't be. That's what I hoped for." Corlis turned back toward the shingle. "This place is a front. Gambling dens have them all the time, too. They don't want returning customers who might catch on that something's afoot. I'd bet anything the so-called patrons inside were all lookouts."

Thessa tilted her head back. The tower must have stretched fifty yards into the sky, and the fake tavern was only the bottom floor. There definitely was ample space in between for any purpose.

"Can we get in at all?" she asked.

"Not through here. But I bet most guests come don't in this way, either. That can attract attention, especially on an otherwise empty street. My money's on another entrance at the back."

"There's no side alley." Thessa scanned their surroundings. "The houses here are built right next to each other all the way around the block. But sometimes they have an open yard in the middle for delivery carts and the like."

"Let's find the way into that yard, then."

They hurried down the road, turning left at each corner to trace the outline of the city block until they came to an opening between two of the buildings. It led them into a shoddily paved inner area, enclosed on all sides by the backsides of the houses, which were even less well tended than the fronts. A mess of barren clotheslines swung in the chilly winds above, while the floor was littered with broken wheels, cracked washbasins, and other discarded items.

Thessa and Corlis meandered between the scrap heaps, careful not to knock anything over as the buildings shut out whatever light lingered at the edge of the sky. As they worked their way back toward the Belfry, however, they were only met with a solid brick wall, twenty feet high.

"Dead end," Corlis said.

The wall ran the whole breadth from one building to the other. By all accounts, it gave the impression that the yard ended there. But it didn't quite feel right.

"There should be three different buildings here back to back," Thessa said. "This is a single wall. They must have put this here later to cut off part of the yard."

"And that part probably has a separate way in." Corlis nodded. "They really are secretive, whatever they're up to in there."

Forced to retreat, they retraced their path to the alley and continued along the street. Thessa fidgeted anxiously with the buttons of her uniform. This wild goose chase was costing them precious time, and Ida could have been in any amount of trouble.

After the next two turns, the block continued on the Street of Canopies. Life at this hour was well underway here, making their job all the more difficult. Not only did they need to keep their eyes open for an entrance, they had to do so while dodging the flood of revelers milling about, as well as the numerous decorative statues and braziers that stood by the walls.

It was so distracting, Thessa nearly missed it.

"There!"

Wedged between a dance hall and an inn, scarcely two feet in width, was a shabby gate cobbled together from some splintered planks. If Thessa hadn't been purposefully searching for it, it might as well have been invisible to her—but there it was, covering up an alley just wide enough for a person to pass. She felt around on the back side for a latch, shuffled in, and waved Corlis through.

The walls on each side were so close, Thessa had nothing but her sense of direction to tell her if she was headed the right way. She followed the twists and turns of the alley until she reached the same wall they'd hit before, but now from the other side. The remainder of the yard opened up ahead, and to their right rose the towering mass of the Belfry with its entrance at the bottom.

"Don't go yet." Corlis grabbed Thessa by the shoulder. "That door is the only part of the yard that's lit. They must be watching it. If we walk up there like this, they'll sound the alarm before we knock."

"Then what?" she asked. "Do you see another way in?"

"Not that we can take. The only windows are way up there."

Thessa followed his finger. On the entire height of the tower, there were about five openings, each about the size of an arrow slit. The lowest of them was ten feet above the roof of the neighboring house. Climbing up there was humanly impossible.

Good thing she was wearing her trousers and not a dress. She pulled off her boots, tied the laces together, and hung them over her neck.

"Have you done anything like this before?" Corlis asked, sensing what she was up to.

"I've climbed a lot of trees, and that was easy enough,"

Thessa said, doing her best to mask her uncertainty. "How different are they, really?"

Corlis withheld his opinion. "Take off your uniform jacket. If they notice you in it, they'll know where to find you later. For that matter, take this." He unwound his scarf and handed it to her. "Wrap up your face so they can't see any of it. I've never dealt with bloodsuckers, but if they have this kind of security, they'll hunt any intruder to the ends of the earth."

Thessa tied the scarf around her head until only her eyes were exposed. "Aren't you going to tell me what a stupid idea this is?"

"We've wasted enough time already."

He folded her jacket around his arm, then moved back to give her room for a running start. Thessa lowered her hands to the ground, rocked on her knees a few times, and with a shiver of heat along her body, she lost herself in the transformation.

Her eyes clouded over before the dark of night turned clearer than ever. She fixed her gaze on a low eave of the nearest building, and after a couple more tentative steps in place, she bounded off.

As it turned out, climbing walls was strikingly different from climbing trees. While she made it to the eave smoothly enough, the following leaps from one outcropping to the next were a deal less graceful. At one point, she lost her footing altogether and tumbled backward onto an overhang, dislodging half a dozen clay tiles in the process. Corlis was far away at this point, but Thessa was sure he was drawing a long, slow breath through his nose.

Regardless, she persevered, and though it took her a minute longer than she intended, she was up on the roof. Now came the real challenge.

She paused only briefly to gauge the distance. The dusty shingles jiggled under her feet as she bolted straight along the ridge. Once she was a few feet from the tower, she pooled every ounce of strength into her legs and shot herself into the air.

She didn't quite reach the window, but she had not expected to. The claws of her naked feet dug deep into the outer plastering, which let her take hold long enough to scamper up before crumbling away from the bricks underneath. Thessa's hands raced along the sheer surface, inch by precious inch, until her fingers found purchase on the windowsill. In one final effort, she hoisted herself sideways through the opening and tumbled to the floor inside.

Or so she would have, if there had been a floor.

As Thessa's head bent down, she was met with a gaping blind abyss. Her hands clawed at the wall in an attempt to slow herself, but the momentum of her legs coming over the edge was too much. She had to think of something before she plunged into the darkness, while the only thing that faced her was the terror of certain death below.

In a panic, Thessa whipped her head back up and caught sight of a wooden staircase along the other wall, another ten feet away. That was her only rescue—if she could make it. As soon as one of her feet was inside, she shoved it against the wall in a desperate push. Arms shot forward, she stared unblinking at the edge of the stairs, as though she could will them into coming closer. Feet turned to inches, inches turned to half-inches, then thirds, then quarters, each increment seemingly taking longer and longer until Thessa hung in midair for an eternity.

She clutched the uprights of the banister, and time caught up with her. Her chest slammed into the boards, while her legs danced frantically over the hungry void. Thessa flung herself up onto the staircase and collapsed on her back, clasping both hands over her heart that threatened to shatter her ribs from the inside.

It really was a stupid idea.

When she no longer heard her own blood screaming into her ear, Thessa coaxed herself back into human form. She put her boots back on and adjusted the scarf that her muzzle had shifted loose. After she nearly fell to her doom, it only made sense to continue up.

The stairs ended shortly in a door that, fortunately enough, the owners had not bothered to lock. No sound or light came from behind it. The handle relented with a rusty creak under Thessa's palm and gave way into a densely stocked storage room. A tumult of scents ambushed her nose, from wine to beer to exotic spirits and more. She felt her way past the rows of casks and bottles until she hit another door. This time, the keyhole shot a spear of light at the ground as Thessa slid the cover, and the air on the other side was rife with chatter. Slick from sweat, her hand nearly slid off the knob as she turned it.

The storage room opened into the back corner of a tavern, tucked out of sight of the tables. Thessa pushed the door open by a foot and slunk through, searching for her next cover. The tavern hall had a number of square pillars that were close enough to the wall to keep her out of sight. Ducking from one to the next, she crept her way around the edge of the room, all the while stealing glimpses of the guests when she could.

She was a good two-thirds into a whole lap when she spotted Ida. She was seated at a table next to the stage, in the company of three Sallician men—two of them notably young and scantily clad. All of them had full cups, laughing and talking as they drank, in a perfectly cordial mood and not under the remotest hint of threat.

Thessa sunk to a crouch in her hiding place. So, this was what she had risked her life for: to see that Ida was not only alive, but enjoying herself. And really, was that so awful? After the ordeal Ida had suffered these past days, the least she deserved was an hour of carefree merrymaking. Why had Thessa assumed she was in trouble to begin with? Come to think of it, the only danger was that if Thessa were discovered, the owners of the Belfry might accuse Ida of bringing an intruder.

Defeated, Thessa tightened her scarf again, and set out to make it back to the storage room or the nearest exit undetected. At the same time, a chair by the nearest table slid back, and a dark-haired woman got up. Thessa jerked behind the pillar and pressed her back flat against it, while the woman came up to the other side of it and fussed with her hair at length. Thessa held her breath in an attempt to disappear from the world, but the dread weighed so heavy on her chest that she couldn't help herself.

When she inhaled again, she didn't want to believe her senses.

It was a scent she'd only ever smelled once, a full year before, but she remembered it as intensely as if it had only been a day. It was the scent of eternal forests, icy clear water, and frosted-over grass. It was the unmistakable scent of a Midorean.

The curiosity was far too much to resist. Thessa slid her head out from her cover to catch sight of the woman. She had her hands on front of her face, running her fingers along what turned out to be a dark-colored wig, tucking stray strands of platinum blonde under the tight lace. Once finished, she nervously smoothed out her dress and looked up before Thessa had a chance to hide again.

They only locked eyes for a heartbeat. The woman's expression turned from unease to utter horror. She stumbled backward into her chair, drawing the attention of everyone at the table, before turning straight to the exit.

Without another word or thought, Thessa dashed along the outer edge of the hall, taking only enough care to stay as much in the shadow as possible. The woman had a shorter distance to cover, but she had to dodge the tables and other patrons on the way, while Thessa ran mostly unimpeded next to the wall. Now and then, she cast a quick glance to the side to see if the Midorean had changed her course. At this rate, Thessa could beat her to the door or follow close enough to catch up to her in the stairwell.

Less than two yards away from her goal, an iron beam swung out from behind a pillar and caught her square under the ribs. Thessa crashed to the floor in searing pain, then staggered back to find that the iron beam was, in fact, the Sallician giant's arm.

"I'll give you exactly one chance to give me a good enough excuse." His knuckles cracked as loudly as shattering bricks.

Thessa got up, while a hundred thoughts darted through her frenzied mind. *What now?* She had to follow the Midorean. She couldn't hope to fight this man. *Could she transform in here?* No, that was too much of a risk. There had to be another way out. *What about Ida?* From what she could tell, Kolos didn't suspect Thessa had anything to do with her. That could be an advantage. First, however, she had to answer.

"I only need to speak with her," she said and gestured at the exit the woman had fled through. "I have no other business here, I swear."

The tattoos on the Sallician's cheeks twisted into a sneer. "That's for damn sure. No one crosses this threshold without an invitation." He reached behind his back and pulled out a knife the size of Thessa's arm. "Not more than once."

She shuffled back toward the corner, running her eyes around the room in search of something to aid her escape. All she found was an end table with a heavy brass candlestick on top and a dimmed quartz lamp hanging over it.

In its fevered rush, Thessa's mind dredged up another memory from the year before. Lokenn had explained to her that thaumaturgic items—such as quartz lamps—were created by trapping pure elemental energies in crystals. Not long after that, she had born witness to the terrible force that erupted when such a crystal containing a fire spirit was shattered. She didn't know firsthand what a light spirit would do, but she was about to find out.

In one swift movement, she snatched the candlestick from the table, and with her eyes closed as tightly as possible, she brought the weight of the brass smashing into the lamp.

There was no sound to the ensuing flash, but it pierced her eyelids like staring into the sun. The giant screamed and cursed, as did most of the guests nearby. Taking her one chance, Thessa dropped the improvised weapon and sprinted to the door.

Behind her, Kolos shouted, "GET HER!"

The Midorean's rapid footsteps echoed up the stairwell. Thessa risked a hundred neck-breaking falls trying to catch up, calling after her in vain. If nothing else, the monotony of the long run was enough to let her mind slow down and think further ahead. These stairs must have led to the Belfry's back entrance, which in turn opened onto the yard. With any luck, she'd be able to catch the woman in the narrow alley before she ran out into the Street of Canopies and vanished in the crowd.

The only thing she'd forgotten was the guard at the door, who closed and blocked the exit behind the Midorean precisely as Thessa reached the final flight of steps. At the same time, a jumble of shouts came from the top of the tower, where Kolos and the others had set out to hunt her down.

Caught between a rock and a hard place, the only way out was another stupid idea.

Thessa withdrew enough to stay hidden from the bottom guard's eye, then she transformed again and came down, snarling and growling as menacingly as she could. The performance did the trick, and the man scrambled out of her path with a shriek. Thessa tore open the door, then darted across the lit yard and into the concealing shadows of the alley, where at last she turned back and yanked the scarf off of her head.

As quickly as the cramped space between the buildings allowed, she followed the path to the boarded gate and burst out into the main street. Out of nowhere, a hand reached under her arm and dragged her off. Thessa turned around, ready to fight or flee, but she was only met with Corlis's face, holding one extended finger over his thin lips.

"Over here," he said and guided her to an alcove. "I believe you two have a misunderstanding to clear up."

Trembling head to toe from fear and exhaustion, the Midorean woman stood with her back against the wall, staring at Thessa.  Her hands were white in the knuckles, clutching the dark wig that must have come loose during the chase, leaving her real blonde hair in a disheveled mess over her otherwise regal features.  She was surprisingly old—or appeared that way, mostly due to the dark circles under her eyes.

Her speech was equally weary when she asked, "Were you not sent to kill me?"

"No!" Thessa lowered her voice. She moved to step closer, but seeing the woman's shudder, she kept her distance.  "I don't even know who you are."

"Then why did you come after me?"

"I saw you're Midorean, and I thought you might know—" Thessa tried to collect her thoughts. "Someone like you was murdered at the Garden of Lilies two nights ago. My friend and I are trying to find out what happened, and I hoped maybe you knew her."

The woman's face momentarily shifted from fear to doubt. "You don't look like you're with the city guard."

Corlis let out something halfway between a scoff and stifled laughter.

"No, we're not," Thessa said. "I only want to help Beldora however I can."

"You're a friend of Beldora?"  Much like Corlis, the Midorean's reaction lay somewhere between two wildly different emotions.

The only thing Thessa knew for sure was that she recognized the name—but whether she was happy to hear it was anyone's guess.

She saw no choice but to be honest. "Yes, I am. If you go to the Garden, you can ask her yourself. My name is Thessalona

Kalou."

There was a brief silence, and Thessa wondered if she should have been more cautious. Then the woman slowly lowered her hands, her pale blue eyes shimmering with the mist of sadness and relief.

"I believe you," she said. "And yes, I did know the woman who was killed there. My name is Taëminn Vei Ruola, and she was my lover."

# V

# Part Five

# Chapter 21

Nel rang the bell again, letting it echo in the empty entrance hall. She'd already done so twice, pausing several minutes in between, but there was no sight of the innkeeper. The only sign of life in the building was the murmurs from behind a curtain near the counter, which presumably led to the tavern. Most likely, the host was busy in there. If no one showed up after she rang for a fourth time, she would go and check herself.

In the meantime, she let her eyes wander around the richly decorated room. On the outside, The Twin Stags wasn't much to write home about—on the inside, it sought to stand out among the hundreds of inns of New Montres by masquerading as a hunting lodge. One wall was taken up in its entirety by a river-stone hearth, while the rest featured board and batten panels with dozens of mounted candles and other trinkets. The seating area in the corner boasted the inn's namesake: a pair of stuffed stag heads above the stained-glass windows, locked into a staring contest neither of them would ever win.

All things considered, it did not strike Nel as a cheap place to stay. The Midorean High Court took good care of their officers.

Right when she picked up the bell for the fifth time, the curtains parted to reveal a portly man with lightly peppered hair and a heavily waxed mustache. He hastily wiped both hands on his apron and took his place at the counter amidst a stream of apologies.

"I am most terribly sorry, Officer. Things are frightfully busy in the tavern—we get one sunny day in two months, and everyone in town pretends it's summer again." He nodded toward the window, where the beams of sunlight cast colorful patterns on the bear hide rug. "Now, how may I be of service?"

"I'm here to see one of your guests."

"Oh, dear." The man wrung his stubby fingers. "Has there been a complaint? I assure you, we take great care not to disturb the peace after sundown. I can—"

"No, nothing's wrong," Nel cut him off. "We've simply arranged a meeting here. His name is Mainu Eph Daëlin, from Midorea." As most of their plans for the day were in the Upper and Lower Court Districts, it had seemed reasonable to start there.

The innkeeper's face melted into a relieved smile. "Oh! Of course. He mentioned as much, in fact. It's the room furthest to the left on the second floor." The man gestured at the rough-hewn staircase by the far wall.

"Can you let him know I'm here?" Nel asked. "I'll wait." She had been inside many strangers' homes over her years of service, but something about an inn room felt more intrusive than usual. Especially if that room belonged to Mainu.

"The gentleman expressly said I should direct you upstairs." The innkeeper bowed with the kind of humility that didn't take no for an answer. "Please, go ahead, Officer. If you'll pardon me, I'm needed in the back."

Nel didn't pardon him, but he was nonetheless gone before she could consider saying so. Left on her own, she climbed the two flights of stairs and followed the corridor to the end, all the way to the last of seven identical chestnut-colored doors.

Unlike the bell at the counter, her knock was answered immediately.

"Who is it?"

"Nel. Nella Dormanni," she clarified for no reason.

"It's unlocked. Open carefully."

Unsure what to make of the instruction, she pushed gingerly on the handle and cracked the door open inch by inch. As there was no resistance on the other side, she ventured further until the opening was wide enough for her to step through. Once inside, her gaze fell directly on the bed. It took her two looks to fully comprehend what she was seeing and not slam the door shut with a shriek.

Mainu lay on his back, mostly dressed from the waist down, but wearing only an undershirt on top. One of his hands was tucked under his head, while the other one rested between his legs and, at first, appeared to be scratching his groin. That was, until Nel checked again and noticed the scrawniest, scruffiest, shaggiest alley cat she'd ever seen, curled up on Mainu's lap and purring in complete bliss.

"Perfect timing," Mainu said. "I had hoped I could introduce you to someone."

Nel had to laugh. "Are you talking to me or him?"

"Whichever one of you is listening." He fished out his watch from a pocket and opened the cover. "Ten minutes early, as always. Normally, I'd be happy to head out, but today I'd like to petition not to leave this bed until necessary."

There was a playfulness to his voice, so far removed from

the cold efficiency he otherwise tended to speak with. Had Nel walked into any other man's room and found him on his back with both arms and most of his chest exposed, she would have turned around in a heartbeat. In Mainu's case, the more details she picked up on, the more different the picture became. His trousers were fully buckled, his feet lay flat on the ground, and his hair was undone in haphazard locks under him. The window was wide open with the branches of a sycamore not two feet away. All clues hinted that Mainu had been on his bed getting ready when the cat came to visit, and he instantly forgot about everything else.

"I suppose I can sit down," Nel said. "I wouldn't want to interrupt such an important meeting."

Mainu gave her a rare smile back. "You're welcome to join. He's much softer than you'd think."

Nel pulled up a chair and, with some hesitation, reached forward to pat the cat on the end that lay closer to Mainu's stomach. The matted and somewhat patchy coat of fur wasn't especially inviting, but upon actually touching it, Nel had to admit he was right. Her fingers slid through the tufts of hair, while the warm body under it rose and fell in contented slumber. Mainu kept his hand at the cat's head to scratch it behind the ears, and having thus divvied up the animal between them, they continued in silence.

There wasn't much in the room to distract her. Besides the few garments flung across the back of a chair or hung from the wardrobe, there was little proof of Mainu's presence. The only telltale sign was an empty cup on the nightstand alongside a satchel of his reviled licorice tea and, as expected, a jug of honey.

Mainu had his eyes closed, and his face was completely still, save for the occasional twitch of the lip when he swallowed. Whenever he did, the knot of his throat slid upward and bulged out the mysterious jagged scar that spanned the breadth of his neck. Some of it was getting harder to see, as his finely trimmed beard, now left to its own devices, had set out to reclaim its territory on Mainu's cheeks and jaw. If he were to ask, Nel would have said it suited him better.

With a satisfied groan, the cat uncurled itself and stretched indulgently, eliciting another smile from its newfound patron. The scene reminded Nel of her parents back home. They too would spend many a peaceful evening by the fire with the family's ancient bloodhound at their feet, or more likely spread across their legs, soaking up their affection.

Nel paused. Was she comparing Mainu and herself to her parents? Her *married* parents. . . ?

Lost in thought, her hand crept gradually up the cat's body, until her motions grazed Mainu's wrist. His thumb, in turn, weaved between her fingers. Nel slowly drew them back toward herself, and he followed.

That was when she accidentally touched the cat's belly, and the formerly docile creature sprung like a bear trap, sinking twenty claws and as many teeth into the trespassing appendage.

Mainu bolted upright. *"Naël! Restill! Res-till!"* he chided the animal in Midorean while he unhooked its paws from Nel's hand.

The cat leapt from his lap and bounded out the window, scampering away among the branches with nary a hiss at either of them.

"I'm sorry," Mainu said. "I should have been more careful. Let me treat that for you." He produced a vial from his bag and soaked a handkerchief with a pungent brown liquid. "Tincture of seaweed. It stings a little, but it's better than cat scratch fever."

He gently took Nel by the wrist so he could clean her bite and claw marks. The tincture stung arguably worse than the bite itself—but perhaps not as much as her own disappointment at the abrupt end to their shared moment.

"Is that the one you thought to name Two-Face?" she asked to break the awkwardness of the situation.

"Mm. He earned his title today." Mainu put away the bottle. "I suppose we might as well get to work."

"All right." Nel rubbed her hand where Mainu had held it. "I'll wait for you downstairs."

"Thank you. I only need a minute to get dressed." While he spoke, he observed his face in the mirror. "I should shave one of these days, though."

Nel considered for a moment, but, in the end, she decided that didn't quite qualify as asking for her opinion.

* * *

While it wasn't exactly summer again like the innkeeper had said, the rare, clear day made a significant difference. Under the clouds, the slick coat of water that lingered after the rain made everything slimy, but when the sun got to shine through again, the roads and rooftops sparkled in a dazzling gleam of gold. After the last two months, Nel wouldn't have blamed anyone who forgot altogether what color the sky was, and she, too, appreciated the reminder.

The change in the air permeated the streets as well. Everyone walked a little slower, held their heads a little higher, and acted noticeably less irritated. Nel and Mainu fell in with the rhythm of the street and marched along at a comfortable pace, taking in the renewed spirit of the city.

Now that she saw more of the surrounding faces, something else caught her attention. Her officer's jacket always garnered her a foot of respectful distance from passersby, but otherwise, no one paid her much mind. The sight of a uniformed Midorean, however, attracted a great deal of interest, especially from the women. That in and of itself wasn't unexpected—what Nel picked up on was how many of those women's eyes, after stealing a glimpse of Mainu, would turn to her in a distinct shade of green.

They wound their way through the streets of the Lower Court District with a break every now and then to orient themselves. Like most of the city outside Ilvior Island, this wasn't a neighborhood Nel knew intimately. The only building she recognized from a distance was the head office of the Messengers' Guild, with its famously gaudy statues and reliefs. As they approached, a railcar trundled past them and rang its bell in quick succession to clear the road ahead. It was gone shortly after, but the ringing persisted—only it didn't come from the rails.

*"Boo! Boo to the lapdogs of the aristocracy!"*

Across the street, a small group had set up camp on the corner and blocked the pavement in both directions. They hadn't noticed Nel, as they were busy yelling at those going in and out of the office. The loudest among them was their leader, a sizable woman with a face as round as the moon and as red as the sun. She was in charge of ringing the bell and leading them in their chants, while the rest followed along and waved their blue rags.

"Are these the infamous bluebells?" Mainu asked.

"Unfortunately, yes." Nel fidgeted with her whistle, not yet daring to blow.

The woman with the bell was too much for her to handle, let alone the entire group. Should she bother at all? It would only be more of a hassle, and getting Forley moved to the Ilvior guardhouse had delayed their work already. She shouldn't abuse Mainu's patience any more. If only she could catch sight of some patrolling guardsmen, she might call them over, but none were around.

While she dithered aimlessly, a messenger coach turned the corner behind the office. At the woman's behest, a boy of no more than ten years reached into the pouch around his shoulder and proceeded to pelt the coach with eggs, cackling and jeering, along with the rest of the group. He aimed the final one deliberately at the coach driver, who narrowly avoided getting hit square in the face.

Nel whistled the traffic to a halt and strode across the road. Outnumbered or not, she was going to put an end to this, consequences be damned. What kind of officer—no, what kind of *sergeant* wouldn't dare to stand up against some louts? If Mainu truly thought she might be captain someday, then she wouldn't stand meekly by like some helpless girl who couldn't defend herself from a cat.

The sound drew the attention of the whole bunch to her, along with most of the people nearby. Nel's skin prickled under the dozens of gazes, but there was no turning back now.

"What's going on here?" she asked. As there wasn't a morsel of room on the pavement, her feet were on the road, leaving her already modest height a solid four inches below the bluebells.

The group's leader loomed over her. "You tell me." She put both hands on her hips. "What crime are we committing by being in a public place?"

"You're loitering for a start, and you're causing a disturbance."

"What disturbance? Because you don't like what we're saying?" The woman turned to her audience and swung her bell in a wide arc. *"Hooray! Long live the guilds! Long live the prefects! Hooray to the city guard!"* she shouted, then faced Nel again. "Is that also disturbing you? Or is it only when we speak against your masters, you hound?"

A few onlookers snickered.

Nel steeled herself. "Don't pretend you're standing here doing nothing. I saw your boy throw eggs at that coach. That's property damage."

"And I saw a man take a piss right on the side of my house. Will you be taking him in, too?"

Another round of chortles. It was becoming clear that this was far from the first time the woman had this confrontation. She likely had answers ready for questions Nel hadn't thought of yet. Her watery eyes squinted in condescension, daring Nel to press forward.

"Why is that boy even here?" Nel asked. "It's the middle of the morning. He should be at school."

"He's *my* boy. I decide where he goes and what he learns."

"Learn? What does he learn standing around here with you?"

The woman pulled in her son by the shoulder. "You heard the officer's question. What are you learning here?"

"I'm learning who our enemies are," the boy replied eagerly.

"The traitors at the beck and call of the aristocracy, who'd sooner burn down the country than grant common folks the same rights they have!"

"That's right." His mother pointed her bell at Nel. "The rights they never earned nor deserved. And he's learning not to trust those who'd put their own kind behind bars, while we're the ones fighting for a better life for *you!*"

At the last word, the audience burst into cheers and applause.

The woman held her bell high and led the group in chants of, "*Common rights now! Common rights now!*" The others soon joined and closed in around them.

Nel was hopelessly defeated. She pushed her way back across the road before the crowd fully engulfed her, finally landing at Mainu's side again.

"Are you all right?" he asked.

"Yes," Nel said, trying not to let her voice tremble with embarrassment. "Yes, I'm fine."

"I think your colleagues are on the way. Maybe it's best if we leave this to them."

Over the ruckus, a series of whistles sounded from down the street, where indeed a band of officers rushed toward the commotion. While Nel's presence alone had done precious little to intimidate anyone, half a dozen men with clubs proved much more effective.

Within a minute, a scuffle broke out as the guards set out to disperse the crowd. Most of them were reasonable enough to leave on the first warning, but the bluebell group was determined to stand fast and be dragged away by their heels if needed. To Nel's dismay, that also included the boy, who clung to his father with both hands while cursing out the guards who tried to pry him off.

The scene was over as abruptly as it had started. The street cleared out, the gawkers returned to their business, and there was nothing else for Nel and Mainu but to do the same. For the remainder of their walk, her mind ran in circles about the encounter, and her cheeks burned in shame over her failure.

# Chapter 22

Thessa counted the buildings on her left. Unless she was mistaken, the third one after this was her destination. She had to trust her recollection along with the directions she received, as there was nothing else to go by. This part of the Miller District lay so far on the outskirts and so far outside the council's interest, even the major streets barely had official names. The one she rode along was only so lucky to be named Railway Road, thanks to the tracks it followed eastward. Such things like house numbers were nothing short of a frivolity.

Two more left. At the heart of the city, that would have meant less than a minute. Here, a single block stretched nearly to the horizon. Massive warehouses and silos stood as far as the eye could see, along with the borough's namesake, mill after mill after mill. All told, this would've been the last place Thessa expected to find a Midorean. She had no choice but to soldier on and hope Vei Ruola hadn't misdirected her. That hope sparked up in her when she reached the third corner and spotted Ida.

"Is this the right place?" she wondered aloud.

"Either it is, or the two of us both made the same mistake," Ida said. "I suppose we'll know for certain when Corlis gets here."

Thessa hopped off of Snake Eyes, then stepped back to examine the building. There weren't many houses in the neighborhood, and this one wasn't much to call a home. About a third of the windows were boarded up, while the rest sported a thick coat of dust from disuse. The crumbled arch of the entryway led into an open space that had stopped pretending to be a garden long ago.

"You're not working today?" Ida asked, indicating the dress Thessa had on.

"No, I am. Corlis said I should change clothes before I come to make sure the uniform doesn't give away where to find me."

"I thought we were supposed to trust this Vei Ruola."

"There are few people Corlis trusts until he's proven wrong," Thessa said.

"Then I hope he's wrong. I'd hate for all that trouble last night to be for naught."

Thessa's cheeks flushed as she tied Snake Eyes to a post. When the three of them met up outside the Belfry the previous night, Ida was—rightfully—not very pleased at the commotion Thessa had caused.

"Does anyone suspect you had anything to do with it?" she asked Ida.

"They haven't said so. Which in and of itself doesn't guarantee anything."

"But if they do, will you be all right?"

Ida crossed her arms. "I've been making do as a bloodsucker for fifteen years. I'll figure something out if I have to."

With the horse secured, Thessa joined her on the lookout for Corlis. He was still nowhere to be seen, either on foot or by coach. The modest traffic here consisted almost entirely of carts and wagons, marching alongside the freight trains that thundered past every so often.

Knowing they'd likely have a few minutes to themselves, and that there was no one around to overhear them, Thessa plucked up the courage to ask, "How did you get turned?"

Ida faced her, but she didn't answer right away.

"Was it of your own accord?" Thessa added.

"Are you asking if this was my own fault?" Ida brushed her veil with the back of her fingers. "Yes, it was."

"I'm sorry. That's not how I meant it." Thessa put her hands up. "I was only curious, and—I wondered if you might have some advice."

The question had weighed on her since she and Ida first met. It wasn't the most opportune time to discuss the subject, but as far as Thessa could tell, there never would be one.

She inched closer. "I became a werewolf against my will. It's been over a year and a half, and I'm still not sure how I feel about it. There have been times when it was a boon; other times, it's the most dreadful curse I could imagine.

"The worst part is how alone I feel. Corlis is a wonderful friend to me, and he does more than he should to help, but he can never truly understand what it's like to live with something like this."

It was in no way Ida's responsibility to console her. She had enough worries of her own. For that matter, it might have been wrong to compare their situations in the first place. Both of them were afflicted by the result of some long-lost necromantic experiments, but how similar were they, actually? Perhaps it was foolish to bring it up. At the same time, the mere act of saying it lifted a weight from Thessa's chest.

Ida regarded her for a while over the cloth that hid her deformity. Eventually, she said, "I know what it's like. A few years ago, Forley and I were thrown out of our home and had to move to a different town again. For nearly a month, I had to live on nothing but animals. It made me so ill I was at death's door.

"He insisted that I drink his blood, but I refused. In the end, he got angry at me for being 'unreasonable.' I told him that, if he were in my place, he'd understand—but he never will be. And to this day, he doesn't."

A freight wagon rolled past. From the perch, the driver and another worker gave them a series of whistles, along with some barely concealed remarks about what they'd like to do under the hay they were transporting.

Ida waited for them to disappear around the next junction before she finished. "If you want advice from me, this is all I can give you: you'll never truly stop feeling alone. You may find people you trust or people who are like you, but you can't always be around them. And whenever you aren't, every face on the street will remind you that you're not the same. The sooner you get used to that, the more bearable life will be."

Harsh words, spoken by a woman whose world had been shaped over years fraught with challenges Thessa could only imagine. None of what Ida said, though, was anything that hadn't occurred to her as well. The same way putting her feelings in words gave her relief, hearing her own thoughts back from someone else came with a whole new weight. After all was said and done, she was back where she started.

There was no time to dwell on that. The next minute, a rent-coach appeared at the far end of Railway Road and pulled up to their corner at an unhurried pace.

"City folks joke all the time about the Wall District practically being in the countryside," Corlis said as he landed beside them. "This may as well be another country to them."

Before either Thessa or Ida could answer, a door opened in the side of the building, and a rough-hewn man in patchy overalls stepped out. Without a word, he motioned for them to come in, then disappeared again at once.

The door led into a dim stairwell, where the man took them up several flights on the creaking steps. On the top floor, they followed an open hallway around the desolate inner yard, and at last, they came to a minuscule apartment. There, the man pointed them toward the next room, then slouched into a rickety armchair and clasped both hands over his belly.

Taëminn Vei Ruola awaited them at a round table with a haphazard array of chairs and a steaming pot of fruit tea in the middle. She was in no better or worse shape than the night before. Her hair may have been more neatly brushed, and her dress properly buttoned, but her eyes were weighed down far more than her age warranted. Nonetheless, she greeted them with the same dignity as if they were at the Jade Hill palace.

Ida took the chair farthest from her, leaving Thessa and Corlis to seat themselves on either side of their host. She offered the pot to Thessa first and proceeded around the table, pouring sweet-smelling red tea into each chipped cup. Considering their surroundings, the scene should have been nothing if not ridiculous, but the woman's dedication to hospitality spoke volumes. Thessa had seen her own mother in such a state before, on the day she received news of her brother's death. Despite the family's insistence that she rest, she conducted an entire dinner gathering without the slightest hitch.

"I apologize for making you come all the way here," the woman began. "I hope you understand I'd rather not invite you into my home yet."

"I'd have been more suspicious if you did," Corlis said. "But I also have to say, the fact that you know where the Miller District is, let alone have a hideout here, is telling."

"Then you should be relieved to know it's not my hideout."

Corlis blew on his tea, but once again, he withheld his response.

"I've met the two of you before," their host continued before she turned to Ida. "But I don't believe we're familiar."

"No, we aren't." Ida's veil covered up most of her face, but not her measured tone. "And I consider myself fairly well acquainted in the Belfry. I thought I'd have heard about you."

"Let's take things one at a time," Corlis chimed in. "Who exactly are you?"

The Midorean drew herself up. "My name is Taëminn Vei Ruola. I live in Namahil, but I usually spend a few months each year in New Montres."

"Doing what?"

"Patronizing the arts. I seek out talented artists and help them find sponsors to support their work."

Ida scoffed and gestured at the filthy window. "Where else would you find either of those if not here?"

"You'd be surprised," Taëminn replied, unbothered by the jab. "Talent cares nothing for wealth or station. All it needs is a fertile mind and the chance to flourish."

"That's a lovely discussion for another day," Corlis said. "Who's the dead woman?"

While Ida's purposeful mockery did nothing to shake the

Midorean, Corlis's blunt choice of words noticeably did so. Part of Thessa wanted to chastise him for it, but she was far too eager to hear the answer herself. Half the city had been agog with curiosity over the mysterious murder victim who, to date, had not been publicly identified.

"Her name is Kalevi Soù Eivarn. We met last winter, a few months before I came to Ardonne. She was such a beautiful soul. Widowed at a young age, with so much to live for and so much love in her heart. In my mind, I made it my mission to find someone who would make her happy. But the more I got to know her, the more I wanted to be that someone.

"Before I left for New Montres, I confessed my feelings to her. I wrote to her every week while I was here, and she wrote back. As the fall approached, I thought more and more about how glad I would be to return to Midorea and get to see her again."

"In Midorea?" Corlis asked. "She wasn't planning to come here?"

"No. Not that I ever knew of. When I heard she was murdered here, I was beyond distraught." Taëminn's cheeks glistened in the faint sunlight. "All I wanted was to see her smile again. To hold her hand. When we were together. . . I could see the life she'd lost coming back to her."

She produced a handkerchief to dab her eyes.

Thessa lifted her cup and took a discreet sip to give her some time. The tea was wonderfully delicious, as if she had freshly picked each berry that day. Taëminn must have brought it with her specifically for their meeting. Along with her impeccable manners, the gesture spoke most highly of her in Thessa's view.

Corlis, however, was less impressed. "And could you see

yourself returning to your husband?" He pointed at the slender bracelet that had slid out of Taëminn's sleeve.

The Midorean tucked the silver band back under the fabric. "My husband, Yanne, is a good man, and I cherish him dearly. My love for Kalevi did not diminish that. But to answer your real question, I never told him about her."

"That's hardly the only way he could have found out."

"And he arranged for a bloodsucker to murder my lover?" Taëminn regarded Corlis with stern disbelief. "I can assure you he'd never be capable of that."

"Not four months ago, me and Thessa witnessed two murders in a house filled with people who'd never be capable of it. Somehow, someone always is."

"My husband is thousands of miles away. The killer is here in the city," Taëminn said.

"Let's talk about that, then," Ida spoke up across the table. "How did you get into the Belfry, and what were you doing there?"

"Braselius used to be one of my sponsors," the Midorean answered. "I haven't been to the tower in years, though I make sure to maintain relations with some of the members. I was able to use my proper name at the entrance to get in, but I disguised myself on the way up." She glanced at Thessa. "Evidently, I didn't do a very good job.

"I mostly sat and listened in on conversations to find out if anyone might have known Kalevi, or had any reason to harm her—"

"But let me guess," Corlis said. "No one there was capable of it."

Taëminn shook her head.

"I did my own share of listening, too. Turns out, Violet

applied for membership," Ida said.

Thessa frowned. "Didn't you say she couldn't possibly be a bloodsucker?"

"You don't have to be one. After all, we can't drink each other's blood, and they wouldn't want us bringing new guests all the time."

"Do you know why she was turned down?"

Ida gave her a frosty look. "I didn't have time to find out after that scene you caused. But I can only imagine they didn't trust her enough to keep a secret, and given my own experience, I'd say they made the right call."

As surprising as that revelation was, it didn't bring them much further ahead. It proved Violet had *some* connection to the Belfry, and she must have known a member there—but nothing about whether she had anything to do with Kalevi's death.

A lull settled over the table. Taëminn stared out through the one clean spot on the window. Ida drummed on the splintered wood of the table. Corlis swirled his cup and kept his eyes down, the way he always did when he was working hard to make sense of things. So much had been said in that cramped room, yet so much more was missing.

"When we met, you recognized the name of Beldora. Are you also a friend of hers?" Thessa asked.

"We move in the same circles. I know her to be a woman of refined taste and character. She regularly invites musicians to perform at her establishment and mingle with her wealthy guests." Taëminn poured out a second round of tea as she spoke.

Thessa couldn't help but think it was an excuse to avoid her gaze.

"Why was Kalevi in the Garden?" Corlis asked.

"I have no idea," Taëminn replied. "To my knowledge, she'd never been in New Montres before."

"I can think of one reason," Ida said.

Taëminn set down the teapot. She hadn't displayed any reaction to Ida's remark about the dingy apartment, nor to her direct questions regarding the Belfry—but upon this, she glared straight at her. "What are you suggesting?"

"Nothing you haven't thought of yourself," Ida said. "If you're prepared to cheat, be prepared to be cheated on. I have some experience of my own on that front."

"Why would she cheat on me at the Garden, of all places? Even if no one recognized her, word would have gotten around to me sooner or later." Taëminn's hand remained in a tight grip on the pot's handle.

Above the veil, Ida's eyes narrowed—not in malice or mistrust, but in pity. "I know that kind of thinking. You're not thinking with Kalevi's head. You're looking for a reason to doubt your own fears. Over my years, I've seen plenty of men ruin their marriages or engagements, and all of them should have known better. But the truth is, once you're foolish enough to be unfaithful, it's only a matter of time before the other mistakes follow."

One by one, Taëminn's fingers relinquished the ceramic pot, and she folded her hand back in her lap.

"Thank you for your insight. I believe I've told you everything I can."

* * *

Corlis sucked his tooth. "She didn't tell us half of it."

The scream of a train whistle cut the dusty air, followed by the deep rumble of a dozen wagons loaded with timber. Thessa and Corlis stood at the western tip of Railway Road, where the inner half of the Miller District rejoined civilization. Ida had gone off to find a rent-coach, while the two of them waited by a lamppost on the corner.

Thessa patted Snake Eyes on the neck and reflected on what Corlis said. "You think she's lying?"

"Not as such." Corlis picked at a fingernail with his pocketknife. "Did you notice she didn't deny she's married, but she didn't say it upfront, either? She was very careful about how much she told us."

"Her lover was murdered. It makes sense she'd worry about who she can trust," Thessa responded. She wasn't truly trying to argue with him. When Corlis's mind was racing as it was now, her job was to feed him questions to disprove one by one.

"That's the thing, though." Corlis punctuated the thought by poking the air in front of him with the knife. "Her lover died, what, three days ago? Three days, and she already has a safe house set up?" He shook his head. "No, she's been afraid for a while. More than that, she's been *prepared* to be afraid."

"Afraid of who?"

"She said it herself: she's got connections from the upper crust to the bottom feeders. The senate, the Werrish syndicate, the Belfry, her husband—anyone and more could be after her."

While Corlis turned back to his nails, Thessa stroked the horse's mane again. "Sounds hopeless."

"Maybe not. Arranging things like this meeting place isn't something she can do on her own. Someone's helping her. If we figure out who her friends are, that could tell us who the enemy is."

It made enough sense, but it didn't bring them further ahead. Once again, all they could do was keep searching for answers in the same places as before.

Overhead, a cloud drifted lazily by and blotted out the precious sunlight that had briefly tempered the autumn chill. Thessa pulled in her shawl around her shoulders. According to weather-watchers, there wasn't much promise of things getting any brighter soon. It felt true in more ways than one.

"How about your other concerns?" Corlis spat a piece of nail into a sewer grate. "Have you given any thought to joining the noble fight for common rights?"

"Not in the last few days," Thessa said. "But when I went by at the office before coming here, they told me there was a fight between some bluebells and the guard this morning, right across the street."

"Was there any reason?"

"They said someone threw a whole basket of rocks and rotten eggs at a messenger coach. When a guard told them to stop, they jumped at her and almost beat her to death. It took twenty patrolmen a half hour to break them up."

Corlis said nothing, merely chewed his thumbnail and raised one eyebrow.

Thessa shrugged under her shawl. "It's what my colleagues said."

Gossip was gossip, and she was no stranger to it—nor to how much the truth was colored by who told it. Perhaps it wasn't a whole basket, perhaps it wasn't twenty men. But however the story slanted, *something* had happened on that corner.

Whatever it was, it had to wait. Ida returned with the coach, and Corlis got in, so they could head to the dockyards in the hopes of getting some answers about Violet. Thessa had an afternoon's work left to do, so she got back on Snake Eyes and parted ways with them at the next crossroads, promising to meet up at The Lame Mare that evening. For now, Thessa had to heed Corlis's advice: think about today's problems today, and leave tomorrow for tomorrow.

# Chapter 23

Argiey scratched his sideburns and observed his reflection over the railing. Despite the abundance of sunlight, the ripples of the water reduced his image to little more than a formless blotch upon the river's surface. With each wave that rushed by, bits of him broke off on one side and rejoined on the other, swirling around in a dizzying dance—as if they wanted to scatter in a hundred directions but were forced to barely hang together. That reflection felt truer to his being than if he had simply stared in a mirror.

He tightened his coat and went back under the bridge. The clatter of hooves and wheels echoed down from overhead, and together with the water's low murmur, melded into a blanket of sound that seemingly came from everywhere at the same time. Yet instead of disorienting him, it settled on Argiey with a smooth comfort, as though the river flowed through his very mind. Perhaps instead of walking over the Broken Bridge, he might try staying under it for his daily thought fasting.

Sadly, on that day, it wasn't an option. Prompt and punctual as always, Mainu trotted down the stairs to the riverbank and accompanied Argiey beneath the immense stone arch. Up above, the peaceful folk of New Montres basked in this precious day of mild weather, and not a soul would think of wasting it in such a cold and shadowy spot.

The lieutenant stood next to him and faced the river. "I can't stay too long. Nel thinks I'm at the consulate, so I have to make sure I'm seen there in case she asks later."

Argiey gave a nod of acknowledgment, not getting bogged down by how Mainu continued to speak of the officer on first name terms. Not yet.

Mainu went on, "Is she back now?"

"She is."

"What happened?"

"Last night, she snuck out to break into some sort of bloodsucker hideout in the Riverside District." Argiey kept his sight straight ahead and addressed his recount to the damp stones.

"She broke into a place filled with the likes who killed Kalevi?"

"Can't say I blame her, frankly. She's been holed up in that safe house for weeks. Cabin fever can take a toll on a person like her. Couple that with the guilt and frustration over Kalevi's death, and it was only a matter of time."

"I'm not sure how pleased her husband would have been with that answer if I had to return to Midorea and tell him his wife was killed," Mainu said.

Argiey wouldn't have claimed to be a friend of the lieutenant, but based on their brief acquaintance, he had gotten a fairly straightforward impression of him. If Mainu resorted to being sardonic, he must have been nothing short of furious.

"Did she manage to learn something useful?" he asked.

"Yes and no," Argiey said. "No leads about the murder as such. But, as it turns out, she wasn't the only one looking.

She ran into some others who are also trying to track down the killer."

Mainu turned briefly toward him. "From the city guard?"

"The opposite, you could say. One of them's the main suspect in the murder. A Laerithian bloodsucker who worked at the Garden of Lilies."

"Laerithian? You mean Ida Nawoale?"

"I don't know her. Do you?"

"Not her, only her son." The lieutenant paused to remember. "Forley, I think his name is. He was arrested yesterday morning for attempted robbery when he tried to get money for his mother's release bond."

Argiey scratched his sideburns again. "You think it might be worth talking to her? You could reunite her with her son for the perfect excuse."

"He doesn't want his mother to know where he is. Nel had him moved to Ilvior Island for that very reason. If I speak to Ida, I should do it alone."

"How—" Argiey began.

Mainu raised a hand to cut him off. His gaze was fixed on the stairs that led up to the bridge, from where a series of rapid footsteps sounded.

The feet in question belonged to a group of well-dressed young boys hurrying down to the river in excited chatter. Once they were all in place, the oldest one held out a tattered burlap sack, while the others huddled around him and loudly dared one another to reach inside. Eventually, one of them wrapped his hand in a handkerchief, stuck it in the bag, and yanked it back out almost immediately. The boys recoiled in a gale of laughter as the Brave One raised aloft his catch: an old, fat rat that squirmed and flailed wildly, hanging from its naked tail in the boy's grasp.

After waving the animal at each of his comrades, who reacted with gleeful disgust, he turned toward the river. In a chorus, they counted the swings of his arm, and upon the fourth one, he released the rodent's tail from his grip. The furry body flew high up at a sharp angle, nearly reaching the road level of the bridge, then some five yards further, it splashed into the grayish-blue water. On the shore, the boys peeled their eyes watching for it to emerge from the waves and struggle some more for their delight.

"I'd hate to be that rat," Mainu muttered.

"It's not as bad as it looks. As far as death goes, at least." Upon the lieutenant's slightly raised eyebrows, Argiey added, "If you fall from high enough, water or rock makes no difference. Your bones turn to gravel on impact either way, so you don't get a chance to worry about drowning. Can't say for sure about rats, of course." He raised his hands in humility. "But over twenty years in the job, I've had some customers who fell from a comparable height."

After a minute or so, the boys came to the same conclusion. Amidst some indignant pouting over their entertainment being cut short, they filed back up the stairs, now trying to wrestle the empty sack over each other's heads.

Mainu rubbed the base of his right hand, which had a series of faint red scratch marks on it. "What made you choose to become a coroner?"

A nostalgic smirk spread across Argiey's lips. "My mentor asked me that selfsame question on my first day, and I didn't have an answer. A few months into my apprenticeship, he asked if I figured it out yet, and I told him, 'I think what I really wanted to be is a butcher, but I like animals too much.'"

He had no idea what Midoreans considered a joke—or if they had a word for it to begin with. But he had an inkling that the noise Mainu made was not merely him clearing his throat.

"How about you?" Argiey asked back. "How does one become a lieutenant of the Midorean high court?"

"Family ties," came the plain reply. "I have a pair of cousins a few years older than me, and they both served. My parents would always send me away to spend the summer with them. Eventually, it only felt natural I'd follow their example."

"You know, that's something I noticed. How little thought folks put into choices that decide their entire lives. We care about today's problems today, and leave tomorrow for tomorrow. Then, before you know it, it *is* tomorrow, and you're stuck with whatever you left for yourself."

Mainu tilted his head. "And what are the problems of today?"

Argiey picked up the thread from earlier. "How's your work going with Nel?"

The slight emphasis he put on the officer's name didn't escape Mainu's attention. He adjusted his shirt sleeve over his hand. "She had a run-in with your people this morning. Nothing serious—not for her, at least. But it did cause enough of a commotion to get some patrolling guards involved, and it upset her a great deal."

"Do you still trust her?"

The lieutenant lowered his gaze toward his own reflection, much in the way Argiey had before their conversation. "I trust her as a person. But if she knew about my real purpose in New Montres, I don't think she would trust me."

That much had been as good as self-evident. The real

question, if it ever came to it, was which one Mainu would choose: his pledge to Vei Ruola or the trust of his officer friend.

"All the more reason to wrap things up as fast as possible," Argiey said.

Mainu's mouth twitched in the corner. "You said there were others with Nawoale. Who were they?"

"No idea. A Sallician girl and some scrawny, wall-eyed fellow. Friends of hers, for all anyone knows."

"It might be worth finding out more about them, to be sure. Can you do that?"

"I need to be back at the deadhouse. Not much digging I can do from there. And—" Argiey trailed off in his attempt to be as diplomatic as he could, before concluding, "I believe I've made my stance clear when it comes to knowing things."

The lieutenant regarded him with his usual inscrutable expression. "Yes, you have. I recall you saying you're happy to play your part for a better tomorrow, but only if you can live to see it. In one way, I understand your reasoning. In another, it feels like you're trying to. . . What's that saying you have? Eat your cake and still have it?"

"Have your cake and eat it, too. Though the way you put it does make more sense," Argiey replied.

"In any case, reward doesn't come without risks."

Argiey waved at the bridge above them, its centuries-old bricks resounding with the bustle of traffic. "There are millions in Ardonne who aren't taking any risks. If the bluebells succeed, they'll reap the rewards, nonetheless."

Mainu brushed a hand along his coat sleeve. "True. But if you'd rather be one of them, and simply wait for others to do all the hard work for your benefit—you ought to make that decision soon." He then strode away and disappeared up the stairs.

Argiey lingered a while by the railing. Up high, the city carried on as busy as ever, absorbed in an unending racket, oblivious to his existence or his concerns. Down the river, a hundred yards away, floated the broken remains of a rat. And in between, there was he, wondering which side he'd end up on. A stiff breeze swept the water, and his reflection splintered into more minuscule fragments than before.

# Chapter 24

Solluri Hill hadn't changed in the last three days. The clearer sky did nothing to brighten the houses, only made their frigid opulence more conspicuous. The cease of wind didn't bring peace with it, but instead made the silence more overwhelming. And however mild the air may have been, it couldn't warm Nel's body against the icy weight on her chest. With leaden steps, she approached the house she and Mainu had visited earlier—the one where his gentle greeting had been such welcome music to her ears. This time, she came alone, while Mainu was at the Midorean consulate.

Or that was where he said he was going.

She shouldn't doubt him. She didn't want to. But there was nothing to be done against it. Like a splinter in her palm or a rock in her shoe, doubt pained her no matter how minute it was. It wedged into her mind the day before, when the coroner came by at the Ilvior Island guardhouse, and stung her relentlessly.

Romer Bornessi opened the door and greeted Nel with the same deference as earlier, mixed only with a slight puzzlement when she asked to see Vei Ruola's apartment again. Regardless, he obliged without hesitation and led the way up, his trusty ring of keys jingling by his side.

"Has anyone come by since we were here?" Nel asked.

"No, Sergeant. Neither your colleagues, nor any visitors. I believe by this point, word of her absence has gotten out."

That it had. Nel and Mainu had been making sure of that for days, going down the list of friends and acquaintances provided by Vei Ruola's husband. None of them had anything meaningful to offer, and many were caught unawares by her departure.

The apartment was, at a glance, in the exact state they had left it. Nel asked Bornessi to wait for her downstairs, as she would be taking a long time. In truth, she needed less than a minute. As soon as the door closed behind the landlord, she went into the day chamber and headed for the writing desk.

Three days earlier, while discussing their theories of horses and zebras regarding Vei Ruola's disappearance, they found a stack of letters in the locked cabinet. Nel thought they might be proof of the woman's infidelity, but Mainu leafed through them and stated that every last one was from her loving husband. Not knowing a word of Midorean, Nel had to believe him—so they put the letters back and spoke no more of it.

The previous day, the coroner visited her at the guardhouse and asked for Mainu. He said he had some paperwork to file regarding the murder victim at the Garden, and he figured it would be quicker to cross the bridge to Ilvior than to wait his turn at the consulate. However, Mainu wasn't there, so Nel had to send the coroner trekking back the way he'd come, with no choice but to go with his original plan.

At the time, the situation had struck Nel as comically unfortunate. *Good thing Mainu isn't the only person in New Montres who knows Midorean*, she thought. But as the hours passed, that thought refused to leave her head. It compounded a nagging feeling she couldn't place, that something was odd about Mainu's behavior. She had told herself she was overthinking, that she was being irrational. . . and that she should trust him.

And then, that morning, Nel had a confrontation with the bluebells outside the Messengers' Guild. That was when her doubt took root in earnest. When she had faced off with her colleagues at the Upper Court guardhouse, Mainu leapt in to help her with some quick thinking, whereas now he merely stood by. It wasn't his duty to rescue her, and she had no right to begrudge him for it, but it was odd. Especially after the moment they shared in his room minutes earlier.

Nel sat on the floor by the writing desk, flipping through the pages upon pages of unfamiliar handwriting and unknowable words. She folded up the stack and tucked it away in her bag. With a single-minded determination, she left the apartment, then the building, then Solluri Hill. Whether or not the letters were proof of betrayal, she would have to see for herself—as well as whose betrayal they were proof of.

# Chapter 25

*he sinkhole of New Montres.* As someone who had borne her own share of unflattering nicknames, Ida held some sympathy for the Wedge—as much as one can be sympathetic toward an island. That being so, she also knew that malicious or not, nicknames were never given without a reason. Back at the Garden, Violet had a reason to dub her "Teeth," and the greater island of the Ryonne delta had undoubtedly earned its moniker as well. As she and Corlis trudged along the miserably filthy streets that wound through the maze of factories, Ida shifted her compassion from the Wedge itself to those who had to live on it.

Judging by his permanent scowl, Corlis wasn't preoccupied with any such concerns. Whenever he wasn't covering his face outright, his nose twisted up in a struggle between the need to breathe and the revulsion it caused him. Ida couldn't fully know how that felt for him, but she wasn't entirely without a clue. Similar to the choking clouds of Braselius's lair, the Wedge air pressed thick and heavy against her lungs, at times with such an acrid burn that she had to cough. It made her wish for the rain to start again, so it could soak up the miasma and wash it out into the river. It only went to show, some parts of the city couldn't be helped by fair weather.

Corlis held out a hand in front of her to wait while they let a cart pass, then resumed without further instruction. He'd been similarly quiet the whole time since they got here, his concentration taken up by their common goal, as well as his own repugnance at the factory district. Not that he'd struck Ida as personable before. The two of them had been on somewhat shaky ground since the day before, when Ida took issue with his indifference in leveling accusations against both Forley and Mendel. They hadn't broached the topic since, and Corlis appeared in no rush to do so.

On the other hand, he also didn't object to Ida accompanying him on the hunt after Violet, and that was good enough for her. She was in no way thrilled to be here, but it was better than sitting on her hands doing nothing—and, for the time being, it was her only hope for finding Forley.

He hadn't shown himself in two days. Not to see Ida at the guardhouse, nor at the Garden, and he hadn't been to work. The ground might as well have swallowed him whole. It wasn't like him at all. He could be foolish and pigheaded and irresponsible, especially since he decided he was a grown man, but he'd never abandon Ida like this. Not when she needed him the most.

Worst of all, she didn't know where he lived. That one frustrated Ida more than anything. Week after week, he badgered her to visit him in the shabby little room he rented, and she always refused. She remembered it was somewhere in this part of town, but that "somewhere" was several square miles of labyrinthine city blocks. If only he'd tried harder to persuade her.

Another brief stop, while Corlis squinted at the unmarked buildings around them. Much like in the Miller District, the council left its citizens to fend for themselves when it came to finding their way in this area. Aside from the three main roads that ran lengthwise across the island, virtually none of the streets were designated. Corlis pondered for a moment, then darted forward into an alley. Ida had no idea where he led her, but he showed enough confidence.

"You know your way around here pretty well," she said to his back.

"Me and my aunt used to do a lot of business with the underbelly of the city. I spent years running back and forth around here as her messenger."

They emerged into a wider street, where he pointed at another crossroads further down. "That corner right there? That's the place I almost got stabbed for the first time."

"What a memory," Ida said.

"It made for quite the twelfth birthday gift, that's for sure." He continued in the opposite direction from the sentimental spot. "Anyway, I left that behind when my aunt died. Haven't been here for almost a year. Didn't miss it much to tell the truth."

"Yet here you are, on the trail of a killer."

Corlis dodged a row of overturned slop buckets on the pavement. "Thessa needs my help."

*Thessa.* Not the Garden, not Ida, not that Midorean. Not anyone with real stakes in the situation. Corlis wasn't there for their sakes—he was a friend of a friend of a friend. Ida had no right to expect more from him, but it also meant his loyalty extended as long as Thessa's desire to help and not an inch further. If the girl withdrew, he'd vanish like a mule in the fog.

All the more reason to wrap things up as fast as possible.

One more stop. This time, not in between buildings, but in front of one. Three stories of draped windows, peeling red paint, and a hanging lantern with the smashed remnants of what once had been red glass. Above Ida's head, a battered old shingle squealed as it rocked on its rusty hooks, welcoming guests to *"The Peach and The Cobbler."*

Inside, they found the owner in a dressing gown and half-done makeup, who made no secret of her annoyance at the two of them turning up this early.

Corlis shoved a generous tip in her hand and asked her for "the new woman" he'd been hearing so much about, who might teach "his wife" a thing or two in bed.

"I'm told she has a specialty," Ida chimed in for good measure. "Something she calls 'the bridge and the towers.'" The phrase had quite the notoriety back at the Garden, and she had no doubt Violet would rely on it to establish her new reputation.

Sure enough, the owner's eyebrows raised in recognition. "Word gets around faster than I thought," she croaked, then waved at the stairwell. "Second floor, third on the left."

Upstairs, Corlis and Ida stood on the two sides of the door so only he would be visible if it was cracked open. He then gave her one last glance and knocked.

From inside, a crow-like voice screeched, "What do you *want?*"

"That's her all right," Ida muttered.

Corlis knocked again, but before his knuckles hit for the third time, the door jerked open so violently it almost tore out the chain on the latch.

"Who are you?" Violet demanded. "It's not even six o'clock."

"I wanted to beat the crowd."

"Oh, I'll tell you what you can beat. Why did that hag let you in? Is she drunk already?"

"Here's why." Corlis raised his purse. "If you're not up for it, I can go and take this with me. Or you can get a head start on the day. Your choice."

Without seeing Violet's face, Ida had no trouble picturing her distorted grimace as she wrestled between her laziness and her greed. The door closed enough to unhook the chain, then opened again to allow Corlis in. He nodded for Ida to follow.

Violet was off in a corner with her back toward them. While one hand fiddled with her undergarments, the other one pointed sharply at the nightstand. "Money upfront," she barked. "Prices are on the door; you can read them for yourself. If something's scratched out, it's scratched out, got it? And I haven't had time to perfume, so don't let me hear you complain about that. Now—"

She spun around and froze at the sight of Ida. Her inky black hair, which Ida had only ever seen brushed to a perfect sheen, hung in a frizzled heap atop her head. The powder she would so carefully apply was also absent, laying bare her true age and her emerging crow's feet. And the shy demeanor that had been her trademark at the Garden decidedly did not carry over to her new place of work.

"Give me a damn reason not to scream the place down."

Corlis bolted the door. "We know you tried to become a member at the Belfry."

That sufficed. Violet's lips and neck twitched, but she merely snatched up a robe and threw it around herself. "Yeah, so? Then you also know they didn't let me in. Did you come here to rub that in my face, Teeth?"

"We're here to ask why," Ida replied.

"What are you, the city guard?" Violet snapped back. "How is it any of your business?"

"It's my business because you're the reason I was arrested, and I'm still under suspicion. So, you can either explain to us, or you can explain it to the guard when we tell them your little secret."

While they were colleagues, Violet's tantrums were little more than an annoyance if anything. After her backstabbing, it would have been a lie to claim Ida didn't relish watching her seethe in impotent fury.

"All right, fine. Yeah, I wanted to join. I was hoping to get turned. Already lost my career as a dancer to old age—didn't want to lose my career as a whore, too."

"After the hard time you gave me about my condition, you were going to risk ending up like me?" Ida asked.

"I know most of them aren't like you. Figured it was just your rotten luck, like with everything else in your life."

"Did the Belfry say why they didn't accept you?" Corlis asked from behind. "Or was your personality reason enough?" He checked the room while Ida and Violet spoke. He didn't have a difficult job, as the entire space was about the size of a broom closet. Besides a single bed, a nightstand, and a chest of drawers with an assortment of beauty products on top, there was little else to see.

"They tracked me down and found out I had a fling with some guardsmen outside of work. Said it's too much of a risk." Violet sneered. "As if it's my fault men have a thing for me."

"I'm sure they do." Corlis poked around the pile of cheap paints. "Enough to buy you Sallician rosewater, I see."

"You keep your grubby mitts off of that!" Violet shoved him

aside and wrested back the delicate crystal bottle Corlis had picked out.

"I can see why you're upset. It's a mighty expensive perfume. Nearly full, too." He ran his gaze around the squalid room. "Which one of your illustrious new customers got you that?"

"I bought it myself." Violet held the prized possession to her chest.

Corlis leaned forward. "With the money you extorted from. . . ?"

Yet again, Violet's face screwed up in frustration. This one appeared to be a detail she was much more reluctant to give up. She rocked in place while she considered her answer until at last she lowered herself onto the ragged mattress. Her features smoothed out, and she leaned back with a complacent smile.

"Beldora."

Ida balked. "Why would Beldora pay you off?"

"So I didn't tell the guard that she was the last one to see the Midorean alive." She flicked the hem of the robe over her reddened knee. "While she wandered around the Garden, I caught her in an alcove to ask if she was looking for someone. She said Beldora had a message for her, so I sent her to the office, where she usually is."

Next to Ida, Corlis crossed his arms in thought. There was no way to tell if any of this was true. It certainly didn't sound like it, what with how easily Violet gave it up. But, at the same time, it was equally unbelievable that Violet had applied to the Belfry, or that Thessa had found Taëminn there, or that a murder would had occurred at the Garden of Lilies. Whether or not Ida wanted to believe those things didn't make them any less true.

"And you ratted *me* out?" she asked. "When you knew I couldn't have possibly done it? What do you have against me?"

Violet tutted. "It wasn't about *you*. I was scared, all right? Pointing the finger at Beldora wasn't gonna do me any good. She's not a bloodsucker, and she had no ties to them, either. There wouldn't be an excuse to arrest her. The guard would start digging, and I had no idea how deep they'd go. You two managed to find out about me and the Belfry, so why couldn't they? If you got away—which I knew you would do—I could have ended up being the suspect." She concluded her speech with a disdainful purse of the lips. "Someone was going to take the fall. Better you than me."

Ida stood over her former housemate. Knowing all she knew about her now, the greatest shame was how much better they could have gotten along. All that pettiness and strife that sullied their relationship had not only been unpleasant but unnecessary.

There was nothing to do about it anymore.

"You really are a heinous bitch," Ida said plainly, then walked out of the room and shut the door on her and Violet's past.

# Chapter 26

Nel sat at her desk in the empty office. Almost everyone else, including Captain Pomeno, had called it a day and gone home. The evening patrol wouldn't be back for hours, and the night shift meant to relieve them hadn't come in yet. She had the entire second floor to herself. By her right hand towered a hefty backlog of paperwork: equipment orders, wages, testimonies, reports, and a whole host of others. All the aspects of keeping a guardhouse in operation that no one cared for, but everyone would miss.

She didn't touch any of that. For the past hour, her eyes were locked solely on the other stack in front of her. Ordered neatly from oldest to most recent, it held the letters found in Taëminn Vei Ruola's apartment—letters which, as Nel learned from the scribe she'd hired at the Crescent Bay market, had not come from her husband.

A series of measured steps echoed up from the stairwell in the back. Nel's fingers tightened around the papers. She had awaited this minute all afternoon, but now that it arrived, she wanted to run away. With each knock of Mainu's heels against the floorboards, her heart rammed against her chest until he was beside her.

"Good evening." His voice floated low and soft. "I got your message at the consulate. You said you found something?"

Taking one last deep breath, Nel steeled herself and rose to her feet. "I went back to Solluri Hill."

A hint of confusion flashed across his face. "What for?"

"These." She passed the letters and waited for him to recognize what they were. "You said these were written by Yanne Vei Ruola."

Mainu didn't move his eyes from the papers. "I did."

"Are you still saying that?"

He folded the stack lengthwise and handed it back to her. "I won't insult your intelligence."

And like that, it was out. The weight of one uncertainty rolled off of Nel's shoulder, only to be replaced by a dozen others. Once a single lie was exposed, it opened a floodgate of questions that threatened to drown all the trust she had carefully nurtured over the past year. Restraining them was fruitless. The best Nel could hope for was to take them one at a time.

"This Kalevi that the letters are from—she's the victim of the Garden murder, isn't she?"

"She is."

"Why didn't you tell me?"

"I couldn't tell you then, and I can't tell you now."

"Why not?" Nel gripped the backrest of her chair for support. "What are you really doing here?"

Across the desk, Mainu stood as unwavering as the pillars of the Broken Bridge. "I'm here to take Taëminn Vei Ruola home. I have no orders to hurt anyone or to interfere with the interests of Ardonne. I can swear that much is true."

Of all the reassurances he could have given her, that

mattered the least. If he had told Nel four days ago that he was an assassin sent to murder half the senate, she would have been horrified. Now, she would have minded that less.

"This whole time, I couldn't understand why you asked for me. All you had to do was walk into the city guard's head office, and they would have assigned you the best, most experienced investigator the city has to offer. If this woman was truly so important, that's what you should have done. Did you think that. . ." Her voice buckled. "That I wouldn't be clever enough to realize?"

"No." Unlike all of Mainu's previous answers, this one came immediately and with a resounding confidence. It should have been a relief, but it only hurt her more.

"Then why?"

"Because I wanted to be close to you."

Nel turned to the window. The last streaks of the early autumn sunset faded on the horizon, tracing a thin border of pink around the gathering clouds. Down on the main square, street lamps flecked the darkness with motes of gold, which shifted and danced together in the mist that fogged Nel's vision.

"Nel, I promise." Mainu's warped reflection hung over the cityscape in a ghostly apparition. "As soon as Vei Ruola's on a train home, I'll explain everything. Until then, I can't take any risks."

She wiped her cheeks. "If you can't be honest with me, then I'm afraid I can't in good conscience continue to supervise your work. . . Lieutenant Investigator Eph Daëlin."

The finality of her words hung heavy between them. For a while, the two of them stood facing the window, looking where the eyes of the other one's reflection should have been, but instead there was only a blur in the smudged-up glass. Like the Twin Stags, locked in a staring contest neither of them could win.

Nel waited for his footsteps to fade and returned to her desk. Her bastion of security, next to which her old life welcomed her back in the comfort of routine. She uncapped her trusty pen and set out to make up on the work she'd so carelessly neglected.

There was nothing to mourn. As the saying went, "You can't lose what you never had." What did she have in Mainu? A colleague. An acquaintance. A sweet tooth who always stained his shirt. Someone who loved cats and was the reason Nel's hand got mauled. Someone who tended to her injuries. Someone who teased her about her honorary title. Someone who believed she might be captain. Someone she'd confided in about the nightmares she had after the incident and who responded with utmost compassion.

Someone who'd been lying to her this whole time.

Downstairs, the main entrance creaked open, and a jumble of voices poured in as the evening patrol shuffled inside. The men groaned in exhaustion, joking and laughing on their way up to stow away their gear before heading home. Nel set aside the ledger she'd been reviewing and got out the logbook in preparation for the report. Before she found the page with the current date, a flurry of surprised shouting broke out below.

*"Jailbreak!"*

Nel slammed the log shut and bolted toward the stairs, right as the patrol leader came sprinting up.

"Sergeant!" he panted. "It's the boy. The one you brought over from the Upper Court. He's escaped!"

# Chapter 27

Thessa reared her head at the sound. She could have sworn she heard shouting, only she wasn't sure if it came from within or from the street. It must have been outside. There was no one there with her. At the end of a grueling workday, Thessa was always the last to be done with her administration, and on this evening, she counted on being alone. She didn't need anyone asking questions.

On a loose piece of paper, she wrote a few words. *"Ida is all right. Forley is missing. Will bring more news as soon as possible."* She then slid it into an envelope, addressed it to Lord Mendel Scolsessi, and headed to the sizable tome in the corner of the office.

Aristocrats, ranked officers, and other dignitaries often needed to send letters to one another, but they rarely could be bothered to know exactly where those letters needed to be delivered. For such occasions, the Messengers' Guild kept a registry of all eminent names who might regularly appear on envelopes with no further direction. Thessa flipped through page after page until she arrived at the letter S, then ran her finger along the margins, scanning the names one by one. At last, there it was.

*Scolsessi*
~~*Lord Huberto*~~ *D*
~~*Lady Ilvia*~~ *D*
*Lord Mendel*
~~*Arsenal Hill, 3rd W Bank Rd X Cascade Rd*~~
*Montres, 29 General Trunio's St*

Thessa copied down the address for herself, but she left it off her envelope. She then sealed it with the guild's own wax and insignia, as well as stamped it both *"URGENT"* and *"REC. EYES ONLY."*

It was a stretch to think Mendel would know anything about Forley's disappearance, but it wasn't a possibility they could afford to ignore. Moreover, there was the whole issue of what really had happened when Forley broke into the money box and why Mendel let him off so easy. Granted, if the boy had indeed blackmailed him into doing so, as Corlis suggested, then he wasn't likely to offer much detail on that, either. For all Thessa knew, her whole plan could be moot. Regardless, she had to try speaking with the young lord, and for that, she needed an excuse.

Ida said Mendel didn't want them to be seen together while the investigation was ongoing. In that case, walking up to his doorstep and introducing herself as Ida's friend might only get Thessa turned away. With an urgent and exclusive delivery in hand, she had a plausible reason to come calling and maybe a chance to see him. If she got that far, she could reveal herself in confidence—if not, the note was innocuous enough not to raise suspicion to any outsiders. Mendel might have been on Ida's side in private, but there was no telling about anyone else.

She was forced to leave Snake Eyes at the stable upon her return, so there was no choice but to make the trip to the Montres District by herself. Railcars ran few and far between in the evenings, so she headed out on foot along the tracks, mulling over the past days' events.

The meeting with Taëminn Vei Ruola raised more questions than it answered. She revealed the identity of the murder victim, but little in the way of a strong enough motive. Corlis said they had a better chance of finding her enemies if they figured out who her friends were. It made sense as a line of thinking, but did that take them any further?

Her thoughts kept coming back to Beldora. Taëminn was cautious to choose her words when she spoke of their acquaintance, but she was willing to trust someone who claimed to be a friend of hers, and that told plenty already. And while Kalevi had been the victim of the murder, the Garden was the victim of its consequences. Who benefited from that?

Beldora had spoken of Sergeant Vendriane's vendetta against her, but was he merely taking advantage of the opportunity, or would he go as far as killing an innocent woman? Provided that Kalevi *was* innocent, for which they had nothing but Taëminn's word. Thessa would have loved to snoop around the Upper Court District guardhouse, but forging a letter to an officer of the city guard was much more of a hazard. For now, she had to make what she could of her own options.

Halfway along, Thessa managed to hop on a railcar that dropped her off at Montres Main Square. From there, it was a short walk to General Trunio's Street, where the number 29 stood in bold brass digits upon an impeccably maintained townhouse. There was no plaque beside the entrance or any other indication of the owners. That was promising. Unless they erected a monumental country villa in their family's honor, aristocrats rarely liked to advertise their residence. Anyone who had business with them was expected to know where to come calling.

Thessa grabbed the knocker and banged it against the polished door, the sound of which eventually lured out a sharply dressed manservant. His pair of pencil-thin eyebrows bunched up in disapproval as he looked her up and down.

"Good evening." Thessa bowed. "I'm sorry to disturb you this late, but I have an urgent delivery for"—she produced the envelope—"Lord Mendel Scolsessi." She articulated the name slowly to drive home the image of a fresh-faced and modestly competent messenger.

"A delivery at this hour? Do you people not carry watches? That would explain a thing or two," the servant drawled, smirking at his own wit.

"I apologize. It's all my fault. I went to the Arsenal Hill address first by mistake." Thessa bowed again and made a deliberately ungracious curtsy.

The thin brows now twisted into haughty frustration. "You lot are hopeless. I spent a whole day trekking to your office last year, so I could report that address change. As if I didn't have anything better to do with my time, between the funeral arrangements and tending to the young lord! And you're still getting it wrong? Your guild will hire anyone nowadays."

Thessa's eyes glinted. This was the perfect reaction. If there was one thing she'd learned in her father's court, it was that everyone was prone to gossip one way or another—it was only a matter of knowing how to poke it out of them. Some responded to flattery, some to envy, and some gave it readily without asking. Lord Scolsessi's manservant revealed himself to be the kind who could best be annoyed into spilling the truth.

"Anyway, give it here. I'll take it up to him," he concluded.

Before he grabbed the envelope, Thessa stepped back and held it against her chest. "I'm sorry," she repeated. "But the stamp says 'recipient's eyes only.'"

The servant sneered at the indignity. "Do you think I'm going to read it?"

That part was something of a gamble. While the stamp did formally mean the messenger could only hand it to the addressee, in practice, most nobles trusted their staff to not rip open their confidential letters on the way up from the door.

But rules were rules, and she had nothing to lose by aggravating him further.

"No, of course not!" she stammered. "It's just. . . it's an official stamp, and my superiors are very strict, and—"

"Are you daft, woman? What do you expect? That I'll invite you into the lord's private chamber and tuck you into bed with him?"

"If you call him down here, I could hand it over."

The man hiked up his nose. "Well, I'm afraid the lord is currently too occupied with the surgeon to receive your highness."

Thessa dropped her act and gaped in sincere shock. "Surgeon?"

"After the *attempt on his life.*" The servant leaned close in smug satisfaction. "Is that enough of an excuse for you? Or do you insist that he come down to fetch this message of yours while being stitched across the chest?"

"No, never!" Thessa shoved the envelope into his hand. "Please, forgive me. Was it a robbery? Should I alert the city guard? I'm on horseback—I can be there in five minutes." She moved to block the man's view, so he wouldn't notice her blatant lie.

In return, he responded with the same contemptuous scowl as before. "I alerted them an hour ago. They should have that Laerithian hoodlum in cuffs by dawn. Preferably on the gallows by tomorrow."

# VI

# Part Six

# Chapter 28

T he day of sunshine was gone as swiftly as it came.
Once they had their fun taunting the city with the
illusion of summer, the winds rushed in a new front
from the Gray Sea. The sky turned back from crystal to steel,
and the rain dangled its legs overhead, not quite ready to
come down, but hinting it would do so any moment. Noble
and commoner alike turned up their collars, squinted at the
heavens in accusation, and grumbled about fall being fall.

Ida saw none of that. She was stuck in a cell again. This one
had wheels, but beyond that, it was no better than the one at
the guardhouse. It was smaller and darker, jerking and jolting
under her along the pothole-ridden roads of New Montres.
The seats didn't boast much more comfort, either. Most of
all, like in her holding cell, all Ida could do was wait. Locked
away from the world, adrift in a helpless state of in-between,
at the mercy of those on the outside.

She didn't want to wait. She wanted to be there *now*. She
wanted to bang on the doors, to scream out the window,
to stomp the floor until the axles snapped. For over forty
years, in the face of poverty, hardship, and disgrace, Ida had
relentlessly held herself together to weather all the adversity
life had leveled at her. Now all she wanted to do was fall apart.

In fact, she wished she could do that in reality, so she could be in a hundred places at the same time. One part to go to the Garden and demand answers from Beldora, one to do the same with Mendel, and dozens more to visit every single guardhouse and turn over every last rock in search of her son. Ida wished to scatter herself over New Montres and beg all its citizens at once to end this parade of lies and deceit.

But whatever she wished, she was only one person. Her strength was limited, and so were her choices. Right now, that meant further extending her trust to Thessa and Corlis, and that trust was more strained than before.

When the three of them met at The Lame Mare that morning, and Thessa claimed Forley had attacked Mendel the previous night, Ida was beyond insulted. She told Thessa that she must have misheard or misunderstood the servant, but the girl insisted on her story, and the innkeeper—predictably enough—sided with her.

After a prolonged back-and-forth, they settled on a plan. Thessa would visit the Garden to question Beldora, while Corlis would accompany Ida to Mendel's townhouse. The risk of her being seen around the young lord and attracting undue attention didn't matter anymore. Ida deserved to know what had happened, and there were no other sources to rely on.

A sharp wind hit them as they climbed out of the coach. On instinct, Ida raised one arm to shield her face, but it was unnecessary. They stood on General Trunio's Street in the Montres District. There was neither dust, nor fallen leaves, nor discarded bits of paper blowing around here. The pavement was swept spotless, with short and carefully manicured trees spaced evenly to the inch. From behind the colorful facades, the houses on each side stared morosely at one another through slender windows, and even the clops of horseshoes lowered to a whisper.

"Number twenty-nine," Corlis said. "Are you known around here?"

"No. Beldora has a strict policy against house calls. I needed special permission to take Mendel to the Belfry, and being in his home was out of the question."

The innkeeper led the way to the porch. "Yet here you are now."

"If Violet told the truth, then Beldora has more to answer for than I do."

"Fair enough," Corlis said. "Anyway, you take over from here. I doubt my name will get us in."

"And mine will?" Ida asked. "After my son almost murdered the master of the house?"

"One way to find out."

Corlis banged the knocker, then tightened his coat and stepped aside, allowing Ida to be seen first by the sour-faced manservant who answered. Once she introduced herself and confirmed that no, she did not have an appointment or a calling card, he asked them with tentative politeness to wait until he announced their arrival. When he reemerged, his attitude was markedly different.

"Lord Scolsessi is upstairs in his drawing room." He opened the door to its hinges and ushered them into an entry hall, where he helped their coats off. "He regrets not being able to receive you in the day chamber, but the surgeon had strict orders of a week's bed rest."

"How is he?" Corlis asked. "Scolsessi, I mean. Not the surgeon."

A withering shadow passed between the servant's ridiculously thin eyebrows. "*Lord* Scolsessi is in stable condition. His injuries were severe, but the surgeon managed to seal his wounds before the blood loss became life threatening."

Corlis sucked his tooth. "Been there."

When he was done with the wardrobe, the manservant bade them to follow him up the carpeted stairs that ran the full height of the narrow building. They passed through two floors that housed the dining hall and day chamber respectively, both only made all the emptier for their lavish decoration. Up on the third floor, they finally stopped before a set of double doors.

"Ida Nawoale and Corlis Andassi to see you," the servant announced them and bowed out of their way, leaving the path clear into Lord Mendel Scolsessi's drawing room.

From his dressing habits, as well as their time on the Street of Canopies, Ida had some inkling about Mendel's fascination with the maritime history of Ardonne. Entering into his personal chamber, that was beyond any doubt. Above the fireplace, a complete ship's wheel was fastened to the wall, surrounded by plaques and drawings of famous vessels. On the wall across from them, naval maps hung in ornate frames, above shelves laden with scale models and dozens of keepsakes. Near the center of the room stood a massive wooden globe, next to a deep blue recliner, upon which sat Mendel.

Ida's heart clenched. His youthful face was now pale and haggard, the only spot of color being a red blotch around the stitches on his cheek. There were no other visible wounds, but judging by the bumps on his fully buttoned shirt, Ida counted one on his arm and one on his side.

"Ida!" He leapt from his seat and did a poor job of hiding his pained wince.

She pushed him back down. "Please, don't. You shouldn't be out of bed from what I heard."

"I can get up in my own house. I'm not going to drop dead from a few cuts," he muttered, but he leaned against the recliner's backrest with obvious relief. His voice cracked like he hadn't drank in days as he turned to Corlis. "I don't believe we've met before."

Ida motioned the innkeeper to get closer. "This is Corlis. He's—"

"A friend of a friend," Corlis finished for her. "I'm helping Ida figure out what happened at the Garden."

"You are?" Mendel blinked back and forth between the two of them in confusion, then picked up a piece of paper from the end table. "Was it you who left this last night?"

"No, that was Thessa," Corlis said, then clarified, "She's the friend I'm a friend of."

Mendel read the paper. "But is it true, then? Forley's really missing?"

"I haven't seen him in days," Ida replied. "Not since he visited me at the guardhouse after I got arrested."

"The guardhouse?" Mendel echoed. "But he—" He glanced at Corlis again, then back at the note.

"He what?" Ida asked. "What happened? Did he come here last night? Did he do this to you?"

The young lord didn't answer out loud, but instead ran his gaze all over the room, more guilt-stricken than if he'd stabbed someone himself. In the end, he gave a reluctant nod.

Corlis waved at his cheek. "Is that your life-threatening injury?"

"There are others." Mendel cleared his dry throat, this time passing a look at Ida. "I'd rather not show them."

"I want to see." Ida moved in to preempt his protests. "If my son did this to you, I need to know what he has to answer for."

With slow, surrendering motions, Mendel undid the buttons on his shirt and cuffs. He twisted awkwardly in his seat and made a series of clumsy grabs at the collar until Ida realized he was trying to pull off the garment without lifting his arms from his sides. She leaned in and slid the fine white fabric from his shoulders, not unlike their countless times together at the Garden—though on this occasion, her care was a great deal more genuine.

The shirt lay on the recliner, exposing Mendel's soft upper body and the number of dressings upon it. Besides the two Ida had already noticed, a band of gauze wrapped around his torso, holding a strip of cotton across the full width of his chest. Higher on his collarbone was a smaller, uncovered cut, similar to the one on his cheek.

Courtesy be damned, Ida picked the gauze between her fingertips. Mendel's breath shuddered as the bandage peeled back with a sticky noise, revealing a ten-inch gash underneath. The skin on either side clumped up around the stitches, and it bore the dark brown discoloration of seaweed tincture.

She gently put the shirt back on him and waited while he buttoned up. "What happened?"

"I truly don't understand, either," Mendel croaked. "He showed up last night in a state—said you were in trouble and needed help, but I could hardly make out half a sentence. He was ranting and raving. I tried to calm him down, and—I don't know how it got there or where he pulled the knife from. It's all such a blur. I can't—"

He coughed again and reached for a cup of water on the table, forgetting his wounds. With another wince, he jerked back his hand and knocked the cup over. Ida hurried to wipe it up and pour another drink, but the pitcher next to it was empty.

"I'll go." Corlis took it from her. "It's in my line of work. I won't take long."

Mendel rubbed his side, while his gaze followed Corlis on his way out of the drawing room. As soon as the door shut, he grabbed her hands, eyes wide in panic.

"Ida, what's going on?" he whispered. "Why are you here?"

The change sent Ida reeling backward. She couldn't help lowering her own voice, too. "What do you mean? I'm here to see what happened to you!"

"Not *here*"—Mendel gestured at the room—"I mean, in New Montres! Why aren't you with Forley?"

"I told you. I don't know where he is!"

The young man's mouth hung half open, forming the beginning of a dozen words that rushed through his head. "You—you *really* haven't seen him? But then, last night—the whole act, it's—" He rambled like he'd been struck with wound fever.

"What act?" Ida reversed his hold on her hands. "Mendel, tell me what Forley did. If you care for me, then you'll do that. Everyone's been lying to my face, and I can't stand any more. Just wait until Corlis gets back. He should hear it, too."

Gradually, he settled down and fussed nervously with the hems of his shirt until Corlis returned with a full pitcher. Mendel downed a pint of cold water so quickly he almost choked on it. After his coughing fit subsided, he wrapped his fingers around the cup like it was a lifeline.

"You have to understand, I thought you knew all about it," he began. "As I said, Forley came to see me last night and said you were in trouble. He said the guard found some evidence that you were the killer, and there was a new warrant for your arrest, so the two of you needed to leave New Montres immediately.

"I promised to help however I could. The only problem was the release bond. If you disappeared, the guard would immediately suspect me of assisting you, especially if Forley was seen coming to my house. So, we came up with the idea to stage a sham robbery. He cut me in a few places—not fatally, but enough to convince the guard that I couldn't have willingly helped you. I gave him some time before raising the alarm, hoping the two of you would be long gone before they caught on to your trail."

More lies. No matter how Ida turned it, either Mendel was lying to her now, or Forley had lied to Mendel *and* her. If both men had told the truth, then something must have happened to Forley since last night. Each thought more horrifying than the last.

And that wasn't considering the fourth option—that both men had lied yet again, as the foreman had told Ida before.

"Mendel, did Forley ever break into the money box at the tannery?" Ida asked.

He didn't respond. That was as good as a yes.

"Why didn't you tell me?"

Mendel scratched at the rim of the cup. "He wasn't trying to steal the lot. He only needed a silver and a half to pay off a debt."

"What debt?" Ida asked, before the answer came to her on

its own. The promise Forley had sincerely made time and again, yet never managed to keep. "He's been gambling, hasn't he?"

"I always go there after the workday to check on things," Mendel said. "I caught him with the lock open but the lid on. He broke down in tears and said he'd take any punishment, as long as I kept it from you. I agreed to take it out of his wages for the next few weeks and leave it at that. He didn't want you to know, and I. . . didn't want to be the one to tell you."

*So you're both cowards.*

"Any other little schemes the two of you have been up to?" Ida rose from the recliner. "Any plans to run away together while I rot in prison or hang, since you're such fast friends?"

Mendel sat crestfallen, like a boy a third of his age. If that was how he acted, that was how Ida would treat him. And if he hoped to buy her affection or forgiveness with that bond, he had sorely miscalculated.

Corlis, who had been listening with one elbow on the mantelpiece, chimed in, "If I may broker a truce for the time being, we need to find Forley. Preferably before the guard does."

"Where do we even begin?" Ida asked. "If he's in the city at all." As difficult as it was to consider that Forley might have fled without her, nothing was beyond belief at this point.

"Anywhere we can think of. His home, his job, his usual haunts, and any train stations on the way."

"Right." Mendel sprung eagerly from his seat and hurt himself in the process again. "We can take my carriage. It's the fastest way we have to get around. I can have it ready right away."

Ida held out with her agreement. She didn't want to

give Mendel the idea that his deception would be so easily forgotten. Again, she wished she could fall into a hundred pieces and scour the city herself. But, in the end, she was only one person, and so she resigned herself to returning to her cell for the rest of the day. At least this one was more comfortable.

# Chapter 29

For twenty-eight years, Nella Dormanni's life had been, in one word, boring. An ordinary childhood in the countryside with her parents and brothers. Nine years of school, where she excelled at nothing but penmanship. Four years as a scribe for the village judge. Then, finally, the move to New Montres and a position with the city guard, in the place where boredom died of old age. Nel had no sublimely happy memories to speak of, but—with one exception—no dismally grim ones, either. For twenty-eight years, she had trodden a comfortable middle ground, and she never regretted it for a heartbeat.

Not until now. Because if her luck had been a little less even and her days only a little more turbulent, she wouldn't have been so overwhelmed by feeling this miserable in this many ways.

First, there was the plain and simple exhaustion. After the guards raised the alarm about the jailbreak, it was Nel's responsibility as sergeant to lead the manhunt. The recently returned evening patrol was forced to stay on duty and accompany the night shift, scouring Ilvior Island for the fugitive. Besides that, Nel also had to alert the neighboring districts so their officers would be on the lookout as well.

Truthfully, she and her colleagues might as well have gone home after that. Forley would have to be a special breed of idiot to hide on the island when the Broken Bridge was a stone's throw from the guardhouse. Nel knew that, and so did the men, who made it less and less a secret as the chase dragged on, long into the night.

But that was far from the only source of embarrassment for her. After she organized the search parties and dispatched the couriers, Nel had the obligation to notify her superior, even if that meant waking him from deep slumber. And predictably enough, Captain Pomeno wasn't pleased.

"You mean to tell me," he fumed, "that this man—this *violent criminal* you had moved to *my* guardhouse *without* consulting me—is now at large on Ilvior Island? After the years I spent building up our reputation as one of the safest boroughs in New Montres?"

He loomed on his porch wearing nothing but a nightshirt and an expression of pure outrage, berating Nel in front of the whole street.

"What were you hoping to accomplish, Dormanni? Was it all to impress that Midorean friend of yours? I thought he was a bad influence on you last year, but at least that time you only brought it upon yourself. But this?" He waved his lanky arms up and down the road. "Have you grown so bored with your work here? Because if it's excitement you're after, we can always have you transferred to the Wedge. Then you can have all the fun you want, going after roughnecks that'll stab you for a slice of bread. I have no use for officers who cause problems instead of solving them."

This went on for a fair while until the captain yelled at her to stop wasting his time and get back to tracking down Forley.

Nel walked away on the verge of tears, hardly able to put one leg in front of the other. Every part of her shook, and the clutch of humiliation threatened to choke her where she stood. As cruel as the captain's words were, and as unnecessary as it was for half the neighborhood to hear them, none of that made them less true.

She had failed. She neglected her duties at the guardhouse because she allowed herself to get swept up in a case she had no business meddling in. And what indeed had she accomplished? A robber on the loose, and not a single lead in Vei Ruola's disappearance.

If there were any leads to be made on that at all. Which, in turn, led into the fourth way she felt horrible—and without a doubt, this one was the worst.

While Nel had dutifully relayed all known details of Forley's escape to the captain, there was one she left out: that Mainu had been the last person to leave the guardhouse before the evening patrol returned. With all the guilt that already bore down on her, this omission was a drop in the sea. But the thought wedged itself into her mind regardless.

*Did Mainu have anything to do with this?*

The obvious answer should have been "no." He had no connection to Forley and no interest in his transfer to Ilvior. What would he have to gain by helping the boy escape? However Nel racked her brain, each answer was less plausible than the last. There was no way it made sense.

But he had lied to her before. And even if he wasn't involved in breaking out Forley, she still didn't know where his true allegiances were. He swore he had no intention of harming anyone or working against the interests of Ardonne—but how much of a limit was that, really?

Nel's head was close to bursting with questions. Her mind and body were run ragged staying up until dawn on a fool's errand. When she got home at last, tired and ashamed, she was ready to collapse into bed and never get up again.

And that was only the start.

The next morning, news began to trickle in from the other districts, and none of them were pleasant. The Montres guardhouse reported that, on top of attempted robbery and fleeing custody, Forley Nawoale was now also wanted for the attempted murder of Lord Mendel Scolsessi. Once again, Nel forwarded the message to Captain Pomeno, and once again, he was livid.

"Attempted robbery, attempted murder"—he wiped a handful of cheese curds out of his patchy beard—"you're lucky the man's so terrible at crime, except for lock picking. Otherwise, you'd have an even bigger mess on your hands. With this one, you have *some* chance of cleaning it up, if you mean to keep your rank as sergeant, that is."

Nel was left to fend for herself on that ultimatum. The night before, that would likely have been the straw that broke the camel's back. But no matter how short, sleep worked wonders on the mind, and the maelstrom of emotion had since settled into resolve. She wouldn't give up that easily. She was going to prove, if to no one else but herself, that she was a capable officer, and her title wasn't merely an honorary one.

* * *

Naturally, it wasn't going to be that simple.

"I'm afraid Lord Scolsessi isn't available." The manservant's thin eyebrows bent up in an unconvincing imitation of regret.

"He took the carriage and instructed me to advise all visitors to call on him tomorrow."

"He's out?" Nel asked. "Wasn't he gravely injured?"

"He was, and the surgeon expressly ordered him to rest. But I can't tie my employer to the bed now, can I?"

"Did he say where he was going, or when he might be back?"

"Neither.  But I can tell you, he didn't go alone."  The servant stroked his chin. "He received visitors this morning. A man and a woman, by the names of Andassi and Nawoale, respectively."

Nel's mouth was agape. "Ida Nawoale?"

"That's right. They accompanied him when he left. I don't know if they'll be with him all day, though."

Already on her first stop, Nel ran into a wall of confusion. Scolsessi went out with the woman whose son tried to murder him? The woman who's a known bloodsucker *and* the main suspect of the Garden murder?

She visited the Upper Court District next in hope of some answers, but all she got instead was another twist in the tale: namely, that Mendel Scolsessi had been the one who paid Ida Nawoale's release bond. Two thousand silvers in full.

"Left her a letter, too," the freckled young officer told her. "In Laerithian.  Didn't understand a word of it, but it's a touching gesture."  He sucked on his entwood bark with a grin. "Or maybe it held the details of her next murder."

"You didn't get it translated?"

"I wasn't supposed to open it to begin with.  Making her wait while I took it to the bay would have been straight up rude. Not to mention far too much of a bother."

Nel sat down in the guardhouse's waiting area—the same one where, two days earlier, she and Mainu had waited together for Forley's paperwork. No matter what had happened the night before, she wished Mainu were there. If nothing else, then to discuss ideas. Now all she had was herself.

*Horses before zebras.*

Ida Nawoale had been arrested for murder. Forley tried to rob a carriage to get money for her bond, not realizing Scolsessi paid it. Ida was released, while Forley was held at the Ilvior Island guardhouse. Forley escaped, went to Scolsessi's house, and attacked him. The attempt failed, and he fled the scene. The next morning, Ida showed up with a friend in tow, and the three of them headed out in Scolsessi's coach.

The most obvious answer would be that Ida was trying to find Forley, with the help of Scolsessi and the third one. Nel had never seen or spoken to her, but considering Forley was willing to commit a violent crime for her sake, she must have been dear to him. They were mother and son, after all.

But what were Forley and Scolsessi? What reason would the boy have to kill the man who helped his mother walk free? Was it mere envy or hurt pride? Did he think Scolsessi had designs on Ida? Had she been Forley's wife or lover, this would be the plainest horse in the world.

Even so, jealousy was the most probable motive. Boys could be awfully protective of their mothers. In which case, Nel had to find out who Forley wanted to protect his mother from.

# Chapter 30

Thessa banged on the door five more times, but no answer came. The shutters were all closed as before, and the knocks echoed at length with no trace of any other sound. No matter how long she waited, Darno didn't show his face in the peephole, nor did any of the women. The Garden of Lilies might as well have been abandoned. Behind her, Snake Eyes snorted in discontent that, yet again, they were wasting their time here instead of working. She hushed him and patted his neck before rounding the house through the side alley.

If Darno wasn't there to let her in, she'd find a way on her own. After what Corlis and Ida had learned from Violet—that Beldora was supposed to be the last person to see Kalevi alive—Thessa couldn't merely turn around and go about her day. She didn't want to accuse Beldora, but she had to get answers.

The handle on the delivery entrance rattled ineffectually when she tested it. There was one open window on the back wall, but it wasn't any great cause for celebration, as it was on the second floor, almost fifteen feet from the ground. A professed athlete could hardly make that kind of jump, even if there was any way to get a running start in the cramped alley. By all measures, it was humanly impossible.

Unfortunately, it was far too early in the day for her to transform, to say nothing of the risk that would have posed in such a busy neighborhood. But she wasn't completely without help.

Snake Eyes followed her with indifferent steps around the building. Thessa led him directly under the window and fastened his reins to a gutter pipe, so he'd know to stay put. After that, she placed both hands on either side of his muzzle and looked him deep in the eye.

"I need you to stay very, *very* still. Understand?"

The gelding gave no answer either way. Thessa rubbed his forehead to calm him further, then turned back to her goal.

She picked up a pebble and threw it through the window, where it hopefully wouldn't land in anyone's drink or porridge. Considering the Garden was closed, she was at least confident she wouldn't hit a naked body in the middle of something. The room swallowed the rock, which clattered against a floor on the inside, but otherwise had no consequences. Her concerns thus put to rest, there was nothing left to do but commit to her latest stupid plan.

She began by hooking one foot into the stirrup and hoisting herself up, but instead of swinging her free leg all the way around, she rested her calf on the horse's rump. Snake Eyes made an inquisitive noise and pawed the ground in confusion. Thessa hushed him again and stroked his mane to apologize for this unusual arrangement. Now came the hard part.

Leaning both hands flat against the wall for support, she gradually shifted her weight all the way to her calf, so she could unhook her foot from the stirrup and raise the other leg as well. Her hands crept up the surface one inch at a time, straightening herself from an uneasy kneel to a shaky crouch, and eventually to a perilous stand.

Snake Eyes could have turned to marble under her, and her whole body would have quaked anyway. The slightest movement on the horse's part could cost Thessa's balance and more. Falling from such a position was mostly harmless—on grass, in an open field. With brick walls no more than two feet away on each side and jagged paving stones on the ground, it promised a broken neck.

Stretching her arms as high up as they went, her hands reached barely over the windowsill. Not nearly enough to pull herself up, but they did manage to grab on to the frame. She only needed one more boost. A rim of decorative masonry ran along the wall and protruded by about two inches, around knee height from her current elevation. Holding her breath, Thessa rested one sole against it, now only standing on the horse's back with the other leg.

She wanted to take a brief pause and reconsider the idea, but Snake Eyes made the decision for her when he shook his head and swayed forward. In the same instant that her foot slipped on the leather of the saddle, her instincts compelled her to lunge upward with all her strength, and in one heartbeat of maddening effort, she hurled herself through the window. Luckily, there was a floor on the other side this time.

Thessa tumbled into the empty room with a racket that, for all she knew, the entire Upper Court District heard. Pushing herself to a stand on steady ground again, she dusted herself off and went for the door. While the house appeared deserted from the outside, surely the women were still around. If Beldora was out, she could ask them where she was or when she might return.

But when her palm touched the doorknob, she stopped. *What would she tell them if they asked how she got in?*

It couldn't have been an accident that the side entrance was locked. While Beldora had been amicable with Thessa the last time she showed up uninvited, it wasn't difficult to believe she expressly ordered for stricter precautions afterward.

Her fingers tingled on the brass handle. All of a sudden, she felt unwelcome. She was no longer a concerned friend coming to visit. She was an intruder and a spy, accusing the mistress of the house based on some hearsay from Violet—the same woman who readily framed Ida without hesitation or remorse.

But that didn't mean she couldn't be right.

Thessa turned the knob as quietly as she could. If anyone spotted her, she'd explain herself and trust that they wouldn't harm her. Until then, she wouldn't take chances.

She was up on the second floor, a long way from Beldora's office. Moreover, the only path there ran along the open walkway, in plain sight from the courtyard and most of the rooms surrounding it. Thessa got down on all fours to have a chance of hiding behind the lattice grid of the balustrade, and she had to halt several times when voices drifted up from below.

From the main staircase, she ducked into the corridor that ran to the back of the building, where the office lay. It was in exactly the state as when Thessa had last been here: luxurious chairs, end tables with flowers and drink trays, tall plants in gleaming copper pots, and carved wooden cabinets with tinted glass inlays. All the same things in the same places, yet their usual warmth was missing.

Thessa shuddered with a sudden urge to leave, but froze

midway. There were footsteps in the hall, along with shreds of conversation. And they were approaching the office.

Without another thought, Thessa darted to the far corner of the room, where a sideboard and a decorative vase offered the closest she could get to a hiding spot. She tucked her limbs as close in as they came, then clasped both hands over her mouth and gave herself up to fate.

Three pairs of feet sounded behind her. One of them ambled in slow, pompous strides, another followed at a measured pace, and one scarcely so much as grazed the floor in their lithe precision.

"Make yourself at home, Sergeant." Beldora's offer rang more with authority than hospitality. "Can I offer you a drink?"

"You can, and you should." The heavy boots made their way to one of the plush armchairs. "Wine will do nicely. Unwatered." The man's overbearing cadence wasn't familiar to Thessa, but judging by how Beldora addressed him, it could only belong to Sergeant Vendriane.

"By all means. Darno, if you will?"

With catlike steps, the Garden's private guard walked over to one of the tables and set about pouring from the crystal decanter. At the back of the room stood one of Beldora's exotic plants, in a pot three feet tall, whose copper surface was polished to such a sheen that it perfectly mirrored the entire room. Thessa could make out every detail on Darno: from the broad knife that dangled at his waist as he uncorked the bottle, to the white scar across his eye when he unmistakably noticed her reflection.

Thessa pried her hands off of her mouth and folded them into a pleading gesture. Darno pressed a single finger against his lips before turning back to his employer and her guest.

Vendriane sipped the wine and exhaled loudly. "Not bad at all. Astercium?"

"Grabossi. Vintage," Beldora replied.

"I wouldn't have thought a Werrish to have such decent taste. Your folk are much more known for guzzling ale."

"I've lived forty years in Ardonne, and I was married to a trader. I picked up a thing or two."

"I'm sure you did." Vendriane indulged in another leisurely swig. "Well, then. To what do I owe the invitation?"

"I wished to inquire how your investigation's going."

"You hardly needed to drag me all the way here for that. My men are doing everything they can to ensure justice is served. I should think that's a given."

"That depends on whose justice your men are aiming to serve.  From what I've seen, they're not exactly straining themselves."

The sergeant chortled at length. "In fairness to them, they don't always have to. Sometimes, we're fortunate enough to have things fall into our laps. For instance, a little bird told me you spoke with the Midorean in this very office before her tragic demise. You paid her to keep quiet, but the poor thing simply couldn't live with the burden and had to do the right thing." He laughed some more to himself while he took another swig.

So, Violet had betrayed Beldora as well.

The madam remained in her seat beside Vendriane.  In the reflection, Thessa caught mere glimpses of the sergeant's profile, but his slicked-back hair and pedantically curled goatee flawlessly matched his demeanor. He and the other two faced away from the copper pot, with no way of spotting

Thessa, but the sheer tension rendered her incapable of moving. All she could do was sit and listen.

"Yes, it is true," Beldora said. "The woman arrived with the train from Midorea, and there was a message waiting for her at the station. It said her lover wanted to meet her here, and that she should ask for me."

"Then what?"

"I told her no one had arranged such a meeting with me, and she might be in danger. I burned the note she received at the station and suggested she leave through the back exit. That was the last I or anyone else saw of her."

Vendriane's voice dripped with pure amusement. "Fascinating tale. Pity there's no way to prove any of your part. The only thing for certain is that you admit to being the last one to see the victim alive. Which, as it is, only leaves your sordid little establishment under all the more scrutiny." He drank the last of his wine. "You better tell your women to seek an honest job. I'm afraid our investigation will continue for the foreseeable future."

He handed the empty glass to Beldora, who rested it on the sideboard and said, "I believe now's the time, Darno."

Before Thessa got an idea what she meant, the guard was by Vendriane's side. Two heavy thumps came in rapid succession, and the sergeant lay prone on the floor, groaning in pain and impotent rage. Darno rested one knee on the back of his neck to keep him down, shoved a handkerchief deep into his mouth, then laid Vendriane's right hand flat against the floor with the fingers spread out.

All Darno said was, "How many?"

Beldora went to one of the cabinets and unlocked a drawer with a key. "The one with the ring will suffice."

Darno's knife was nothing but a flash of light as it slid from its sheath with a hiss, then thunked into the floor in the same fluid motion. The sergeant's legs flailed helplessly, while the rag muffled his screams into a pathetic whimper. Beldora took the severed finger from Darno and handed him a lit candle, with which he seared the wound. The whole scene was over in less than a minute.

As if she needed one more reason to be alarmed, the beguiling scent of freshly spilled blood slithered into Thessa's nose and sent an unwelcome wave of tingling down her back. The irresistible urge to transform had ceased after the incident during the summer, but its dreadful memories wouldn't fade soon.

Darno pulled the sergeant into an upright position and removed the handkerchief, though he kept his blade drawn and close to his neck.

"You mad whore," Vendriane sputtered, cradling his hand. "You think you'll get away with mutilating an officer? I will have you and every one of your filthy tramps hanged!"

"No, you will not," Beldora said, as calm as when they walked in. "Not unless you want this to get out." There was a rustle of paper while she held what looked like a letter in front of the sergeant.

His tone faltered. "H-how-how did you get this?"

"How I got it is not your concern. Your concern is who I might show it to."

Vendriane swallowed. "This proves nothing."

"It proves enough. It proves the imperial paladins planned an insurrection before the declaration of the republic. And while it never came to be, this proves you knew of it—and agreed to tell no one."

Beldora folded up the paper and locked it away again. "You will cease your farce of an investigation, clear Ida Nawoale of all charges, and formally lift the ban on the Garden. Fail to do any one of those, and this is going straight to Jade Hill."

"You expect me to release an obvious suspect and admit defeat?" Vendriane spat the question. "I might as well hand in my resignation."

"I know the guard has connections to an establishment run by a certain Braselius. You can liaise with them to find an alternative. Or grab someone off the street and put them on trial, for all I care."

The sergeant held up his maimed hand. "And how am I supposed to explain suddenly missing a finger?"

For the first time, the shadow of a smile crept into Beldora's voice. "Tell your colleagues you lost it intervening in a robbery on the street. I can ask the women to act as witnesses to your heroic deed. Now that their livelihoods will be restored, I'm sure they'll be glad to do you this favor."

With that, she judged the discussion to be over. Darno jerked Vendriane to his feet, and the three of them proceeded to the door.

"Mark my words, you Werrish slag," the sergeant sneered, "You've made a dangerous enemy today."

Beldora led the way out of the office. "There's room in my collection."

Thessa didn't creep out from her corner until she was positive they weren't coming back. She lifted one hand to blot out the puddle of Vendriane's blood from her view while she weighed her choices for an exit. The warm and inviting space of Beldora's office was now a deadly trap full of terrible secrets, and she had no intention of staying a moment longer.

Thankfully, it was on the ground floor and farthest from the main street, allowing her to climb out the window unnoticed.

Snake Eyes greeted her in the alley with an impatient stomp of the hoof, and she couldn't have agreed more. Regardless of her past with either Beldora or the women, Thessa only wanted to be as far away from the Garden of Lilies as possible.

# Chapter 31

"How did she end up figuring it out?"

Argiey's hands moved practically on their own, stitching up the body he had just examined. Over on the next slab, another customer waited their turn with endless patience. The blessing of working with those who have put all urgency behind them.

By the desk, Mainu was slumped in a chair, playing aimlessly with a capped pen between his fingers. It was curious how slight of a change it took to make him wholly different. Besides the scruff of his beard growing back, his appearance was the same as any other day before. Rather, it was the absence of his single-minded sharpness that now robbed him of his very essence.

"When we searched Vei Ruola's home, we found Kalevi's letters to her," he said to the ceiling. "They were in Midorean, so only I could read them. I was concerned that if we had such a strong lead that soon, it would be harder for me to get in touch with you. I made a choice on the spot and said they were from her husband."

"And you trusted she'd trust you."

"I should have known she was smarter than that." He twirled the pen and knocked it against the desk. "I knew she was."

Argiey didn't have to be a mind reader to realize the lieutenant was mourning more than his professional slip-up. That, however, would be his own problem to solve. In the meantime, Argiey aimed to keep his head where it mattered.

"How much does she know?"

"Only that I lied about the letters—and she suspects I have a secret purpose. I don't believe she thinks you or your friends are involved."

"That's a lot of believing and thinking." Argiey tied off the thread at the last stitch. "What are you going to do now?"

"Vei Ruola still insists on finding the killer. I can't force her to leave, but without the city guard's authority, my options are limited."

Argiey pushed the rolling table up to the slab, then called Mainu over to help him shift the body onto it. He wasn't used to having company for longer than a few minutes at work, but he didn't mind the additional pair of hands. And to his credit, Mainu wasn't at all squeamish. Argiey had seen senior officers turn various shades of green at the sight of a drowning or trampling victim.

They moved the cadaver to the back room, so it could be picked up later, along with the week's others. After the effort, Argiey concluded the process, as always, with a toast at his desk to the departed.

"If it's any consolation, you're welcome here," he told the lieutenant as they clinked. "There's not a lot I can offer besides my radiant company, except maybe this bottle and some fine reading."

Mainu picked up the paper Argiey referred to. "*Bloodcurdling Tales for the Fearless?*" he read the title out loud with little enthusiasm.

"The highest quality in lowbrow entertainment the presses of New Montres have to offer. I should know."

"You write these?"

"Not all of them." Argiey waved in humility. "Not even most. But I do earn the occasional fistful with a submission. I see all sorts of bloodcurdling things in my line of work—I might as well take advantage."

The lieutenant turned over the page and gave him an askance look. "Will you be writing one about a woman found dead with a bite mark?"

Argiey waved again. "Half of the next issue will be nothing but bloodsucker stories, and a lot more colorful. But these two might make it." He ambled over to the remaining occupied table and drew back the sheet. Underneath was the mortal shell of a middle-aged man, arguably in much worse shape than the woman they'd taken to the back. "The husband found them in bed together and slew them both in a jealous rage— though I'd say he got the brunt of it."

He got out a fresh set of forms and sat down by the desk. "While you're here, why not help me with this? I have to note the external injuries. You can dictate them to me from there."

Taking his newly bestowed apprenticeship in stride, Mainu walked over to the body and listed off, "Stab wound on the chest. Left side, between the tenth and eleventh rib. Bruise on the right forearm, outside, below the elbow."

Argiey nodded along. Couldn't have been more precise himself. At least this would take the lieutenant's mind off of things.

"Bruise on the left upper arm, front, below the shoulder," Mainu continued. "Another one on the left side, above the hip. One on the right cheekbone, and one more on the right side of the neck."

"I'd wager that last one wasn't from the husband," Argiey smirked to himself, scratching his sideburns. "Anything else?"

He kept his eye on the paper, ready to take down what Mainu said, but there was only profound silence.

Next to the table, Mainu stood at the head of the corpse, utterly transfixed. "There's a bruise on his neck."

"Yes, it's known as a love bite," Argiey said, unsure what to make of the comment. "You see, when two people love each other very much—"

"Where's Kalevi's body?" Mainu turned to him, and in a heartbeat, he was his old self again.

"In the graveyard mausoleum north of the Wall District, waiting to be buried." As he answered, Argiey knew that wasn't what the lieutenant wanted to hear. "But I have the picture, if that's enough."

He rifled through the cabinet in a frantic search until he found the lightpaper image he'd made of Kalevi when she arrived. He brought it over to Mainu, who snatched it out of his hand and held it next to the dead man's face.

The difference was plain as day. While the man's neck featured a sizable black spot where his lover had recently dug her teeth in passion, Kalevi's was as pristine as the day she was born—save for the two pricks on the jugular.

"If someone had been sucking on her neck, it would have left a mark around the holes," Argiey said.

"Which means her blood wasn't sucked out," the lieutenant finished. "It was *drained.*"

Argiey bit his lip. *Sometimes, the things that* aren't *there tell the whole truth.* Oh, how disappointed his mentor would have been.

"What better way to remove all suspicion from yourself than to make it seem impossible for you to commit the crime?" he wondered out loud. In some way, he had to admire the killer's effort. "How would you even go about that? It must have been a gallon at least. That's not exactly something you can pour down the sewer out the back."

"The hair." Mainu pointed at Kalevi's shoulder-length locks in the picture. "Do you see how uneven it is? I've spent enough time in a barber's chair to know that can't be intentional. This hair was sliced off with a knife."

"To keep it out of the way." Argiey rounded the table, keeping his gaze on the woman's face in the picture, while his mind filled in the rest. "She was hung upside down."

Mainu set down the paper. "Is there a slaughterhouse in the city?"

"One in the Miller District. But that's miles away from the Garden of Lilies."

"There must be some place nearby where this was carried out." The lieutenant strode to the desk and grabbed his coat. "I need to find where it was."

His eyes were ablaze with a fire that seemed to shoot out of them and burn into Argiey's soul. They both understood the urgency at hand. It had already been over three days since the murder. If they wanted any chance at scrounging up whatever evidence lingered at the scene, they had to do it immediately. Wordlessly, Mainu reminded Argiey of the conversation they had under the bridge, about the choice he had to make between playing his part and waiting for others to do what was needed.

He dropped his gloves on the table. "I should have a map somewhere down here."

# Chapter 32

Situated on the edge of the Brewer District and surrounded by the smell of hops all year round, the public records archive was as undistinguished as it was vital to the city's function. Any onlooker would think it was another apartment-house among the dozen others on the narrow street. Captain Pomeno once called it a defensive measure, since if its purpose was more well known, the local guardhouse couldn't blink twice between arson attempts. Births and deaths, marriages and divorces, companies and private citizens—as the captain put it, "If it can be taxed, it's on file there."

Nel rang the bell on the counter, and like she did back at the Twin Stags, she ran her eyes around the entrance hall while she waited. Compared to the inn, the archives had considerably less to offer. The entire room was the size of a cell and about as well lit, with peeling wallpaper that might have had a pattern once upon a time. About the only thing worth noting was a five-foot stack of the town bulletin's issues in the corner.

The archivist emerged from the back room with all the haste of a groundhog. His beady eyes and front teeth compounded the similarity, the latter of which somehow appeared longer each time Nel saw him. While he may not have been the most eligible man in New Montres, his knowledge of the archives was undeniably vast—so much so that, as Nel suspected, there wasn't a modicum of room left in his head for names.

"Good afternoon, Officer—" he trailed off with a squint.

"Dormanni," Nel said, before he fell back to sleep in trying to remember. "Sergeant Nella Dormanni from the Ilvior Island guardhouse. I need to see some files on an individual."

"Second floor. This way."

He lifted the countertop and grabbed a ring of keys from the wall before shuffling toward the stairs.

"What's with that stack over there?" Nel asked to fill the pause.

"Back issues of the bulletin. We're supposed to take them to the basement, but the cabinets down there are a nightmare. So, I let them pile up a while and then do it all at once."

As far as Nel could say, the entire building was a basement. Despite the numerous windows all around, light had to come from the lamps inside, since the sky was fully blocked by the dozens upon dozens of tall shelves. They reached from floor to ceiling, with nary a space between them, packed to the last inch with documents.

Nel told the archivist to gather everything he could find on Lord Mendel Scolsessi and his immediate relations, then settled in by one of the handkerchief-sized tables that were squeezed into the cramped space. Aristocrats had notoriously overgrown family trees, often going back centuries, with a matching array of financial and other interests. The difficulty was never in finding them, but rather in sifting through the piles to discern what was relevant. Nel braced herself for several hours of quiet time in the dusty hall.

"Thank you," she said when the archivist dropped the first handful of papers before her. "You can bring the rest as you pull them and leave it on this side of the table."

The gangly man yawned. "This *is* the rest."

Nel spread out the documents. There were no more than ten. "Are these only for Mendel Scolsessi?"

"No, these are for the whole family."

Nel had enlisted the archivist's help before, and while he wasn't exactly sprightly, he never skimped on a task. If he said this was everything on the Scolsessi family, then there wasn't so much as a pamphlet anywhere else. With newfound intrigue, Nel took the slim handful of papers.

On the top were a number of ownership deeds: small tracts of land around New Montres, two residences in the city, a tannery, and a trading company. For a noble family, it was nothing extraordinary.

Under that was Mendel Scolsessi's birth record, from the year nine hundred and. . . *thirty-six?* That made him twenty-one years old. If he had designs on Ida Nawoale, it made a lot more sense that her seventeen-year-old son would have objections. *Nel* would have had objections.

She shook off the feeling and continued. After the birth record was the marriage certificate of Lord Huberto and Lady Ilvia Scolsessi, followed by a file that Nel didn't recognize upon first glance. It wasn't one she had often seen, and the formal header revealed why. In the upper right corner, the paper bore the now-forgotten insignia of the Emperor of Ardonne.

*Certificate of Recognition*

*Let it be known by the will of His Majesty Feore Volearte, sovereign ruler of the Empire of Ardonne, that from this day forward, the Sixth to the Wax of Graze, in the nine hundred and thirty-second year of the empire,* **Huba Zholsewic**, *born in Werhen, shall be recognized as an honorable citizen of Ardonne, with the name and title of* **Lord Huberto Scolsessi.**

"That explains the shortage," said the archivist, leaning against the shelf behind Nel to keep him awake.

"Yes, I guess it does," Nel said. "But look at the date. Thirty-two. That was right around the end of the last war. Hardly the kind of time when a Werrish person would be welcome in Ardonne, let alone given a title."

The archivist picked at his teeth. "Must have done something right."

Beneath that, Nel reached the bottom of the pile with two identical-looking papers. The death records of Lord Huberto and Lady Ilvia Scolsessi, deceased late in the winter of the year before, on the same day.

And that was the end of it. The entire history of the Scolsessi family in Ardonne, from the father's naturalization after the war, his marriage to an Ardonnese noblewoman, the wealth he acquired and the son he begat, to his demise at the same time as his wife. They must have died together, most likely in some sort of accident. An accident that left their twenty-year-old son with the family estate to himself.

*Horses before zebras*, Nel reminded herself. But the chill down her spine refused to relent.

"If there's anything you want to take with you, I'll need you to sign off on it," the archivist said as Nel stacked the papers again. "The rest you can drop in the basket, and I'll put them away."

"I don't think so," she replied. "But I do need to trouble you some more. And I'm afraid it involves the nightmare of those cabinets downstairs."

* * *

He had not been exaggerating. The upstairs archives might have been dim and airless, but they got some semblance of daylight. The basement, meanwhile, was a single, pitch-black void. That in and of itself wouldn't have unnerved Nel—her own childhood home had a windowless cellar, and by the age of five she'd grown out of her fears—but this was different.

Upstairs, though the shelves were packed in tight rows across the floor, they had enough room between them for one person. Down here, they were in a solid block without two inches' worth of a gap. Wherever Nel turned the flickering lamp, there were only the cabinets that towered above her on both sides, immobile and imposing, yet at the same time threatening to crush her between them.

*Don't be ridiculous*, she chided herself. *It's only furniture, standing perfectly still.*

Then a rumble came from behind, and all the monoliths started to shake at once.

Right as Nel found the time to wonder how they were supposed to get anything out of here, the archivist started down the line with a crank in hand. Stopping beside each cabinet, he stuck it in a hole on the side and turned it with a series of resounding metallic clanks. Each time, the enormous case then slid forward, freeing up some space between it and the next one, revealing the pair of rails underneath that they were attached to.

One after another, the archivist shifted the cabinets in this way until he caught up with Nel and granted her access to the row she had asked for.

"See, this is what I meant," he said, setting the handle aside. "I hope you won't need any more than this."

"No, it's just one," she replied.

With a reminder to herself that she wasn't four years old any more, she sidled into the narrow alley. In front of her, the dozens of identical drawers were each marked with a year and month. She pulled out the one for the month of Calve, year nine hundred and fifty-six, and thumbed through the issues inside. Once she got to the right date, she flipped it all the way to the back.

*The city of New Montres mourns the tragic and untimely passing of Lord Huberto Scolsessi and his beloved wife, Lady Ilvia, in a devastating fire that laid waste to their home on Arsenal Hill.*

*Lord Scolsessi, born Huba Zholsewic in Werhen, earned his title from Emperor Feore for his contribution to Ardonne's victory in the last Werrish conflict, where he delivered invaluable military information to the Ardonnese legion. Lady Scolsessi made a name of her own in recent years, as a vocal proponent of the republic and common rights among the aristocracy.*

*Their accomplishments will forever be remembered in the annals of history, and their legacy lives on in their son Mendel, who risked life and limb to rescue his parents from the blaze.*

Nel skimmed over the rest of the article, which detailed the funeral arrangements and the couple's final resting place, for all those who wished to pay their respects to the deceased.

The lantern rocked gently in the archivist's hand, shifting the pool of light it carved out of the all-encompassing dark of the basement. The shadows of Nel's hands over the paper shrunk and grew with each sway, seemingly distorting the ink around them, as if the truth of the writing skewed in one direction or the other with each movement.

"A bluebell in the aristocracy, eh?" the man muttered in vague amusement over Nel's shoulder. "I wonder how many of their peers were really sorry to see her go."

"Or her husband," Nel wondered. "By the sound of it, he was essentially a traitor to Werhen. There are plenty of people in New Montres with strong enough ties to their homeland to bear a grudge."

The archivist made a sound of unenthused agreement, then posed the much more pointed question of whether she needed help with anything else.

Truthfully, Nel wanted to answer yes. There were a lot of things she needed help with—the case of Forley Nawoale, the murder at the Garden of Lilies, the disappearance of Vei Ruola, and her own confused feelings about Mainu, to name a few. Outwardly, she merely thanked him for his time and assistance.

Back out on the street, the overcast autumn day almost blinded her. Nel made her way back to Ilvior in a bemused daze, reeling after the morning's events. Somehow, she was closer and further from the truth at the same time. None of what she learned went any length to explain why Forley attacked Mendel Scolsessi, but it must have explained something.  It was as if Nel had her nose up against the individual pieces of a mosaic she was yet to make out in its entirety.

Worst of all, she had to report to Captain Pomeno about her progress.  She had already sent out the warrants for Forley's arrest to all the guardhouses, along with an image of his face that she'd made with the guard's sketch artists, but beyond that, all she or anyone could do was wait.  As the barren poplars around the main square of Ilvior Island came into view, Nel slowly braced herself for another lengthy browbeating, picturing all the ways the captain might deride her in front of the whole office.

She was so absorbed in her thoughts that she was entirely unaware of the footsteps coming up behind her until a hand grabbed her under the shoulder and jerked her into the nearest alley. Her well-drilled instincts kicked in, and before she realized it, she twisted the assailant's arm, ready to move in for the hit—only to stop herself at the last moment.

"No, please," Forley whispered in a panic.  "I need your help.  I think my mother's in danger.  I'll give myself up, I promise.  I'll confess to the break-ins and the robbery, and"—he faltered—"I'll tell you what I know about the Garden murder."

"The murder?" Nel repeated. "How do you know anything about that?"

The boy's large brown eyes glistened in remorse. "Because I'm the reason it happened."

# Chapter 33

Noise. That was all the world meant to Ida. Meaningless, indiscernible, oppressive noise. And it wasn't only in her ears. The city around her reduced to a colorless, grayish haze that seeped into her head and filled it from the inside. She rested her elbows on the table and rubbed her throbbing temples, for fear they might split open.

"Try to eat. It'll make you feel better, I'm sure of it."

Mendel's words cut through the blur to briefly remind her where she was, but not much else. In front of her lay an untouched plate of food—a roasted lamb rack dripping with fat, alongside herbed lentils and thick slices of emmer bread. To anyone else, a feast fit for an emperor. To Ida, more noise. She forced down bite after flavorless bite, and while each morsel melted in her mouth, she may as well have been eating snow.

Over on the other side of the table, Corlis had no trouble taking full advantage of Mendel's invitation, and he was already done with most of his meal. After they'd driven around for endless hours, the young lord suggested they stop at an inn on the Street of Canopies to regain their strength and lift their spirits. Ida should have appreciated the gesture.

"We can leave whenever you feel ready," Corlis said from behind his wine cup, then ran his eyes around the room.

Ida had chosen to face the wall so as not be overwhelmed by the bustle of the inn, and Mendel took the seat next to her. That left Corlis to sit on the opposite side, and from his vantage point, he kept watch the whole time. For exactly what, Ida didn't know. Forley wouldn't come strolling into a place like this.

"Give her a minute. She needs to eat," Mendel said to him, then turned to Ida. "Come to think of it, have you drank at all these past days? Maybe that would be better for you."

"I'm fine," she replied. "I don't need to drink."

"Are you sure? We can—"

"I *said* I don't need it."

Guilt swept over Ida for snapping at him, but she said nothing else. Fixing her gaze on her plate, she continued to poke around aimlessly in the mound of lentils. Mendel did the same next to her, doing everything he could to prolong the remaining two mouthfuls of his own supper.

After a while, Corlis excused himself and left them alone. The noise of the world blared relentlessly around Ida, now joined by the deafening silence between her and Mendel.

"I'm sorry," she said at last. "I'm so sorry. I had no right to speak to you like that. I should be thanking you for all you're doing—for all you've done for me and Forley."

"Never mind me," Mendel said. "You're worried about him. No one can blame you for how you feel."

She buried her face in her hands. "I don't even know how I feel. All day, I've been asking myself: where did he go? How could he do this? Why didn't he say anything to me? I can't comprehend any of it. That's what frightens me the most."

"There must be a reason for all of this."

"But who should know that reason, if not me?" Ida blurted out. "Who should understand him, if not his mother? I raised him. From the moment I first held him in my arms, I thought I knew everything about him. But I don't anymore. All those times he got into trouble, I blamed it on the other boys he'd been around, and I kept trying to find the right place for the both of us. I trusted him to know how much I wanted him to have a good life. That as long as I kept him close, he'd grow out of it.

"Then we had that fight last year, when he almost stabbed someone over a game of dice. I had never been so angry with him before. For the first time in seventeen years, I had no idea who he was. I used to know everything about my boy, but the man in front of me was a stranger. It made me worry that all those influences from before had taken hold on him."

Ida's breath shuddered. Mendel refilled her cup from the water jug, and she took a shaky gulp. Her stomach was so badly knotted that she struggled to keep it down.

"And now, to learn that he's been keeping all these secrets—gambling again, stealing from you, disappearing without a trace—it's tearing me apart." Her thoughts ran in a circle, back to the question she started from. "What else have I been unaware of? If I didn't know about any of this as his mother, then what *am* I?"

There was no putting an end to the words that poured out of her, fueled by years of doubt she never had the chance nor the willingness to share. Throughout his life, Forley always had her to rely on, but she was never afforded such a luxury.

Mendel placed a hand on her forearm. "Forley is smart enough to realize how fortunate he is to have you. He can't abandon you so easily. I promise you, everything will be all right."

He spoke with such eagerness that, if only for a moment, Ida might have believed him.

"You truly are kind." She took his fingers between hers and gave him a weary smile. "One day, you'll make a woman very lucky."

Before Mendel could respond, Corlis turned up and asked if they were ready to resume their search. Seeing as how she'd be unable to swallow another crumb anyway, Ida pushed out her chair and led the way outside, with the young lord in tow. The innkeeper joined them in the carriage shortly after, and they were off for the hundredth time.

By the end of the day, their list of destinations had grown lamentably short. They had already checked the Upper Court District guardhouse, where Mendel demanded to speak with Sergeant Vendriane, but he was out somewhere. They'd been to the Garden, the tannery, the nearby taverns, but no one had seen Forley in any of those places. Corlis also led them to some gambling dens on the Wedge he was familiar with. These in particular filled Ida with a mixture of hope and dread. As much as she wished to find her son, the idea that he'd sunk this low terrified her above all else.

Hour after hour had gone by on their blind chase, where Ida would see nothing but the inside of Mendel's carriage until they emerged in yet another part of town. Each time, it was a dead end, and they retreated into the rolling cage. Ida felt worse and worse, as the last slivers of her perseverance slipped away from her, and her body gradually gave in to despair.

They'd given up on talking long ago. When they were on

the road, the only words they exchanged were about where to head next. Beyond that, Ida kept her head down and her gaze pinned to the floor. The carriage was built to be as comfortable as a carriage could be, but there wasn't a cushion in the world that stayed pleasant after a whole day of travel. Ida shifted and fidgeted around in a struggle to make herself at ease, which only frustrated her more.

The other two weren't much better off, either. They sat in the same arrangement as they did at the inn, with Mendel next to her and Corlis having the whole back-facing seat to himself, but he evidently had the same struggle as Ida. He leaned forward on his knees and picked at his fingernails with a pocketknife, which resulted in him cutting himself when the wheels hit a bump in the road.

*"Son of a—"* Corlis swore as the knife flew out of his hand and clattered on the floor, right between Ida's and Mendel's feet. Before the latter offered to pick it up, Corlis was already down on all fours, fumbling around their legs and having to steady himself against the seat.

"I can't see a damn thing in this darkness," he grunted.

That was when Ida noticed the motes of yellow light outside as the streetlamps were lit. The day had run away from them, and evening descended on the city.

Corlis found his knife and shoved himself back up onto the seat, shortly before the carriage came to another stop. He climbed out and held the door open, but Ida only shook her head.

"You two go inside," she told the men. "I'll wait here."

"I'll wait with you," Mendel said. "Corlis, can you handle this one on your own?"

"I can try," came the flat response. "But in all honesty, I'm running out of ideas. And I really should check on the inn."

"We've checked a hundred inns already," Ida said in exasperation.

"I meant my own. Thessa should be waiting there, and she might have news. I'll go fetch her, and the two of us can meet up with you in an hour. There are a few more places on the Wedge that only open at night. Wait for us at the Port Road bridge."

"Wedge. Port Road bridge. One hour," Mendel repeated. "We'll be there."

He closed the door and knocked for the driver to start. Ida's stomach lurched together with the seat under her, and it was all she could do not to get sick over the carpeted interior. Thoughts rattled in her brain like so many marbles, and amidst the despondence, one of them bubbled up to demand her attention—that she didn't want to find Forley.

It was ludicrous, but she couldn't resist it. After the ordeal of the past days, all she yearned for was an end. If they learned somewhere that he had left the city, or taken a boat overseas, or whatever else happened to him—if Ida got some definitive answer to her myriad questions, she could give up. It was an appallingly selfish idea, but it refused to remain in the depths where it belonged.

And Ida was glad it did. Because by entertaining the thought and seeing her own horrified reaction to it, she got all the reassurance she needed that she was still herself. She was still Forley's mother, and she was going to find him, no matter the cost.

The driver opened for them, and Ida climbed down the steps onto the filthy streets. She tightened her shawl to shield herself from the evening chill and breathed in deep. The mercifully odorless air was heavy and damp, presaging the rain that the skies had been promising all day.

High above them, the night domed over New Montres like an upturned bowl, shutting out the moon and stars. Against its backdrop, Ida barely made out the silhouette of the flat, blocky building next to them, and the faded lettering over the formerly red bricks that spelled out the name Scolsessi.

They were at the tannery.

Weren't they supposed to meet Corlis on the Wedge? Ida looked to Mendel in confusion, but she was only met with the driver, who had climbed down from his perch. The two of them stood a mere foot apart, possibly closer than they ever had been since they embarked on their journey that morning.

What a curious feeling it was to see a face that was entirely unfamiliar, and at the same time be equally certain who it must belong to. The scant lights of the Brewer District streets revealed to Ida a man around fifty, bald as an egg, with the biggest birthmark she'd ever seen, right above his lip. The exact description of the man who Mendel suspected of stealing his ribbon at the Garden.

That was her last thought before a soaked rag smothered her nose and mouth, and the darkness closed around her.

# VII

# Part Seven

# Chapter 34

Ida drifted in a serene emptiness. The outside world and all it included had ceased to exist. There was neither light nor sound accosted. Her body was immaterial, free from the pain and nausea that bore down on her all day. Nothing hurt her. Nothing troubled her. All her concerns had fallen away, out of mind and out of memory. There was no past or future, merely the peace of the present.

It wasn't right.

*"Where is he?"*

Voices bubbled up from an unknowable depth and seeped into her ear, piercing the comfort. Ida's mind rebelled against the sensation. She didn't want to hear. She didn't want to be aware. But she couldn't help it. She *needed* to hear.

*"He said he'd be here, sir."*

*"Then why isn't he? We've been looking for him all day."*

Her instincts latched onto the scraps and ripped her out of the void. With each word, her senses became clearer. Soon, she had arms and legs again, and they all ached. Her insides churned. Her skin chafed against something rough, and her tongue was swollen and dry. Lastly, the feeling returned to her throat, and she burst into consciousness as she began to heave.

She was tied up. One length of rope pinned her arms to her sides while two others bound her wrists and ankles together. She wriggled around on the hard, flat surface, helpless to remove the wad of cloth that made her gag. Eventually, a rustle came from the side, and someone pulled it out of her mouth.

Ida blinked the haze out of her eyes. Above her hovered Mendel's face, its soft outline rimmed in the fluttering light of a lantern.

"Be quiet," he said.

"Mendel, what's happening?" Ida asked. "Where are we? Who are you waiting for?"

"Quiet!" He sounded nothing like himself. His lukewarm tone was gone, replaced with a strained, guttural whisper.

It was a frightening contrast, but not enough to suppress Ida's desperation for answers. "Is it Forley? Please, tell me it's not him. Tell me he isn't a part of this. Please, Mendel—"

"I said be quiet!" Mendel raised a hand to strike her, but his fingers curled into a quivering fist instead, and he merely pointed at her with a sneer. "You've already ruined everything. But if you make it worse, I swear you'll regret it." He backed away and barked at the driver beside him. "Go back out and keep watching. Don't go far."

While the bald man trotted out of Ida's view, her eyes slowly got used to the environment. They were inside the tannery, next to one of the enormous tubs, where she'd been laid out on a wooden board. As the darkness gradually relinquished more and more details, there was a trail of faint glimmer that ran upward from her feet and vanished among the rafters. It was a metal chain.

Mendel paced up and down, wringing his hands and tugging

at the strings of his beloved naval coat. Despite the situation and the cold contempt with which he spoke, his movements hinted more at fear than anything else. The contradiction only scared Ida more.

"What are you doing to me?"

"Shut up," he spat back.

"I don't understand." Tears streamed down Ida's temples. "I don't understand anything. You lied for my sake at the Garden! You paid my release bond!"

"And how did you repay me?" The anger exploded out of him. "All you had to do was hole up in that whorehouse and wait a few days, but you had to go snooping around where you didn't belong. Why couldn't you stay put, like I told you to? Vendriane and I would have fixed everything!"

"Sergeant Vendriane? He's in on this after all," Ida not so much asked as said. He was the one Mendel was so anxiously waiting for. On the one hand, it assured her—to a degree—that Forley wasn't involved. On the other hand, it also led to an inevitable conclusion. "*You* were behind the murder?"

Mendel said nothing.

"Why? Why there?"

The young lord's mouth twitched. "How naïve you are." His voice cracked in his struggle to retain control over his overflowing hatred. "You have no idea who you're working for. What kind of business that woman truly deals in. You think the Garden's a simple brothel? I'll tell you what it is: a front. A gilded mask, covering up the plague that's defiling this country with their perverse ideals. Those who want to take from us what's rightfully ours! Those who took my father away from me!"

With each sentence, his fury took greater hold over him.

Having no other escape, Ida shut her eyes, opening them only when the echoes of his accusation faded between the walls of the deserted building.

"You said your parents died in a fire."

Mendel's face changed at once. His rage released, leaving behind an unnerving calm that killed the very light in his eyes.

"They were dead to me long before that."

He drew back into the darkness, beside one of the narrow windows to gaze out into the street in search of Vendriane. A low, slow rumble descended from above, where the rain beat the roof with a million thick drops.

"It was all Beldora's doing," Mendel said. "Father knew her through their shared Werrish background. They were no more than passing acquaintances, and it should have stayed that way. But he made the mistake of introducing her to Mother.

"Beldora tainted her mind. Convinced her that our title—our honor, that my father earned by risking his life—was undeserved. I watched my mother turn from a sensible, respectable woman into a traitor. First advocating for this travesty of a republic, and then for the abolition of our own dignity.

"I pleaded with Father to divorce her, but it was too late. She had corrupted him, too. No matter how I tried, there was no reasoning with them. At the end of last year, they both announced their plan to support the bluebells' cause.

"That was the day I lost them. The fire was merely their funeral. If they were prepared to burn down everything my father built up with his deeds, then they deserved to witness it from the inside."

He walked back to Ida's plank, his breath shuddering like

he was afraid of his own thoughts. "I did what I had to do. I swore I'd have my revenge.

"Beldora was too well protected. I couldn't get to her directly, but after some digging, I heard about a Midorean that lived here in New Montres. She helped the bluebells with money and connections. I knew I could cripple their organization if I got her, but I wasn't careful enough.

"I sent her an anonymous threat, and she went into hiding. I was sure she was still in the city, though I had no way of knowing where. But I could send a message to her, to Beldora, and all the other traitors."

Ida listened in terrified silence. So, this was the reason Vei Ruola's lover had to die. Not out of jealousy, nor for any wrongdoing of her own. It was nothing but the price she paid for loving someone's enemy.

The side door creaked open, and the driver trudged back inside. "I checked all around. Vendriane's nowhere to be seen."

Mendel fiddled with the trim of his coat for reassurance— the coat he had modeled after the uniform of a legion he'd never been part of. His plain features twisted in a wild stampede of emotions, straining to work up the courage to follow through on his honorable plan.

"What are you going to do with me?" Ida asked, knowing full well he wouldn't let her walk away right after he confessed to murder. "Mendel, please. I have a son. I need to see him."

The young lord shook his head, at once reverting to his accusations. "None of this was supposed to happen. I planned out everything. The Garden would have closed down, and you'd have been free. I would have taken care of you."

Up in the distance, a pulley rattled as the driver wound up

the chain, and Ida's legs rose into the air. Before she could scream, Mendel stuffed the handkerchief back into her mouth. She thrashed wildly to break free from her bonds, but the ropes' deadly grasp refused to relent. Foot by foot, she was lifted off the wooden boards, upside-down like a butchered animal.

Mendel brought a leather strap under her left arm and over her right ear, then tightened it to force her head onto her shoulder, exposing the side of her neck. Another series of grating metallic noises came, this time when the driver slid the pulley along the rail overhead, dangling Ida over the vat of reddish-brown liquid.

Eyes wide in horror, Ida watched the young lord take an ice pick from his lackey and lean over the tub to grab the back of her head. For a heartbeat, the two of them stood barely an inch apart, and she saw nothing but Mendel's watery eyes, flashing with a madman's resolve.

"We could have been so happy."

# Chapter 35

Nel wiped the side of her neck where the rain trickled under her uniform, then ran her quartz light over the building again. The beacon coming out of the cheap crystal was already patchy and uneven, and through the haze of the downpour, it was nearly useless—but it sufficed to make out the faded lettering over the red bricks.

"Scolsessi," she said. "This is the one."

"Ugh." One of the officers behind her screwed up his face. "Smells like piss and dung."

"Imagine what it must be like when it's hot," said the other one.

"Quiet," Nel hushed them.

"This should be the locals' job," the first one grumbled, making a token effort to lower his voice. "Why are *we* here?"

Why, indeed. Nel had several answers to that question, and none of them sat well with her.

After she returned from the public archives, Forley dragged her into an alley and begged her to help find his mother. He insisted that Mendel Scolsessi wanted to kill her, and that he'd most likely do it at the tannery—which was also where, according to him, the young lord had committed the Garden murder. His story bled from numerous wounds, to say the least. He couldn't say how or why Scolsessi had done any of the things he accused him of. He babbled something about breaking in and stealing from a letterbox, or money box, or some other box, but it made neither heads nor tails.

Despite all this, he spoke with an earnest conviction Nel couldn't ignore, and more than that, he offered to give himself up and confess to everything he'd done. That alone could have saved Nel's position in the guard and put her back on Captain Pomeno's good side.

Unfortunately, things weren't that simple.

If Nel had walked directly into the guardhouse with Forley in tow, the captain would have thrown the boy back into his cell and called it a day. Granting an escapee's plea for help was absolutely out of the question. Nel's job would have been safe, but Ida Nawoale wouldn't, not to mention potentially letting a murderer get away, or worse. That wasn't a thought Nel was prepared to live with.

After some heavy deliberation, Nel came up with arguably the most reckless plan she'd ever hatched. She told Forley to stay in hiding on Ilvior Island, then waited for Captain Pomeno to leave for the evening. At that, she grabbed the first two officers she saw and had them accompany her to the Brewer District, under the pretense that Forley had been sighted there.

And so, the three of them stood, huddled under the overhang of a warehouse across the road from Scolsessi's tannery. Nel cased the surroundings. If Scolsessi was in fact behind the Garden murder, *and* he was trying to harm Ida Nawoale, *and* he did so at this place, then this act of blatant insubordination could earn Nel both her job and her peace of mind. If not, she was certain to get demoted, if not discharged outright.

All or nothing. The odds weren't to her taste. Nothing odd was to her taste.

After one last check up and down the street, she led them out of their hiding spot to circle the building and count the exits. As they passed the tannery's refuse vats on the side, a shattering noise sounded over the officers' stifled heaves.

"Watch your step!" one of the men grunted behind his hand. "If you spill any of this on you, you can forget getting back in that wagon with us."

"It wasn't me." The other one waved. "It came from back there."

"There's no one there, idiot. Mind your two left feet."

"Enough!" Nel hushed again and ran her light along the ground. "There, it was a loose tile on the roof. Now stay sharp and keep your eyes ahead."

"Wait, who are those?"

Amidst chastising the men for not looking where they went, Nel neglected to do precisely that, so she didn't notice they had reached the building's corner. As she spun around to face where her colleague pointed, she stumbled over her own feet in surprise.

Two figures shimmered through the haze of rain outside the tannery's main entrance. One of them was hunched over and fiddled with the padlock, while the other one held an umbrella over the two of them, scratching his sideburns with his free hand.

Nel hurriedly ducked back behind the corner before they could spot her.

"Isn't that the coroner from the Broken Bridge?" one officer whispered.

The other one added, "And that's your Midorean friend!"

He frowned at Nel in puzzlement. "Did you call him here, Sergeant?"

No, Nel had decidedly not called him, which raised a host of questions. Why were these two here, and why together? Had they also found some clue to indicate this was where the murder took place, or did they have some other agenda? Some part of her wanted to go and confront Mainu, while another part wanted to see for herself what he was up to, without giving him a chance to make up excuses.

She wavered just long enough for Mainu to finish picking the lock and peek through the crack of the door. What he saw, Nel had no way of knowing, but the next moment, he barged in amidst a series of shouts. A cold lump in Nel's stomach told her she had made the wrong call by waiting. By the time she darted out from her hiding spot and reached the equally shocked coroner, it was too late.

From within the building came Mainu's voice in a sharp cry of pain, before he yelled, "Argiey! They're getting away!"

Nel whipped around to the officers in a panic. "Block the exits! Hurry!"

To their credit, as much as the men moaned and groaned the whole way, they knew their job. On her orders, they sprinted off in opposite directions toward the side doors they had noted during their lap around the block.

Meanwhile, Nel ran past Argiey and into the tannery, having no idea what to expect inside. The massive hall was completely dark, save for the light of a single lantern left behind. In it, she could barely make out Mainu's outline, slumped on the ground next to one of the foul-smelling vats. Further away, the rushed steps of unseen feet echoed from the blackness.

"Mainu!" Nel pointed her torch at him. "Are you all right?"

He was not. The lieutenant sat upright, leaning with his back against the tank for support, while his hand clutched a frighteningly large dark stain on his thigh.

"Nel?" He squinted at the sharp light of the quartz. "Is that you?"

"Don't move!" she said and pushed on his shoulder to keep him from standing. "You're hurt. Keep it flat, and let me dress your wound."

"I'll be fine. Get her down, quick!"

He waved upward and behind him. Confused, Nel followed his hand with her torch and had to suppress a scream. Seemingly hovering in midair above the vat, tied and hooked upside-down like a hog in a slaughterhouse, was an un-conscious Laerithian woman that could only have been Ida Nawoale.

Shaking off her initial horror, Nel found the pulley and safely lowered the body to the ground, where she pressed one ear on her chest. As difficult as it was to hear over the mad thumping of Nel's own heart, Ida held on to life by a hair.

Next to her, Mainu had removed his coat and ripped a shirt sleeve to tie off the bleeding. His face was stern as always, but the beads of sweat on his brow made it obvious he was in great pain. Nel turned her attention back to the woman and the wounds on her neck, struggling to keep her sight focused. Mainu could have been killed in here, and it was because she doubted him.

"We got them, Sergeant."

The officers' triumphant voices pulled her out of the guilt. Nel hastily wiped her face and rose to find her colleagues sporting drawn swords and pleased grins, while a few feet before them were two other men, kneeling on the ground with their hands up.

"This is a misunderstanding," the younger and more well-dressed man said. "I am Lord Mendel Scolsessi, and I am the owner of this facility. I caught this man breaking in and tried to stop him."

"Oh, rot in the cold depths, you scum-sucking weasel." The bald man spat. "You think you can throw me under the cart?"

Scolsessi ignored him and kept his eyes on Nel. "I swear on my honor as a nobleman, I had no knowledge of this."

"You can sort out your stories at the guardhouse," Nel said before the mud-flinging continued. She instructed the officers to handle Scolsessi and the Laerithian, while she unhooked the cuffs from her belt and went to the bald man.

With a disdainful scowl, he lowered both hands and held them out to the front. As soon as Nel clapped the first ring on his wrist, he grabbed her by the arm and twisted her into a headlock.

Nel reacted on instinct before the guardsmen cried out in shock. She raised one elbow to ram it into the man's side, but at that point, her muscles ceased to work. Every sinew in her body stiffened at once, so much that even her lungs refused to expand. She didn't understand why until her senses caught up. Digging into her neck, right under the jaw, was the cold tip of an ice pick.

# Chapter 36

Thessa scoured the roof in search of a way in. She'd prowled around for minutes in the rain, struggling to keep her foothold, but to no avail. She wasn't ready to give up. Ida was in there, and she needed help.

Corlis had been right, as was his habit.

Thessa had waited all evening at The Lame Mare for him and Ida to return. When Corlis was the only one who showed up, she already suspected something had gone wrong. All he said, in turn, was that Ida was in trouble, and they had to go to the tannery as quickly as possible.

When they arrived, a guard wagon was already stationed a block away, and as they crept closer, they spotted three uniformed officers surveying the building. At that, Corlis suggested they leave the rest to them, but Thessa insisted on seeing it for herself. After all, it had been the same guard that falsely imprisoned Ida without any real proof, and whose sergeant was intent on driving the Garden of Lilies out of business. And while the scene Thessa had witnessed in Beldora's office left her doubting the madam's intentions as well, the lesson she learned was to trust her own eyes first and foremost.

Leaving Corlis and her boots at a safe distance, she transformed and climbed up onto the neighboring warehouse, from where she could leap over to the tannery. As she did, she sorely misjudged how slippery the roof would be in this downpour, and she narrowly avoided tumbling down into the alley. In her scramble, she dislodged one of the clay tiles, which fell directly behind the guards below and caught their attention—fortunately, not enough for any of them to look up. They continued their tour on the ground, while she proceeded to sniff around for an opening above.

At last, one finally revealed itself to her, in the form of a ventilation gap where the slope of the roof met the front wall. She squeezed through the hole and into the rafters, methodically placing one foot in front of the other along the narrow beam.

The tannery was steeped in darkness, save for a lone ring of light in the middle. As much as she could, Thessa kept her gaze upon it, turning away only to ensure she stayed on balance. The air didn't help in her concentration, either. It was laden with dozens of smells, each more revolting than the other. Bile, ammonia, burnt hair, scalded fat, decaying hide, to say nothing of all the sweat, and—

Thessa froze. *Blood.*

It wasn't like the other scents in there. All of those were old and stale, but this was freshly spilled, much like Vendriane's at the Garden. But it was different from that, too. It was different from any blood Thessa had ever smelled. Thick, intense, and almost sweet, it flooded her mind and sent a ripple of heat down her body. She had to lower herself on the beam and sink her claws into the wood, lest she swoon from the overwhelming sensation and plummet from the breakneck height.

Overwhelming. That was the word for it, and as the first rush ebbed away, she understood why. It wasn't the scent of *one* person's blood—it was the scent of *hundreds*, blended into one. Her tongue lapped against her elongated fangs, dripping with glistening strands of drool, while her insides rumbled with a hunger like never before.

Deep beneath the monstrous urges, Thessa's reason fought tooth and nail to regain control and disperse the red fog that had descended on her. Splinters dug into her palms and feet as she pressed against the musty wood, straining with all her might not to succumb to frenzy.

"They're getting away!"

The main entrance swung open, and the desolate building filled with shouts. The commotion was enough to shake Thessa out of her trance, if only to be aware of her surroundings. She shook off the sensation and crawled further along the rafters to get a clearer view of the events below.

The guards had since burst in from the side and had Mendel and his lackey surrounded. Ida had been lowered from the chain, and a man leaned over her to dress her wound. The two in the middle spoke over one another to shift the blame, while the sergeant tried to keep them in order.

It was Nel Dormanni. Thessa had seen her countless times at the guardhouse when she ran letters to Ilvior Island. Why was she here? Had she taken over from Vendriane, or was she part of the same conspiracy? Was she on Beldora's or Braselius's side? After the last few days, it was impossible to tell.

At Nel's instruction, one of the guards grabbed Mendel, while she went to shackle the other one. For all intents and purposes, it seemed to be over—but right when Thessa was about to back away, the bald man grabbed Nel and pointed an ice pick at her throat.

"Drop your weapons."

One of the officers stepped forward. "Don't be an idiot, man. It's not worth it."

"Drop your weapons, or she's dead."

The guards exchanged a series of glances, and after a pause, threw their swords in the dirt.

"No!" Nel cried. "Don't let him do this!"

"Get back. Away from the door," the bald man shouted over her, then grimaced at Mendel. "You can keep him. Make sure he hangs."

Running his eyes back and forth over the guards, he shuffled toward the side exit, one step at a time. None of them tried to stop him. None of them could. Not from the ground.

Thessa breathed in deep and let the hunter take over. High up in the rafters, she locked her prey in sight, matching her own pace to his. It was only a few more yards to the door, where he would have to release Nel before running out into the street and disappearing into the rainy night. A single moment was all she had to leap safely down and catch him.

Catching them was never the hard part. Letting them go alive was. Especially with the tantalizing aroma of Ida's blood on her palate.

*Five more steps.* Thessa slunk along the beam in time.

*Four steps.* The men stayed where they were, now hopelessly far from him.

*Three steps.* Nel stumbled, but didn't throw her captor off balance.

*Two steps.* There wasn't going to be a last one.

Thessa jumped at the wall and sunk her claws into the

mortar, momentarily slowing her fall and allowing her feet to catch up. From there, she kicked herself away, exactly when the bald man shoved Nel forward. The arm that held the ice pick swung to the side in a wide arc, giving Thessa the perfect target.

Blood filled her mouth, and screams filled her ears.

"What is that?"

"Is that a werewolf?"

"Sergeant!"

"Help me! Get it off!"

"Get back!"

The fury erupted in Thessa with the blaze of a wildfire. This wasn't a badger, or a snake, or some other pitiful creature. This was human flesh and human blood. A taste above all others. A taste she'd already known, one year earlier. Her first kill.

The memory struck her like a club to the temple. She unhooked her jaw from the man's arm and reeled backward, staggering into the corner. Her eyes filled with stars, and she doubled over, shaking her head in defiance of her instincts.

She wouldn't kill again. She wouldn't allow herself to do it. Not here, nor anywhere else.

"Nel, are you all right?"

A voice split the mire of chaos in the room and pierced Thessa's mind.

"Don't move. Don't provoke it."

A man's voice. A familiar one. But where from. . . ?

"Does anyone have anything silver?"

That's right. From one year ago. It wasn't as hoarse, but it was the same.

Thessa's eyes opened, and before her was the Midorean.

The one who'd been in that loading yard on the Wedge, along with Nel.  The yard where Lokenn was about to find the evidence he, Thessa, and Corlis needed to save their lives from the paladins. Nel was the one who interrupted him, but it wasn't her fault Lokenn died. It was his.

And now he was right before her, wounded and helpless.

The man stared back at her with a blank expression. His body tensed up with anticipation, holding out his arms before him, struggling to get up on his injured leg. His right hand lowered ever so slightly, reaching for one of the discarded swords. In response, Thessa bent down, ready to lunge.

"No!"

Nel's weight rammed into her before she could duck out of the way, and the two of them tumbled to the muddy floor. Thessa forced herself out of the woman's grip, rolled off of her, and prepared to attack again.

The sergeant clambered to her feet and stood in front of the Midorean with her arms spread. Her cheeks were pale and gleamed with tears. Nel's stocky body quivered in every limb, but she refused to budge. In spite of her visible terror, the message was clear. "If you want him, you'll have to go through me."

The memory of killing Estrum might not have been enough, but that at last got through to Thessa. Nel's reaction washed over her in a tidal wave, and her thoughts cleared up in an instant. Around the room, the guardsmen reached for their weapons, but they didn't dare come nearer. Everywhere Thessa turned, she saw faces looking at her and seeing a monster.

She sprang to the exit and fled out into the rain, as fast as her feet could carry her.

# Chapter 37

Nel stared at the door the monster had left through. There was nothing else in the world. The ringing in her ears blocked out all sound, and her body was wholly numb in its petrified stance. She might as well have stayed in that spot for the rest of eternity. There were neither minutes, nor hours—only she and the door.

The first shreds of her environment she picked up on were the hesitant questions of her fellow guards.

"Do we go after it?"

"If you want to, you do it. I'm not going anywhere."

The men shuffled back to work and set about getting the bald man in irons, all the while decidedly leaving Nel well and alone.

Then, after however long, something else made its way into her world. One hand on her left arm and one on her right, gently lowering them to her sides. Their touch awakened her blood and sent it coursing through her veins once more, and with it, the feeling returned to her legs. Slowly, Nel turned around to face Mainu.

She didn't know who spoke with her voice, but she said, "Are you all right?"

He stood above her, somewhat unsteady, and answered as

matter-of-factly as ever, "You tackled a werewolf to save me."

Nel's newly flowing blood rushed into her cheeks. "I had to do something. I was so ashamed I let myself get taken hostage, but—when he held that pick to my throat, I simply seized up with fear."

Mainu didn't reply immediately, only frowned in thought before he raised one forefinger to the jagged scar across his neck. "I never told you how I got this, have I?"

Nel shook her head.

He continued, "Two years ago, I was in the same place as you. A man we went to arrest got me in a chokehold and held a knife to my throat. The difference is I tried to be a hero. I tried to get out of it, and he cut me open.

"The surgeon said it was sheer luck the attacker did such a terrible job and missed both of my neck veins. Had the blade gone half an inch further to either side, I'd have bled out in minutes. Now, once again, I rushed in without thinking, and look what that got me.

"You were exactly right to do nothing." He moved his hands to her shoulders. "I don't know what I would have done if I lost you."

For a second time, the world vanished from around Nel, and there was nothing but warmth. It was in the strong, steely arms that enveloped her, the chest that pressed against hers, and the fingers that ran through the mess of her undone hair. Most of all, it was on her lips, with the sweet taste of licorice and honey.

There were neither minutes, nor hours. She might as well have stayed in that spot for the rest of eternity. But, regrettably, even an eternity had to end at some point.

"Sergeant." One of the officers cleared his throat.

Nel unfolded from Mainu's embrace and gathered herself. "How are they?"

"Scolsessi and his accomplice are clapped and ready to go. The latter will need a surgeon pretty soon."

"And Nawoale?" Nel remembered. "Is she safe?"

"She lost a lot of blood, but I believe she'll recover," Mainu said. "I'm not altogether sure how her physiology works, but I've heard bloodsuckers are quite resilient."

"Good." Nel collected her thoughts. After the madness that shook the place since they entered, the banality of a routine arrest bordered on the surreal.

She stepped up to the young man and said, "Mendel Scolsessi, you're under arrest for one count of murder, as well as the attempted murder of Ida Nawoale."

Scolsessi, with all of his twenty-one years, made a valiant effort to exude noble indignity. The outcome was diminished by the numerous mud stains on his fine naval coat after his panicked scurrying on the floor.

"I'm not guilty of anything."

"You can explain that to the judge," Nel said and nodded toward the lackey. "And you'd better start working on your story, because something tells me we'll have quite the testimony against you. As well as one from your former employee, Forley Nawoale."

"Forley?" Scolsessi scoffed. "The serial gambler and delinquent, who was caught trying to steal from this very office? Hardly the most trustworthy witness." He sneered in contempt. "That's assuming this one makes it to the trial. And you have no proof the Midorean was killed here."

"Well, I wouldn't exactly say *none*."

Nel, Mainu, Scolsessi, and the officers all turned to the side exit, where Argiey walked in. Nel had entirely forgotten the coroner was anywhere near the building, but here he was now, strolling in as leisurely as if he was out on Crescent Bay. His appearance, though, told a markedly different story. From the neck down to his toes and fingertips, he was caked in a thick layer of sludge and offal.

Paying no mind to his state, he whistled a carefree tune to himself and walked over to a water faucet. Instead of washing himself down, as Nel—or any sensible human being—would have done, he only held out his hands and rubbed the length of black slime that hung from it.

Despite her judgment, Nel's morbid curiosity got the better of her, and along with Mainu and the others, she joined the coroner by the tap. He kept whistling and rubbing away at the sticky mass, which gradually dissolved to reveal a foot and a half of platinum blonde hair.

"You should empty your refuse vats more often, young lord." Argiey smacked Scolsessi across the face with the wet locks.

Once the officers had their fill laughing, it was time to head back. One guard picked up Ida, and the other hoisted the lackey on his shoulders. Nel led the young lord, still protesting along the way. The coroner offered that, for the sake of everyone's noses and general well-being, he'd take a separate route home.

Nel and Mainu guided the strange procession to the guard wagon a few blocks down. Around them, the downpour continued exactly as it was before their arrival, reducing the city to a blur. Houses were no more than formless masses against the sky, and the only stars were the street lamps that seemed to hover in midair, their posts hidden in the inky night. The whole landscape shifted from one instant to the next, like there could be anything waiting beyond the shimmering mist.

New Montres, the center of the world. Whatever happened within its walls, the capital lived on, changing year after year, yet forever the same. Sitting behind the window of the wagon, Nel knew her own world would never again be what it used to.

# Chapter 38

*We could have been so happy.* Those were the last words Ida heard before she was almost murdered by one of the few men she'd come to trust since her marriage. Lying in her bed at the Garden, recovering from the ordeal, there was little else she could do but roll these words over and over in her head, thinking about all the ways her life could have been happier—*if* it could have been happier.

Would she have been happier if she'd never worked for Beldora? She wouldn't have met Mendel, only for him to betray her. But he was far from the only evil in the world. She had dealt with plenty of it over the years. No matter where she went, there would have been another Mendel waiting for her somewhere.

Would she have been happier if she'd never become a bloodsucker? If she hadn't buckled under the fear of losing her youth and beauty, and with it, her and Forley's livelihood? She wouldn't have ended up accused of murder. She wouldn't have been at the mercy of Braselius and his circle of interest. But she could as easily have ended up like Violet—tossed aside by the world like a forgotten toy, only to grow bitter and resentful, stabbing whoever she could in the back to get her way.

Would she have been happier if she'd stayed faithful to her husband? If she hadn't given in to the temptation of that old flame and the memories of long summer sunsets under the trees in the garden? She could have remained an honest woman and a devoted wife. Together they could have built a happy home for their own children. But none of those children would have been Forley.

Was this, then, as happy as her life could get?

Either way, what could have been hers didn't matter. All that mattered was what she had, and that was herself and her son. Except now she was about to lose him, too—not to any malicious force or any grave mistake of her own, but the uncaring march of time.

Once Ida was awake, Beldora saw to it that she got to eat and drink, then filled her in on everything that happened after she passed out. How Mendel was caught red-handed, how his lackey nearly got away, and the mysterious appearance of a werewolf that stopped him from doing so. The latter in particular caused quite a stir, as the guard chose not to publicly acknowledge the event, which naturally gave rise to a dozen rumors across the city.

Other than that, the morning rolled by in solitude while Ida gathered her strength. After lunch, Beldora came by again, this time to announce that she had visitors. Before she finished the sentence, Forley barged through the door and threw himself on his knees by the bed, where he locked Ida in an embrace and buried his face in her hair.

"I'm sorry." He shook violently as he wept. "It's all my fault. Everything's my fault."

Ida hushed and patted her boy, crying with him until both

their tears ran dry. While they did, Thessa and Corlis joined them and took a seat on the other side. The former wiped her eyes now and then, whereas the latter merely stared into the distance, unbothered as ever.

Eventually, Forley sniffled his last and sat up.

Knowing full well why the three of them had come to see her together, Ida pointed the question, "What really happened?"

Thessa and Corlis deferred to Forley, who shuddered at the attention, but he mustered the courage to speak.

"After Mendel hired me at the tannery, I fell back into playing. He paid so well, I thought I could afford it. I got careless with the bets and ended up owing a silver and a half. I was scared that if I borrowed, you might find out, so. . . I broke into the money box in the office during the midday break. But I felt awful about it. After work, I snuck in again to put it back. That was when Mendel caught me.

"I said I'd take responsibility for it, only begged him not to tell you. He said he wouldn't do it, but two weeks later, he called in the favor. Took me up to Solluri Hill in the middle of the night and made me break into an apartment there."

Corlis chimed in, "Taëminn Vei Ruola's apartment."

"What did you steal?" Ida asked Forley.

"I didn't touch anything," he protested. "All I did was pick the door. He was the one who went in."

"Mendel stole a letter." Thessa picked up the thread from him. "I looked it up in the guild's logbooks. Almost all letters from outside Ardonne are registered—at least, if they're sent to someone important.

"A week after Taëminn went into hiding, Kalevi wrote to tell her she was coming for a surprise visit. The letter was delivered, but Taëminn wasn't home to read it by then.

Mendel found it and left a message for Kalevi with the station attendants, telling her to come to the Garden and speak to Beldora.

"When she did, Beldora suspected something was wrong and told Kalevi to leave through the back. That was exactly what Mendel expected. His lackey waited in the alley, grabbed her, and took her to the tannery to kill her. Then, he brought her back, and Mendel snuck his ribbon out to him, so they could put it on her wrist and tie the murder to the Garden."

Word by word, everything slowly fell into place. Yet, at the same time, the clearer the story became, the less sense it made.

"What was the point?" Ida asked. "Why did Mendel go to all this trouble?"

"He had an oddly decent number of reasons," Corlis said and proceeded to count them off on his fingers. "By killing Kalevi, he sent a message to Taëminn and the bluebells. By leaving the body here, he incriminated the Garden and forced it to close. By making it look like a bloodsucker, he could ensure he'd never be suspected, in case the collusion with Vendriane didn't work out. And by coming to your rescue after you got falsely accused, he could pressure you into owing him a favor, not unlike your son."

The image of Mendel's delirious eyes floated before Ida. *"We could have been so happy."* A taste of bile spilled into her mouth.

"You're good at thinking like a cold-blooded killer," she noted to Corlis.

He showed no emotion at the comparison. "I'm no better at it than anyone else. Only less afraid."

Ida's remark was mostly playful, but it wasn't completely

without truth. As briefly as she'd known the innkeeper, he had been as sly and calculating as Mendel. It was only luck that he had ended up on Ida's side.

"But what happened to you?" she asked Forley. "Where were you after I was released?"

The boy hung his head and fiddled with the fraying edge of the bedsheet. "I tried to steal a carriage to get money for your bond," he mumbled. "But I got caught and arrested. They almost put me in a cell at the Upper Court guardhouse, but a woman from Ilvior Island offered to have me moved there. Then"—his words became nearly indiscernible—"Then I picked the lock on my cell and slipped out when no one was looking."

Too exhausted to chastise him, Ida only asked, "Did you really try to kill Mendel?"

"No!" He snapped upright like a spring. "That was a lie. I only wanted to talk to him. To ask why he paid your bond and what he meant to do with you. And I said I would confess everything to the guard if he tried to hurt you."

"You *threatened* him? When you knew he was capable of murder?"

"No! I mean, yes, but—I didn't think—" Forley tripped over his words, stumbling into the correct ones by accident. He hadn't thought indeed. All his life, he would act first and hope that things would sort themselves out. He never did so with malice, and never to hurt her—but goodwill without wisdom did little good.

Ida turned back to Corlis. "How did you find me, then? After we drove around all day, you told Mendel to meet you on the Wedge."

"I did tell him that." Corlis leaned back. "I wanted to be

sure he thought me and Thessa would be far, far away.

"See, the first thing I wondered was, how did Forley know where Mendel lived to begin with? *You've* never been there, the house isn't marked, and I doubt he invites his employees for coffee and cakes every weekend. Made me think the two of them might have had business together before.

"Then there were the scars. Mendel had made sure to cut himself spectacularly across the chest, as well as the cheek and the arm, then said it was Forley's idea. I grew up watching tavern brawls, and I know this much: you don't *slash* in a knife fight. You *stab* in a knife fight, preferably in the soft parts." He imitated the motions on himself and gestured across the bed. "Your boy being the troublemaker he is, he would have known how to make those scars believable."

Forley gave a small nod, at once wanting to confirm his innocence and being embarrassed to admit his familiarity with the matter.

"But the real warning sign was you," Corlis said to Ida. "And how you got sicker as time went on. Sure, you were worried, but you've also faced a possible death sentence before, and you took that much better.

"When we left the inn after dinner, I stayed behind to check your water cup. I don't have the same nose as Thessa, but I picked up on a hint of spirit. Inside the carriage, I dropped my knife and prodded around the seat for a while. Sure enough, I felt a hip flask tucked under the cushion, and I noticed the same smell on Mendel's sleeves. He'd been slowly poisoning you all day."

Ida listened with mounting aggravation. Everything he said offered a clear explanation of the dreadful state she was in the past day, not realizing it wasn't simply her nerves. But the relief of learning the truth was far outweighed by another question.

"You figured out all this and didn't say anything?"

Forley joined in, "You let her sit in that carriage with the man who wanted to kill her?"

Corlis sucked his tooth. "I'm not saying it's the best choice I ever made. I'm saying I had to make a choice, on the spot.

"I've been around gamblers. When I got back into the seat after finding that flask, Mendel gave me a look I've seen at the cards table. It was the look of a man who knew the game was up. I'm a great many things myself, but useful in a fight is not one of them. My best bet was to get help and come to the most likely place we'd find you."

"The *most likely* one?" Ida echoed. "You weren't even sure you'd find me?"

"But we did find you," Thessa piped up. "And it's not as if he was blindly guessing. Corlis never does anything without thinking it through."

Not knowing what Ida thought minutes earlier, Thessa couldn't have meant her words as an intentional jab about Forley's habit of rushing into things. But the contrast didn't escape Ida, and it didn't make her any happier.

Corlis crossed his arms. "If I confronted him then and there, I had no idea what he might do. We were in his carriage, driven by his man. You could hardly sit up straight. Even if we got away, he'd know we were a threat, and it was clear he'd stop at nothing. Without any proof, we couldn't ask the guard for help, either."

"So, you used me as bait?" Ida asked. "We could have fled! We could have left New Montres, or Ardonne altogether!"

The innkeeper rose from his chair. "Did you forget the part

that your son was missing? And either way, *you* two could have left New Montres. But not me, nor Thessa—who, may I point out, risked her life more than once for your hide."

On that, he left the room with his friend in tow. Forley remained by Ida's bed, still picking at the threads of the sheets. Outside, the last night's rain had not relented in the slightest, battering on the glass with a thousand minuscule fists to be let in.

"Do you want me to go after them?" Forley asked.

"Why would I want that?"

"Ma, they helped save you."

"They put me in danger to begin with!" Ida waved at the door. "They badgered me into going along with their little investigation. If they'd kept their noses out of it, none of this would have happened. Mendel wouldn't have tried to kill me."

"But he wouldn't have been caught, either!" Forley's petulance bubbled up. "Vendriane would've let him get away, and who knows how many other people he'd have killed?"

"What does that matter? There are killers everywhere. You need to worry about not getting mixed up with them like you did."

Forley gave her a bewildered stare. "I know you don't trust other people," he said, "but do you really not care about them at all?"

Ida grabbed his hand. "I care about *you*. About *us*. That's what I've done for seventeen years."

He didn't answer that, but Ida knew he wanted to. He wanted to protest and rebel against her, and deep down she wished he would. Sooner or later, it had to be more than the two of them. But for the time being, he knelt on the floor and laid his head on her lap, while she caressed his cheek. Beyond the walls of the Garden, autumn ruled the steel skies—but in some part of Ida's mind, it was forever a warm summer sunset.

# Chapter 39

*"But my love, you're shivering."*

*"It's the autumn chill, dear sir, nothing more."*

*"Then we should make haste. Come, I know a shorter way."*

*He put his arm into hers and, in a manner befitting a gentleman of his breeding, led her with brisk strides toward the next corner, where he directed her to the right. The street they turned onto—nary more than an alley, rather—was dark and barren and unwelcoming, most unlike the path an aristocrat such as him might be inclined to take. Moreover, as they trod along the rough and damp stones, there came a sharp wind, and with it a most malodorous stench struck the lady's nose. As her gaze wandered from one ramshackle abode to the next, she remarked more and more disquieting details about their environment. Many of the bricks bore scratch-marks, two feet in length and an inch deep, alongside large dark stains that, upon closer inspection, revealed themselves to be dried blood. She turned to her noble companion, wishing to express her desire to leave this place and take the longer route—but in the same spot where he had stood not more than a minute ago, was something no longer human.*

Argiey drummed on the table in thought. Ending them was always the hardest part.

His search for the next sentence was interrupted by the doorbell. Figuring he might as well take a break until inspiration struck, he capped his pen and walked to the drawing room window to check on the visitors. Down on the street, by the main entrance, was a cluster of three umbrellas. He ought to have expected as much.

From the cabinet, he procured a tray with four glasses in preparation before he grabbed his cloak from the peg and hurried down the outside steps to open the gate.

"Coroner Madrasco, is it?"

This time around, Argiey could confidently identify the woman as Taëminn Vei Ruola, and she was every bit as regal as he had pictured her—tall and slender, clad in the famous Midorean fashion that impressed with its simple elegance rather than the amount of expensive trimmings. Her face, while darkened by grief, maintained an impeccable grace as she addressed him.

"Argiey will do," he replied and greeted the other two with her. "Lieutenant. Sergeant. Please, come in. I promise I've had a thorough bath."

Back upstairs in the coroner's quarters, he bade them to have a seat on the chairs he hastily moved over from the dining corner, then uncorked his favorite bottle of caraway brandy.

"Are you headed to the train station?" he asked while he poured out.

"Yes, we are." Vei Ruola took the first glass from him. "I'm not leaving for several more hours, but I wanted to stop by and personally thank you for all your help."

"As did I," Dormanni added. "If it wasn't for your strong stomach, we wouldn't nearly have the case against Scolsessi that we do."

Argiey scratched at his sideburns. He couldn't remember the last time—or the first time—he had this many guests up in his room, and he wasn't certain he enjoyed this kind of attention.

"Can't say I'm used to such ceremony," he said, "but I appreciate your kind words. I'm glad you're safe and sound, my lady."

She gave a faint smile in return. "Taëminn will do."

They toasted to a safe journey and to health as per custom. The brandy seemed to agree a great deal more with Mainu than the bitters downstairs had, going as far as to smack his lips at the taste. From the lieutenant, this was as good as a standing ovation.

Over the rim of his tumbler, Argiey regarded him and Dormanni. He hadn't been present for the passionate moment the two of them shared the previous night, having only heard about it afterward. Seeing how close they placed their chairs now, though, hinted that kiss had not been an isolated occasion.

"If you will pardon me," he said in the vague direction of the pair, "there is a certain question I might need to ask."

He looked mostly to the lieutenant for a reaction, but Dormanni was the one who answered. "Mainu told me everything."

Argiey tapped the side of his glass. "Which is that—?"

"That Taëminn is here to help the bluebells organize.

She channeled funding from Midorea with the help of her husband Yanne at the Midorean national bank. And he told me the three of them have been part of a similar cause back home."

For a start, that was enough.

"Well, the fact he's not currently in irons tells me something about your attitude," Argiey said to the sergeant. "But, if I may, so does your measured tone."

Dormanni's summary had been an entirely factual one. It didn't suggest she disapproved of anything she was told, but nothing about the opposite, either. And the way her round, usually pleasant face stiffened at Argiey's remark made it clear that was intentional.

"My position at the city guard doesn't make it possible for me to endorse it," she said. "Not officially, at least."

"And unofficially?"

In place of an immediate reply, she weaved her fingers between Mainu's and clasped his hand. "I trust him, and that he does what he thinks is right. For everyone."

That was about what Argiey could have hoped for. There was a great deal the city guard was known to turn a blind eye to—gambling dens, opium caves, a racket or two. Dormanni being prepared to "forget" persecuting bluebells on Ilvior Island wouldn't make or break the movement's success, but it gave them one safe place to be. If an emperor who erected a broken bridge could settle for as-is, then so could Argiey.

He toasted with the last of his brandy. "To live and let live, then."

With their glasses emptied and the pressing matters discussed, the guests rose to leave. As Mainu helped Taëminn's cape onto her shoulders, his gaze fell upon the papers on

Argiey's desk.

"Is that your latest bloodcurdling tale in the making?"

"That's right. It's about a werewolf stalking the alleys of the city." Argiey picked up the half-written story. "After last night's sighting, it's bound to be on everyone's lips. I thought it'd be nice to be first on the ball this time."

"Does anyone know anything about it?" Taëminn asked, umbrella in hand. "A werewolf in New Montres is bound to raise an alarm."

"Not a trace after it ran away," Dormanni said. "Although, from my angle, it looked more like a 'she' than an 'it.'"

"You got closer than any of us," Mainu said.

"There were rumors about one on the Wedge, too," the sergeant went on. "It was around this time last year. Could it be the same?"

Argiey spread his hands. "We'll have to wait and see—and hope it's not too late when we do."

The group murmured their agreement. Dormanni then bid her farewell and went ahead to fetch the coach, telling the other two to follow her a minute later when it came round to the entrance.

"You know, Argiey," Taëminn said, "if you ever wish to consider making a living off of your stories, I happen to know someone at a reputable printing house."

Argiey bowed his head. "Once again, I am grateful for your kindness, but I'd rather stay with what I know best." He glanced at the door that closed behind the sergeant. "Not to mention I'm more useful to you here."

The woman's expression changed at the hint. "Speaking of which—have any of the packages been compromised?"

"As far as my contact at the graveyard told me, no."

"Good. Thank you."

Argiey scratched his trusty sideburns. "If I may ask—what exactly was in those packages?" He gestured at Mainu and added, "It's usually my policy to know as little as possible, but at your colleague's inspiration, I'm taking steps to rethink that."

After some brief consideration, Taëminn nodded. "All sorts of things. Compromising letters, notes, and other bits of evidence my associates managed to gather. Secrets that need to be kept as safely as possible, out of reach for those who'd try to wrest them back—until they're needed."

Mainu chimed in, "Needed for what?"

Argiey meant to ask the same question, but in truth, he was already certain about the answer. What other use is there for keeping another person's secrets?

"Blackmail," he said. "But who?"

"Whoever is necessary," Taëminn replied. "Ringing bells and handing out pamphlets is all well and nice, but it does precious little to convince those in power to make the right decisions."

She left to join Dormanni out on the street. Mainu followed behind her, but not before he shot Argiey a parting glance— one that suggested this information was equally new to him.

From the drawing room window, Argiey watched the small company climb into the coach and roll off into the rainy New Montres afternoon. For a few minutes, he pondered how much he had truly gained by seeking to know more than he used to.

In the end, that would have to be a problem for tomorrow. He got back to his desk and uncapped the pen, setting out to complete his latest bloodcurdling tale.

* * *

Meanwhile, in the city of Tarnecia, eighty-year-old widow Milda Farelli sat at the newlyweds' table and smiled lovingly at her latest beautiful husband, while the master of ceremonies cried, "Raise your glass in a thousand well-wishes upon the happy couple, Lady Milda and Lord Alendro Benuarte!"

# About the Author

Jerry F. Westinger is a software developer by day, aspiring author by night, pastry chef on the weekends, and mortician by trade.

# Also by Jerry F. Westinger

**Coming soon!**
Bad luck and worse choices continue in 2025